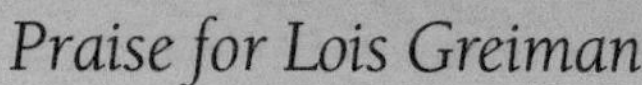

Praise for Lois Greiman

"Da[illegible] anovich

"Lois [illegible] Sayers.
W[illegible] write
[illegible]."

—Kinky Friedman, author of
Ten Little New Yorkers

And

UNSCREWED

"What a marvelous book! I was hooked from page one. *Unscrewed* is a delightful romp . . . a laugh on every page."
—MaryJanice Davidson, *New York Times* bestselling author of the Undead series

"A mystery that has it all, romance, murder, comedy, and a hot detective! . . . *Unscrewed* is a fun mystery that will keep you interested and rooting for the characters until the last page is turned."
—FreshFiction.com

UNPLUGGED

A *Romantic Times* Reviewers' Choice Nominee for Best Mystery & Suspense/Amateur Sleuth Novel

"The second book in Greiman's series even surpasses the superb first book. The writing is sharp and the dialogue realistic, with enough comedy interspersed. Greiman makes you feel for all of her characters. Whether you hate, love or fear for them, she brings forth every emotion."

—*Romantic Times* (Top Pick!)

"L.A. psychologist Chrissy McMullen is back to prove that boobs, brass and brains make for one heck of a good time. . . . It's the laugh-out-loud-funny inner life of this sassy single and clever writing that will make you disappointed when it ends."

—*Mystery Scene*

UNZIPPED

"Fast and fun, with twists and turns that will keep you guessing. Enjoy the ride!"

—Suzanne Enoch, *USA Today* bestselling author of *Flirting with Danger*

"This is an amazingly good book with tons of twists and turns. And it's funny. . . . Plus, the sexual tension between Chrissy and Rivera spices things up but never detracts from the pacing. Greiman has put out a winner that will hopefully become a series."

—*Romantic Times* (Top Pick!)

"Move over, Stephanie Plum and Bubbles Yablonsky, to make way for Christina McMullen. . . . The chemistry between the psychologist and the police lieutenant is so hot that readers will see sparks fly off the pages."
—TheBestReviews.com

"Sexy, sassy, suspenseful, sensational! Lois Greiman delivers with incomparable style."
—Cindy Gerard, bestselling author of *To the Edge*

"Guaranteed to deliver belly laughs; readers will crave more from this wacky new sleuth."
—FreshFiction.com

"Sexy and funny . . . Bravo! Well done!" —*Rendezvous*

"Wholly full of froth, this first contemporary romance-mystery from Greiman introduces an unusual heroine . . . [and] promises madcap mayhem. . . . For a summer vacation read, simple sexy sport may well be just what the doctor ordered."
—*Publishers Weekly*

"Lucy Ricardo meets Dr. Frasier Crane in Lois Greiman's humorous, suspenseful *Unzipped*. . . . The result is a highly successful, tongue-in-cheek, comical suspense guaranteed to entice and entertain." —BookLoons.com

"A crazy, enchanting, funny, great mystery all rolled into one." —*Romance Reviews Today*

Also by Lois Greiman

UNSCREWED

UNPLUGGED

UNZIPPED

AND COMING SOON

UNNERVED

Unmanned

Lois Greiman

A DELL BOOK

UNMANNED
A Dell Book / November 2007

PUBLISHED BY
Bantam Dell
A Division of Random House, Inc.
New York, New York

This is a work of fiction. Names, characters, places, and incidents either are the product of the author's imagination or are used fictitiously. Any resemblance to actual persons, living or dead, events, or locales is entirely coincidental.

Cover art by Ben Perini
Cover design by Lynn Andreozzi

Book design by R. Bull

ISBN 978-0-440-24362-5

Printed in the United States of America
Published simultaneously in Canada

www.bantamdell.com

OPM 10 9 8 7 6 5 4 3 2 1

To Ruth, my absolute favorite daughter-in-law, who is everything a woman should be. Thanks for being brave enough to join our family.

1

A woman needs a man like a tuba needs a cucumber.

—*Chrissy McMullen, tenth grade marching band aficionada—astute but jaded at the tender age of fifteen*

"McMULLEN," RIVERA SAID. I was juggling half an apple fritter, a cell phone, and ten million irate commuters when he called—an average Tuesday morning in L.A.

"Yes?" I steered with my elbow and set the fritter daintily on the napkin covering my just-above-the-knee silk skirt. It was the color of pomegranates, complemented to dazzling perfection by my delicately pleated carnation pink blouse, and absolutely spot free. I'm nothing if not classy.

"Sorry about last night." He had said he would drop by after his shift, but he hadn't shown. Which was just as well. The respite had given me plenty of time to steam my ensemble and moisturize my knees, which I often used to drive so I could finish off my breakfast. The remainder of the fritter waited demurely in its little paper bag on the passenger seat.

"You needn't be," I said coolly, ignoring the fritter's siren song. "I had a myriad of things to do."

There was a pause, then, "A myriad?" Rivera's tone sounded vaguely amused.

"Listen, it's good of you to take the time out of your busy schedule to call," I said, "but I'm afraid I have a good deal of work to do this—"

"You're pissed," he interrupted.

"I'm a licensed psychologist, Lieutenant. I don't get—"

"I said I was sorry."

"Well, you don't sound sorry. You sound—" I stopped.

I had told myself a slew of times that Lieutenant Jack Rivera was no good for my quiet, inner self—or my body mass index. If I had a nugget of sense the size of a germ cell I would have drop-kicked our so-called relationship into the distant-memory bin long ago, but Rivera's got an inexplicable appeal. Something I can never quite put my finger on. It could be his little-boy love for stray dogs or his enigmatic smile, but sometimes I've got a bad feeling it might be something a little less cerebral and a little more . . . well . . . hormonal, like the way he fills out his jeans. Let's face it, every therapist worth her insurance-funded paycheck knows that despite flawless breeding and costly matriculation, we are, under it all, still instinctual beings—and I'm not dead yet, despite the obvious intentions of the cosmos at large and a good part of the L.A. community.

There had been two attempts on my life in the past six

months. Those attempts had taught me some valuable lessons. Specifically, to keep my security system manned, and to stop at Yum Yum Donuts every morning before work. Life is short. I may not make the return trip.

A truck driver laid on his horn as I merged into the middle lane.

"Where are you? Are you talking on your cell while driving again?" Rivera asked.

A little spark of leftover guilt shot through me. I was raised Catholic by a mother who believed shame was the number one component in healthy child-rearing. "What?" I asked.

"Jesus, McMullen, are you trying to get yourself killed?"

I gritted my teeth and zipped into the right lane. My borrowed car was going to need fuel soon. It was a Porsche Turbo Cabriolet, and though it beat my little Saturn all to hell in the sexy department, it couldn't come close in the miles per gallon arena. "While I very much appreciate your concern, Lieutenant, I don't believe I need your lectures at this precise moment," I said.

"Are you on the interstate?"

"No," I said, and gunned the little roadster onto the exit ramp.

"You're lying, aren't you?"

"And this from a man who can't be bothered to fulfill his slightest commitments," I countered.

"It couldn't be helped." Rivera sounded irritable and a little distracted.

"Another fiancée emergency?" I asked, and knew immediately that I should have kept my mouth shut. Intelligent silence isn't a new idea . . . just an underrated one.

The phone went quiet for a moment, then, "You still jealous, McMullen?"

"Please," I said, and accidentally snorted a little. Must have been because my nasal passages were closing up. Classy women with Ph.D.s do not snort unless under grave physical duress.

He laughed.

"Listen, Rivera," I said, tone brimming with education and good solid bonhomie. "It's kind of you to call, but I really must get to work or—"

"I'll stop by tonight."

I punched the snappy little Porsche past a late-model Buick. "I'm afraid I'm otherwise engaged this evening, but I'll see if I can—"

"Yeah!" he yelled, ineffectively covering the receiver, then said to me, "About eight."

My smile was beatific. A shame it was wasted on the bald guy in the Buick who took that opportunity to flip me off. "As previously stated, I'm afraid I'll be unable to—"

"I'll bring Chinese."

My salivary glands tingled at the thought of Asian, but I infused my spine with pride and the memory of a half-dozen broken dates. Rivera was about as dependable as an offshore squall. "That's very considerate of you, but—"

"Don't bother dressing," he said. His voice was low and smoky. My ovaries perked up like a hound on a beef bone scent, but I'd been infused with . . . stuff.

"Listen . . ." I began, gearing up for a snotty answer, but he had already hung up. I stared blankly at my phone until the blare of a car horn yanked me into reality. Jerking the Porsche back into my ordained lane, I snapped the phone shut and tossed it on the passenger seat.

"Don't dress for dinner," I snorted.

Crumbs rained onto my lap from the rest of the fritter.

Did Rivera really think I had nothing better to do than wait panting by my door for him to show up with those sexy little take-out boxes from Chin Yung? Did he think I was desperate?

By the time the low-fuel light clicked on, I had worked up a full head of steam. I swiveled into the nearest gas station, selected a fuel choice that wouldn't require a third mortgage, and dragged a windshield scraper from its receptacle near the paper towels.

Standing there in my pomegranate skirt and classy but all man-made material sling-backs, I scraped ineffectively at the bluejay droppings marring the Porsche's windshield. The car had been loaned to me by a height-sensitive little myope who was dating my best friend and former secretary, Elaine Butterfield. But Laney had recently morphed into the Amazon Queen—long story—and left to film a TV pilot in some remote area of the Bitterroot Mountains. Thus I was left with her rightfully insecure beau and a long string of secretarial applicants who could neither type nor, apparently, think; I dared not be late to work, but there was one particularly large blob on the window directly in front of the driver's seat. It was the color of ripe eggplant, and I was out of washer fluid. Murphy's law had struck again.

"Here. Let me help."

I turned toward the gallant gentleman who had appeared near my elbow. He stood a little under six foot in his scuffed work boots and held a windshield scraper like a broadsword in his right hand. Blue fluid dripped from the netted sponge. A veritable good Samaritan. I stared at him. Good Samaritans are as rare as cellulite in the greater L.A. area.

"Unless you need to prove your independence or something," he added. He wore round, gold-framed glasses over aquamarine, heavily lashed eyes.

"I have a strangulation hernia from carrying salt down to my water softener," I said.

He studied me, head tilted, dark hair receding a little. "Screw independence?" he guessed.

I nodded toward the windshield. "Knock yourself out."

He did so, not literally, leaning over the hood and sawing with vigor. His blue jeans rode low on narrow hips and there seemed to be zero fat molecules hanging out at his waistband.

Turning the scraper, he squeegeed off the excess water and moved around to the other side of the car. His T-shirt had been washed to a soft, olive green and showed the tight flex of his triceps to his advantage.

"Thank you." I was trying to put the irritating memory of Rivera's absence and Asian bribery behind me, but I was still feeling fidgety and a little flushed. "You can leave the rest."

But he was already applying the sponge to the passenger side. "I'd rather commit murder," he said.

My nerves cranked up a little. Maybe it was the fact that I was late for work. Or maybe it was the mention of murder. The thought of manslaughter made me kind of jumpy lately. "What's that?" I asked.

"Leaving a car like this dirty," he said, and grinned at

me over the sparkling windshield. "It'd be a heinous crime."

I studied him more closely. "Are you an attorney?"

"No." He laughed as if it were a preposterous idea. He had an intelligent aura about him, so I suppose I should have known better. "You?"

"A psychologist."

He nodded. "If I had a Porsche I'd swaddle it in bubble wrap and stow it in a climate-controlled garage. Even if I was a psychologist."

Maybe I should have informed him then and there that the car wasn't mine, that my own vehicle was just above rickshaw status, and that I had earned more money per annum as a cocktail waitress than I did as a licensed therapist, but my vanity was already feeling a little bruised. "I'm fresh out of bubble wrap," I said, and checked my watch. It was 9:52. My first client was due to arrive in eight minutes, and leaving Mr. Patterson with my current receptionist, the Magnificent Mandy—her choice of sobriquets, not mine—would be tantamount to cutting my psychological throat. "And functioning garages," I added.

"Tell me you don't leave it out in the elements," he said, and stroked the car's cobalt hood as if it were a cherished pet. Men are weird.

"L.A. doesn't have any decent elements," I said.

Dumping the scraper back into its receptacle, he wiped his hands on his jeans and rounded the bumper. "You from the Midwest or something?" he asked.

"Chicago."

"No kidding? I grew up in Oshkosh. Wisconsin."

I nodded. "Land of the Packers and baby overalls."

"That's right," he said, and, wiping his hand on his jeans again, stretched out his arm. "Will Swanson." His grip was warm and firm.

"Christina McMullen," I said.

He smiled. Little wrinkles radiated from the corners of his eyes. "You miss the cold?"

Nice eyes. Kind. "Almost as much as I miss acne," I said.

"Yeah." The smile fired up a notch. He nodded toward the interior of the gas station. "My brother and I just moved down here a couple months ago."

"Movie script in tow?"

He laughed, ran his fingers through his hair; lightly tanned forearms, well toned. "Guess everyone has one, huh?"

"Not at all," I lied. "I met a guy just the other day who doesn't write anything but poetry."

"Haiku?"

"Free verse."

He grinned at my astounding wit. "We're doing carpentry work to pay for an overpriced apartment in Compton."

Thus the nice forearms.

"Say . . ." He tilted his head again. His hair was straight and a little too long, just brushing the tops of his ears. "You're short one garage. I'm short on cash, maybe we could help each other out."

I gave him an apologetic look. "I'm afraid my cash isn't very long, either."

"We work cheap." He grimaced as he glanced at the scrap of paper he'd just fished from his back pocket.

"Sorry. I guess Hank has our business cards, but I can write down my number if you're interested."

He *did* have nice arms, and I'd shelled out money for worse reasons. I'd once spent a hundred and twenty-seven bucks to have my hall shampooed because the carpet guy used the word "dearth." There's a dearth of guys with decent vocabularies.

Will was already scribbling with the nub of a pencil he'd pulled from his jeans. I glanced at the number as he handed it over. Decent penmanship. A little slanted. If I remembered my handwriting analysis correctly, that meant he had a creative soul. Or was it psychopathic tendencies?

"Are you any good?" I asked.

He nodded, then grinned, hunching his shoulders a little. "Actually, we kinda suck."

Funny. Self-deprecating. Cute. Rivera, on the other hand, was irritating, conceited, and dangerous. Hmmm.

My phone rang from inside the car. I opened the driver's door.

"Call me sometime," he said.

I gave him an understated smile as I slithered onto the Porsche's buttery seats. And for a moment I almost felt sexy.

By two o'clock, sexy was but a distant memory. By six-fifty, I couldn't even remember what the word meant. My head was congested and I felt kind of dirty . . . but not in a good way.

The phone rang in the reception area. I waited for the

Magnificent Mandy to pick it up. She didn't. I answered on the fifth ring.

"L.A. Counseling."

There was a moment's hesitation before the phone went dead. I put the receiver back in the cradle, at which time my so-called employee poked her head into my office. Her face is as heart-shaped as a valentine, her hair short and dyed the color of cartoon lightning bolts.

"Should I have answered that?" she asked.

I tightened my hand on the phone and managed to refrain from lobbing it at her head. Good thing it was time to go home. "That might have been nice."

"Even if it's after six?"

I smiled serenely. "If it's not too much trouble."

"Oh, no." Her eyes were bubble bright behind glasses with little stars at the peaks of the black frames. I had hired her because of the glasses, thinking they made her look intelligent. I've made other equally idiotic decisions, but never in regards to secretaries. "No trouble. That's what you're paying me for, right?"

"I thought so."

She scowled, pressing her lips into an absolutely straight line. "You look tired. Did you have a hot date or—"

Her question was interrupted by the doorbell. She glanced toward it, thinking hard. Maybe it was easier with her mouth open.

"Perhaps you should see who that is?" I suggested.

She nodded snappily. "Good idea." Her platform shoes tapped merrily across my carpet and onto the linoleum. Her tights were Popsicle pink. "Hello."

"Good evening." The voice from the reception area sounded vaguely familiar.

There was a pause, which Her Magnificence failed to fill.

"I have a seven o'clock appointment."

No response, but I recognized the newcomer's voice now. Mrs. Trudeau. She'd been a client for some months. I had a feeling she thought me shallow and unprofessional. I'd spent a good deal of time and my best psychoanalyzing trying to convince her otherwise.

"I called yesterday to reschedule, remember?"

There was another pause, then: "Oh, crapski," Mandy said.

I plunked my head onto the desk and refrained from crying.

It was 8:05 when I turned onto the 210. Despite a good deal of self-loathing, I was nervous about Rivera's impending visit. I needn't have worried, though, because when I pulled the Porsche up in front of my little fixer-upper, his Jeep was nowhere to be seen.

Harlequin greeted me at the door with a series of whines and wiggling spins, thwapping me with his tail at regular intervals. Harlequin is the approximate size of an African elephant. He's bicolored, droopy-eyed, and amusing. If I liked dogs, he would be at the top of my Facebook list.

"No Rivera," I said.

He cocked his boxy head and grinned, showing crooked incisors. I kicked off my sling-backs and hobbled into the bathroom.

"Good thing, too," I said, locking the dog out as I used the toilet. He whined from the other side of the door. "I think I'm getting a cold," I added.

Straightening my skirt, I scowled into the mirror above the sink and reminded myself that wisdom comes with age. I was looking pretty damn smart. And my nose was red. Maybe that was a sign of genius. I sighed, washed my hands, and planned my evening as I wandered into the foyer to arm the security system. I'd eat, slurp down some Nyquil, and drift away into a blissful, drug-induced haze.

But the doorbell rang just as I was about to touch the keypad, and I jumped despite my placid nerves and shrink training.

Harlequin barked and circled ecstatically. He had adored Rivera ever since the dark lieutenant had insisted I take him in.

"Steady," I said. Maybe I was talking to the dog.

Taking a few deep breaths, I checked my watch. He was forty-two minutes late when I opened the door.

"Congratulations, Lieutenant. You're only—" I began, but my words withered as I recognized my visitor. The windshield man stood on my crumbling steps, hands shoved into his back pockets, eyes sincere behind his wire-rim glasses.

"Will Swanson," he said, and gave me an embarrassed grin. "From the gas station?"

"Oh. Yes," I said, witty under pressure.

Strong as a bulldozer, Harlequin squeezed past my leg to slam his nose into Windshield Guy's groin.

"Holy crap!" he said, backed against the stucco. "What is that?"

"Sorry. Harlequin, come!" I ordered. I might just as well have told him to sing the Hallelujah Chorus. He paid me no attention whatsoever. But after a couple more snuffles, he sneezed twice, then galloped loose-limbed down the steps and made a mad circle around my abbreviated yard, past my lone cactus and the two rocks that keep it company.

Windshield Guy watched, eyes wide behind the wire-rims. "Is it . . . a dog?"

Harley's ears were flapping like wind socks and his tongue stretched nearly to his piebald shoulder. "Maybe," I said. "Can I help you?"

"Oh." He looked surprised. "I'm sorry. Weren't you expecting me?"

I may have blinked. Sometimes it's the most intelligent expression I can muster on short notice.

"I called your office," he added.

I waited.

"Asked if it would be okay to stop by. Your secretary gave me your address," he added quickly.

I wished like hell I could believe he was lying, but I'd known Mandy for a couple of weeks now. The girl made Gatorade look like Einstein.

"Oh, shit," he said, and blushed a little, backing away. "She didn't tell you I called. You probably have company. I can . . ." He glanced uncomfortably down the street. "I'll come back later."

"No, it's all right." No company. No Asian ambrosia. Harlequin galumphed back up the steps, nearly falling on his face before plopping his bony rump atop my foot and gazing adoringly into my eyes. If a guy looked at me like that even once I'd have five fat babies and a gas-guzzling minivan by Thursday. Reaching down, I fondled one droopy ear and reminded myself I knew very little about this guy except for the nice forearms. "How'd you get my phone number?"

"Yellow pages. L.A. Counseling. Christina McMullen, Ph.D." He was blushing again. Kind of sweet, but when I glanced toward the street, my suspicions fired up. Maybe they're innate. Or maybe the attempts on my life have had an adverse effect on my naturally trusting nature. "Where's your car?"

He laughed, sounding nervous as he backed down my walkway. "Hank needed the truck. I took a cab over. Cost me an arm and an ear."

Suspicions. Maybe that was why I was sans five fat babies and the ubiquitous minivan. "Did you want to take a look at the garage?" I led him down the steps. Harlequin followed me, over the ragged walkway and through my front gate.

"I'm sorry if I've made you nervous. I was sure your secretary would have told you to expect me," he said.

"Not your fault," I said. "The Magnificent Mandy doesn't like to be conventional." I was starting to feel a little guilty. I mean, yeah, I did need a garage update, but I was far more interested in how his forearms flexed when he cleaned windshields. "Listen, Will, I don't know if I can afford—"

"Shit. I'm sorry," he said. We'd reached the corner of my garage. It canted toward the south as if fighting a stout northwesterly. He glanced down Opus Street. There was no traffic this time of night. "I don't know what's wrong with me. I didn't mean to make you feel like you owe me a job. Man, I'm terrible with hot . . ." He paused, flustered.

My ears perked up, along with my flagging self-confidence. "What were you saying?"

We made eye contact. The sun was setting, casting a rosy glow over the garage . . . and my mood. He shuffled his feet. "Hank can charm the socks off hot girls. But I . . ." Another shrug.

I remembered our conversation at the gas station. It had actually been kind of witty. "I think you do okay."

"You kidding? I'm sweating like a greased pig," he said. "Of course, in Oshkosh they think that's sexy."

I laughed. He exhaled sharply, stared at me for a moment, then turned away. "So this is the alleged garage."

I gave it a jaundiced glance. I'd once parked Solberg's Porsche in it. He had subsequently threatened litigation. "Can it be saved?"

He made a face. "Are you religious?"

"When I have to be."

He tapped a rotted board with his foot. "Now's the time."

"I'll dig out my rosary."

He glanced at me. "You're kidding. You're Catholic *and* beautiful."

Our gazes locked again. "Am I going to have to pay extra for the flattery?"

He grinned a little, looking boyish again. "We don't see a lot of girls like you in Oshkosh," he said, and took a step toward me.

I knew right then that I should step back, but it wasn't as if Prince Charming were waiting in the wings. Hell, Rivera wasn't even waiting in the wings. Still, my nerves were jumping. Nice girls don't make out on the first date. Of course, it had been about a decade and a half since I'd considered myself a girl. And the rules are somewhat less stringent for aging women who have been inadvertently celibate for twenty-one months, two weeks, and six days.

"Thought my heart was going to stop when I saw you across the parking lot," he said, and stepped a little closer, blocking Opus Street from view. He smelled kind of woodsy, like fresh-cut timber.

Harlequin galloped around the corner of the garage, ecstatically chasing nothing.

"Would have sold my kidneys just to see you smile."

Things were heating up rapidly, like the initial pages of one of those erotic novels. I shook my head, waiting to wake up . . . or for him to rip off his tear-away pants.

"Listen, Will—" I began, but then he leaned in and kissed me with mouthwatering sweetness.

"I'll leave if you want me to," he murmured. "Or—"

He stopped, scowled, and glanced over his shoulder toward the street.

"Or what?" I whispered, but suddenly there was a loud pop.

"Fuck it!" he swore, and lurched behind me.

Another pop. I spun toward him, numb, disoriented, and *sure,* absolutely *certain* someone wasn't shooting at me. Not again. Wood sprayed into the air. I screamed. He shoved me forward. I crashed onto my knees. A bullet whizzed over my head. I dropped onto my belly, chanting Jesus' name.

And it must have worked, because the shooting ceased.

My heart was beating like bongos against the dirt. I lifted my head a quarter of an inch. No pinging.

Behind me, something whined and fell silent, and I suddenly felt sick. Sick and shaky.

"No," I rasped, turning on scathed hands and bloody knees.

Harlequin was nowhere to be seen, but Will Swanson was there, sprawled on the ground in front of me. Eyes staring, hands lax, and blood oozing from his head into the parched earth beneath me.

2

Death and taxes—the one don't look so bad when you compare it to the other.

—*Elmer Brady, Chrissy's maternal grandfather, who had refused to pay taxes on more than one occasion*

"SIT DOWN." RIVERA'S TONE was dark and hard-edged. My own sounded kind of squiggly.

"He's dead, isn't he?" I was standing in the middle of my kitchen, dazed and queasy and not entirely certain how I had gotten there. Rivera had arrived before I'd reached the body, had pulled me to my feet. A few minutes later, a cruiser had squealed to a halt next to my garage, lights wheeling crazily.

"Yes," he said.

My hands were shaking, my legs noodley, but I turned toward the door, wondering if I could manage the knob.

"Sit down," he repeated, but I had to see for myself, to

do what I could, to try to make sense of a world gone mad . . . again. The floor felt uneven beneath my feet.

"Sit down!" he ordered, and, yanking a chair from nowhere, pushed me into it. The room tilted. I teetered with it. "Put your head between your legs."

"I'm fine." I can usually lie with more panache, but guys don't generally drop dead in my front yard. Though it's happened in my office. My stomach crunched at the memory.

From outside, I heard the static of a two-way radio. Words followed, but I couldn't make them out—just the tone, solemn and succinct and matter-of-fact.

Rivera kept his hand on my shoulder, holding me down or holding me up. Hard to say for sure.

"What's his name?" he asked, but I was lost in my own morass of self-pity and disorientation.

"He never hurt anyone," I said, and felt a warm droplet drift down my cheek.

"How well did you know him?"

I blinked, glanced up at him, smearing away the tear with the back of my hand. "Harlequin?"

His scowl sharpened for an instant. A tic danced in his dark-stubbled jaw. "Jesus." The scar beside his mouth twitched. "I'm talking about the dead g—the deceased."

I blanched, remembering Will Swanson's eyes, wide and sightless above a growing pool of blood. It had been surprisingly dark, black almost, forming a paisley shape before being soaked into my starved lawn like milk on dry toast. My stomach heaved.

"Head between your legs," Rivera ordered again, and this time I complied, scrunching my fingers in my skirt and breathing deep. "Christ!" He sounded impatient and angry. Shuffled his feet. His shoes were brown leather, scuffed at the toes, just visible beneath his blue jeans, and somehow the sight of them started my tears up in earnest. Harlequin had loved shoes.

I drew in a shaky breath, let my tears drip onto the floor, cleared my throat, and straightened carefully. "Where is he?"

Rivera was silent for a moment as if trying to follow my line of thought, then, "Stay here," he said, and turned away.

"I want to come—" I said, and tried to rise, but he turned back toward me.

"Stay!" he said, and jabbed a finger at me with more venom than he'd ever used on Harley. "Or I swear to God I'll let them haul you downtown."

"He was *my* dog," I said. Maybe I was trying for defiance, but my voice warbled and my chin felt strangely disconnected.

He swore again, but softer this time. "Please . . ." The word sounded funny coming from him. Like he'd never said it before and was trying to figure out how to formulate the sounds. ". . . just stay put for once in your goddamn life."

I considered arguing, but there was something funky going on in his eyes. It almost looked like worry, so I kept silent, trying to work that out. And apparently he took that as agreement, because he was gone in a moment.

Near the cupboards, Harlequin's dishes sat on a plastic mat. Three nuggets of food were scattered across it. I felt my eyes well over again. My throat felt tight. It was stupid. I knew it was. A man was dead, and all I could think about was that lop-eared—

The door opened. Rivera stepped inside, face chiseled into a frown, brows low over deadly dark eyes. I hiccuped between my chattering teeth, and then he thrust the door open and Harlequin stood on the threshold, eyelids drooping, skinny tail clamped between trembling, knock-kneed legs.

"Harley," I whimpered. His head came up and then he was slinking across the floor toward me and I was crying and hiccuping while a dog the size of a buffalo licked my face and tried desperately to climb onto my lap.

When I'd run out of tears and snot I found that Rivera had leaned his hips against my counter and was watching me with thundercloud eyes.

"I didn't even think you liked that damned dog," he said.

I wiped the back of my hand across my nose and tugged at a floppy ear. "I don't. He's just so . . ." I cleared my throat, unable to come up with a socially acceptable superlative. "Where'd you find him?"

"Under the Porsche." There was a pause. "I'm assuming it's Solberg's?"

I nodded, sniffled, pressed my face to the dog's for a minute. He smelled bad.

"You okay?"

"Sure," I said, and cleared my throat again. "What about . . ." I steadied myself. My knees hurt where they'd been scraped raw. "What about Will?"

Watching Rivera, it was as if a light switch clicked in his personality, and suddenly a little notebook appeared in his hand. He scribbled rapidly. "What's his last name?"

"Is he dead?"

His eyes narrowed. "How well did you know him?"

My lips jerked spasmodically. "He was from Oshkosh."

He gave me a look that suggested I might be a few smokes short of a full pack.

"He has a brother," I said.

He nodded. Crazy or not, he still seemed happy to have me talk. "Where'd you meet him?"

"I was getting gas."

"What was he driving?"

"I didn't see his car," I said, trying not to think too hard, to remember too much. "But he liked the Porsche."

Rivera snapped his gaze to me. "You were driving Solberg's car?"

"Mine's in the—"

"Tell me—" He stopped himself. The muscle danced in his jaw. "Tell me you didn't just meet this guy today."

I fiddled with Harlequin's collar. Rivera has an ungodly gift for making me look stupid. Of course, sometimes I give him a hand, just to be neighborly. "He was a carpenter."

This news didn't seem to make him any happier.

"Said he'd fix my garage for cheap."

"Jesus!" Rivera said, and suddenly he was pacing. "You just met the guy this morning and invited him out to . . . to what?" He stopped to glare at me. Harlequin clambered from my lap and clicked across the cheap flooring to gaze up at him. "Don't you think at all?"

"Yeah, I thought." I jerked to my feet. The adrenaline that had gotten me through those first ugly moments was firing up again, leaving the weak-assed nausea behind. "I thought you probably weren't going to show again."

He gave me a puzzled look from the corner of his eye. I've been familiar with that expression since I was four and Dad found me scrunched up on the top shelf in the kitchen cupboard eating Oreos. "So you invite some . . ." He waved in the general direction of my front lawn. ". . . some dead guy over?"

I raised my chin. "He wasn't dead at the time."

"Well . . ." He chuckled, paced. ". . . his chances weren't very good, were they? Not with you in his life."

I gritted my teeth at him. "*You're* still alive."

"Probably just a damned oversight on your part."

"Probably," I said, and traipsed into the bathroom. Rivera followed me. But I ignored him as I yanked open the door beneath the sink and snagged a package of Virginia Slims from behind the box of tampons. I had a little trouble opening the pack, but the cigarette felt good between my fingers. Having it snatched out of my hand didn't feel quite so lovely.

"Hey!" I said.

"You quit." He tossed it in the garbage. "Remember?"

"Well, I started again," I said, and tried to pull another from the neat rows, but I fumbled the pack and it toppled to the floor, spilling cigarettes atop my bathroom rug. And then I started to cry.

But even over the sobs I could hear Rivera cursing. "Come here," he said finally, and tugged me into his arms. I resisted for a moment out of principle, but when I let myself go, his chest felt firm, his V-neck soft against my cheek. I tried to stop crying. Some women look cute when they cry. I look like a horror-flick chick. The one you know is doomed from the moment she steps onto the screen.

"Blow your nose," he said, handing me a roll of toilet paper.

I was beyond arguing. I blew my nose. Then he led me to the couch and pulled me down beside him. Harlequin climbed up and with a heavy sigh plopped his head onto my lap.

"You okay now?" Rivera's voice sounded low and dusky.

"Sure." As lies went, it was shaky, but at least I didn't blubber like a colicky infant.

"Can you tell me about it?"

My lips twitched hopelessly. "You going to yell at me again?"

"I didn't yell."

I gave him a look from drippy eyes.

"Much," he added, and pushed the hair back from my face. At one point it had been coiled up in a stylish 'do. Now it probably looked as if I'd had an unfortunate run-in with an industrial fan. He grinned a little, touched my cheek. "I can't keep the boys at bay much longer, honey. They're going to want a statement."

Honey. The word sounded strange from his lips. Unfamiliar but oddly right. I refrained from crawling into his lap and curling up like a love-starved kitten. I would have had to take the dog with me.

"His name was Will Swanson. He helped me clean my windshield." I told him the name and location of the gas station.

"Why?"

I thought about that for a second. "To be nice?"

He scowled but didn't comment, maybe because he thought I'd start sniveling again. "Where'd he come from?"

"Oshkosh."

"I mean, was he inside the store? Filling his car?"

"Oh. He was just there when I glanced up."

"He introduce himself?"

"Not right away. We talked." I remembered back, swallowed. Will had been charming. Now he was dead. A trend seemed to be forming. "He had a movie script, I think."

"Do you know where he was pitching it?"

I shuddered in a breath. "I was late for work." I cleared my throat. "Didn't have much time."

"Did you see any identification?"

"Iden—"

"Credit card." He made an impatient gesture. "Driver's license. Birth certificate?"

I blinked, lashes fat and heavy from the latest deluge. "Birth certificate?"

His scar jumped. "What made you think he was who he said he was?"

I frowned at the untidy wad of toilet paper still in my hand. "What would make me think he wasn't?"

"Jesus, McMullen, everyone and his brother seems to be trying to kill you. It's time you woke up and—"

I must have been tearing up again, because he stopped himself, drew a deep breath. "I'm sorry."

The tears froze in my eyes. "What?"

He was silent for a moment. His brows shadowed his dark cop eyes. "I've apologized before."

If that was true, you couldn't prove it by me. In the past I had thought it physiologically impossible for him to do so. Maybe my doubts showed in my expression, because he leaned his shoulder into the couch and watched me skeptically. "Have you eaten?"

I stroked Harlequin's muzzle where the fur was as soft

and short as velvet. "You said you'd bring Chinese," I said, trying to sound neither accusatory nor idiotic.

Maybe I sounded childish instead, but maybe he liked it, because he smiled a little. "Listen, I need to talk to Williams for a minute. Will you be all right for a while?"

"Sure," I said, and shrugged, but I wasn't crazy about sitting there alone. Harlequin humped closer, draping a foreleg over my lap. Maybe he felt the same way.

Rivera nodded. "Try to rest. I'll be back in a minute."

It was actually longer than sixty seconds, but not by much. When he stepped back into view I saw that he was holding a bag from Chin Yung.

"I'm going to heat this up," he said.

I fiddled with Harley's ears. "You don't need to go to the trouble. I'm not very hungry." It was shockingly true. Short of the bubonic plague, not much ruins my appetite.

He scowled. "I just about got laughed out of the precinct for bringing takeout to a crime scene, McMullen. Had to tell them you were shocky and hun sui gai was the only thing that would bring you around."

"You're hilarious," I said.

"Rest," he ordered, and went into the kitchen.

I dropped my head back against the sofa cushion and tried not to think. Usually it's not so hard, but usually—well *sometimes*—there's not a dead body within shouting distance. Still, the sweet scent of chicken in dark sauce drifted into the living room, making my quest easier.

I found myself in the kitchen in a matter of minutes. Three pans were arranged in a triangular formation in the center of my table. None of them had matching covers. In my kitchen, food and foodlike substances rarely make it into a pot before they're consumed, so it had always seemed like a waste of time and money to buy any spectacular cookware.

Rivera motioned toward a chair with a spatula. I sat down like a palsy victim. Harley plopped down beside me, head even with the tabletop. Opening the smallest pan, I fed him a clump of rice. He gobbled it down and grinned for more.

"You're going to spoil him," Rivera said, and picking up the pot, spooned a hefty portion of rice onto my plate.

"He's an only child," I said.

Replacing the first pan, he lifted the second. The lovely scent of Asian ambrosia filled my head. After inhaling Yum Yum's finest, I had skipped lunch, and I felt a little weak at the sight of the golden chicken, but guilt had been implanted in my brain in utero and nailed down during twelve years at Holy Name Catholic School. "Shouldn't we be . . ." I winced and nodded toward the outdoors, where dead bodies were probably strewn about like popcorn. "Talking to the police?"

He scooped out the hun sui gai. It was pretty enough to make me tear up again. Replacing the pan, he took a seat at the end of the table. "What would you tell them?" he asked.

"That I didn't kill him," I said.

He gave me his deadpan expression. It was still first-rate. "I found you seconds after the incident, green around the gills and about to fall flat on your face. It seems unlikely you were the cause of his death."

"It was unlikely that I caused Bomstad's death, too, but you still accused me." It might have been a childish grudge, but I didn't think so.

"You looking for another apology, McMullen?" he asked, staring at me.

I shook my head, dropped my gaze to my plate, and fiddled with a lovely hunk of chicken. "I'm afraid forcing another one on the heels of your first might do irreparable damage to your psyche."

He watched me eat. "How did he get here?"

I didn't have to ask what he was talking about. "He took a cab."

"What company?"

"I didn't see."

"You didn't see the name of the company or—"

"I don't know anything!" I snapped, and stood abruptly. My chair bumped backward, rocking against my uncertain knees. "I don't know why he was killed. I don't know who killed him. I don't know what you want."

His eyes were one notch short of deadly. "I want to know if there's someone who wants you dead," he said.

3

There are two kinds of people in the world. Those who enjoy a nice salami and those who have no souls.

—Saul, the deli guy, perhaps speaking metaphorically

MY LITTLE WORLD GROUND to a halt. For some inane reason, I had never considered the idea that someone may have been trying to kill *me.* I inhaled carefully, stared at Rivera for a moment, then turned and wandered into my bedroom. The covers were tousled, the pillows askew, and a bevy of garments were scattered across the furniture, but I didn't care. I crawled onto the mattress and pulled the wrinkly blankets up to my chin. Then I rolled onto my side and closed my eyes.

"Chrissy," Rivera said, but I didn't have time to ignore him before the doorbell rang. There was a momentary pause before he turned and trekked across carpet and linoleum to answer it. I could hear voices, but the words were mostly indistinct.

"Tomorrow," Rivera said.

The other voice countered, rising in volume and agitation, and then the door closed. The world went silent. Rivera had stepped outside, but I didn't care about that, either. I actively sought sleep. I know it seems ludicrous, but there are a limited number of talents at which I am truly gifted. Other than eating, sleeping is at the top of the list.

Harlequin clicked across the floor and heaved himself onto the bed. A kernel of rice was stuck to his nose. His breath smelled like Asian ambrosia. Weird. I closed my eyes again, but after several minutes I still wasn't asleep. And my nose was dripping, so I wandered into the bathroom and dragged down a bottle of Nyquil. Some people have to get drunk to forget. Me, I just need a little bit of green magic. But I couldn't find a measuring spoon, so I slopped half a cup into a glass and drank it down. Moments later I was staggering back to bed, stomach clenched and esophagus burning.

My dreams were an odd conglomeration of weird and weirder. Medication sometimes does that to me. For a while I was flying, gliding along. There were no wings or anything but I was floating over my parents' house. I felt the age-old psychosis rise up at the sight of it, but I calmed myself. I was all grown up now, educated, independent, and . . . Naked!

Shit! I tried to cover myself before Mom saw me and grounded me for eternity, but suddenly I was falling, tumbling ass over ankle until I landed with a plop in my own bed.

All was well. I was safe. Besides, I'd looked pretty damned svelte as I'd fallen through the sky. My legs were freshly shaven and my hair looked great.

Something tinkled musically from the kitchen, and the heavenly scent of waffles drifted dreamily in the air. Someone was making breakfast. Maybe it was Julio Manderos. He's Hispanic, ridiculously good-looking, and tends to frequent my dreams on regular occasions ever since I'd met him some months earlier. True, he was—or at least had been—a gigolo, and for a while I'd considered him a murder suspect, but in my dreamy meanderings, I didn't hold that against him.

I stretched luxuriously. I could hear water splashing and I smiled. Maybe Julio was drawing me a bath, pouring in scented oils, lighting candles. On the other hand, maybe it was Harlequin. He's pretty active in my dreams, too. Then there's Cliff, the "dancer" I'd met at the Strip Please. He was dressed as a pirate . . . for a while.

I love pirates.

And suddenly I was on my feet. I felt willowy and weightless as I floated along in the gauzy morning light. There was a noise in the bathroom. I opened the door.

Lieutenant Jack Rivera stood inside. And he was naked.

He was moving in what I call sexy motion—slow, evocative surreal-time. His hair shone blue-black and was slicked away from his sharp, high-boned features. His body glistened with dew drops, every finely tuned muscle visible and flexing. Below his washboard belly, his skin was a shade lighter, except for his dick . . . his "manhood," as they call it in my favorite raunchy novels. That was the size and color of paprika salami, nestled in his dark curls and lying dormant against his bulging, off-center testicles.

I blinked and stared. I love dreams.

"Sorry," he said. His voice was low and smoky as he reached for a towel with a broad, muscled arm. The room was steamy, but of course it would be. The room is always steamy in my erotic dreams.

"Thanks," I said, my voice smooth as fine liqueur.

He eyed me through dark, heavy lashes as he lifted the towel. But he only patted his face dry, leaving his finer parts exposed—of course. "For what?"

"I only eat waffles in my dreams." His manhood was starting to wake up, reach toward me. I should sleep more often. "Don't have a waffle maker."

He lowered the towel a little. It looked snowy white against the skin of his lean-muscled thighs and did nothing to hide his erection. Naturally.

"They're pancakes," he said. "Mama's recipe."

I nodded, not taking my eyes off his penis. "Rachel was right. You're hung like a breeding stallion." Rachel had been one of his exes. One of his many. But exes don't matter in dreamland.

He took another step forward. Even his damned feet were attractive. But why wouldn't they be? "You okay, McMullen?"

"Never better. You want me to get the syrup so we can get things started?"

His dick throbbed a little. Gotta like that.

But then he scowled and wrapped the towel around his waist.

My dreams screeched to a halt.

"Take that off," I ordered, but my voice sounded kind of scratchy now and my head was spinning.

"What the hell's wrong with you?" he asked, and taking one more step, put his palm on my forehead.

His hand felt suspiciously real. I scowled, then, reaching up, poked him tentatively in the chest.

"Are you on drugs?" he asked, flicking up my eyelid with his thumb.

I blinked. And suddenly I felt sick to my stomach. It twisted hideously and then I knew the truth: The green magic had conspired against me. I wasn't dreaming, I was awake! Lucid. Well . . . awake.

Stumbling backward, I bumped into the doorjamb and ricocheted sideways. I wanted to rush into my bedroom and shut out the world, but my guts were trying to climb up my esophagus.

So I reached out, snagged my fingers in Rivera's towel, heaved him out of the bathroom, and slammed the door behind him. A second later I was yakking into the toilet.

By the time I settled back onto my heels my eyes were streaming but my stomach had been pacified. I turned on the tub tap, rinsed my mouth, and buried my face in the nearest towel as memories stormed in like flying monkeys—gunshots, dead eyes, Nyquil.

"McMullen." Rivera knocked once. "You okay?"

I peeked over the towel, wondering if he'd believe me if I told him I was dead. Probably not. "Don't come in," I said, and then he came in, stepping into the bathroom with a good deal more reality, but no less sex appeal than he'd displayed a few minutes before.

"What the hell's going on?"

I didn't answer. Couldn't. Sometimes humiliation can weld my tongue right to the roof of my mouth. Sometimes that's the best place for it.

He was staring at me. I was staring back. Couldn't help myself.

"Are you drunk?" he asked.

I shook my head.

"Drugs?"

"Nyquil."

"How the hell much did you take?"

I glanced toward the bottle on the sink and winced. "Might have been full when I started."

He cursed, scowled, then sat down on the edge of the tub a few inches away. The towel still looked snowy white against his thighs. "Did you tell me I was hung like a breeding stallion?"

I pulled the towel up over my eyes and shook my head.

"Yes you did."

I snatched the towel from my face. "You're supposed to be a dream! Why the hell aren't you a dream?"

His brows had risen into his hairline. "I guess it's a good thing I told Mandy to cancel your appointments."

I had a nagging suspicion that I should be angry at his high-handed behavior, but if I remembered correctly I had offered to fetch the syrup so we could—

"Did you offer to get the syrup so we could—"

"You're hallucinating!" I snapped.

And then he laughed. "Jesus, McMullen, I can't decide if I should be horny or horrified. Come on." He stood up. "I cooked breakfast."

"I'm not hungry."

"Now I *am* worried," he said.

"Go away."

"Don't make me do something drastic."

I snorted. I'd just propositioned him with syrup. How much worse could things get?

He stared at me for a moment, then shrugged and left.

I closed my eyes, resting my head against the wall behind me and reveling in my victory. Sometimes you have to take what you can get.

"Yes, is Connie McMullen there?"

I heard the words plain as day. My eyes popped open. I staggered to my feet and hurtled into the kitchen. "What the hell do you think you're doing?"

Rivera glanced up casually, covered the mouthpiece with one hand, and stared at me. "You going to come and eat?"

"Don't you dare call my mother," I hissed.

"Already did."

"You're lying."

He uncovered the receiver.

"All right," I snarled, and lumbered into the kitchen.

He hung up the phone and folded his arms across his chest. It was still bare . . . and dark . . . and sexy as hell. Damn him. He'd already pulled on his jeans and they looked ridiculously pristine. My own ensemble was crinkled up like an accordion. Double damn him. I plopped into a chair and glared. "There. You happy?" I asked.

"Ecstatic," he replied, and taking the lid from the frying pan, flipped a pair of fat, golden pancakes onto my stoneware dinner plate. He placed three strawberries beside them, topped them with something that looked like honest-to-goodness real whipped cream, and sprinkled cinnamon over the top.

I glanced at it. Smelled it. Wondered why Harlequin hadn't eaten it yet.

"I'm trying to convince you there's reason to live," Rivera said.

He set a steaming measuring cup of syrup in the center of the table where a half-dozen magazines and two romance novels had reclined the night before. They were nowhere to be seen. I wondered vaguely if Rivera was a neat freak or if he just had some weird-ass aversion to eating on top of reading material. But even that thought sent a little tendril of guilt spiraling through me. A man was dead, what did I care what kind of freak Rivera was?

He pushed the butter toward me. "Everything'll be okay."

I glanced up at him. "Easy for you to say, nobody's trying to kill you."

He didn't respond, but took the chair next to me and poured syrup on my pancakes. I scowled. "Are they?"

"Not today. Do you want some cheese?"

I gave him the tilted-head look I'd learned from Harlequin.

He shrugged. "I like cheese," he said, and settled back in his chair, watching me. "I went to a lot of trouble on those cakes."

I scowled again, cut out a fluffy, golden triangle, and shoved it into my mouth. I realize that witnessing a murder should have made my taste buds go numb, but I won't lie to you: The pancakes tasted like heaven. If heaven is buttery and a little crispy around the edges.

"How have things been going at work?" he asked.

I took another bite. He poured me a glass of milk. "All right," I said, mouth full. Turns out I was hungry. But that doesn't make him smart or anything. I'll probably be hungry postmortem.

"Any interesting cases?"

I took a slurp of milk, stared at him over the rim. "Lepinski decided on smoked turkey on rye." Mr. Lepinski has been my client for over a year. His wife had recently cheated on him with the deli guy, and he was currently ignoring the situation by discussing luncheon options. It was a time-honored tradition with him.

Rivera nodded, not knowing what I was talking about and apparently not caring. "Anything else?"

I plucked a strawberry and twirled it in the white ambrosia. I'd been right, it was real whipped cream. Yummy. Sometimes reality actually *was* better than my dreams.

"What have the police found out?" I asked.

His brows lowered a fraction of an inch. "Anyone threatening you?" he returned.

And suddenly the fluffy ambrosia didn't look so appetizing. I glanced at my lap and cleared my throat. "So someone *is* trying to kill me."

"I didn't say that."

I pushed my plate aside. The cakes were nearly gone anyway. "Yes you did."

"Answer the question, Chrissy," he said. "Has anything unusual been going on at work?"

"I'm a therapist. Everything's unusual."

"You know what I mean."

"You mean you think I've pissed someone off. He tried to kill me and shot Will instead."

Rivera didn't respond.

I tilted my head, feeling dizzy. The price I pay for green magic. "Am I right?"

"I want you to think back, Chrissy. This is important. What do you know about Will Swanson?"

"I told you—"

"He wanted to see your garage. Because he was a carpenter."

"Because he had a garage fetish!" I snapped, then sighed. "Yes, because he was a—"

"With what company?"

"He worked freelance with his brother."

"Whose name was . . . ?"

I thought for a moment, remembering the way Will had smiled, sweet and kind of shy. "Hank," I said.

"So you had an appointment with him?"

"Not exactly."

The muscle in his jaw jerked. "He just showed up out of the blue?" He paused, but not long enough for me to come up with something clever. "And you let him in."

"He said he'd spoken to Mandy."

"Did he?"

"I don't know."

"So you let him in assuming he was telling the truth."

"I didn't let him in at all. I thought he was you . . . late again. I was prepared to slam the door in his face."

He gave me an evil grin. "But seeing it was him, you went skipping outside without any kind of protection."

"This isn't Baghdad, Rivera. I don't go around with an armed guard. I don't see terrorists behind every bush like some—"

"Well, maybe that's because you're so damned—" He stopped himself, stood abruptly, closed his eyes. "So he told you he was here about your garage and you followed him outside."

I wanted to hit him, but last time it had only made me feel guilty when the skin around his eye had turned a metallic magenta color. Well, a little euphoric, but mostly guilty. "He was embarrassed that he'd shown up unannounced. He'd thought Mandy would have told me. He was shy. Thoughtful. I was trying to put him at ease, so I led the way through the gate."

"Which you hadn't locked."

I was about to launch a scathing rejoinder when he raised his hand, fending off my verbal attack. "What time did he arrive?"

"Eight forty-two." My tone might have been a little sullen.

"Exactly?"

"I wanted to see how late you were."

"And he didn't come in."

"No."

"So you stood out on the stoop talking to him."

"I didn't know it was a crime," I snarled.

"Did you know it was stupid?"

"Listen—"

"Men are bastards, Chrissy," he rasped. "Haven't you figured that out yet?" He was standing very close, pressing me back.

I pursed my lips and glared up at him. "I'm doing a case study."

He stared at me, then relaxed a little and almost smiled. "Did you notice anything unusual on the way to the garage?"

"This is L.A."

He ground his teeth. Sometimes my sense of humor makes people do that.

"It was quiet," I said.

"Has there been trouble in the neighborhood? Any other shootings or—"

"No."

"Petty crimes? Maybe just a neighborhood spat?"

"No."

He exhaled carefully. "Do you know of any reason someone would have wanted this guy dead?" He looked angry again. "Think hard."

"I didn't know him."

"You never saw him before, not at the market, not in a parking lot somewhere?"

I shook my head.

"Did you ever hear the name prior to yesterday?"

I couldn't manage an answer.

"How about Elijah Kaplan?"

I swallowed. "Is that who's trying to kill me?"

He paced the limited kitchen space, propped his ungodly lean ass against my counter, and glared at me.

"Is it?" I asked.

"Elijah Kaplan died on your lawn last night."

I shook my head. "His name was—"

"Vince Horst, Wally Hendriks, Nick Walker."

"Will Swanson," I corrected, stomach tilting.

The room went silent.

"His name was Will," I repeated. "He said so."

Rivera glanced out the window toward the Al-Sadrs' lawn. It was groomed to perfection. If my lawn looked that good, I'd raze the house.

"Wasn't it?" My voice was very small.

Anger jumped in his jaw. "He grew up in Amarillo. His father was a small-time grifter. His mother had a drug problem."

"When did he move to Oshkosh?"

Rivera exhaled slowly.

"When did he live in Wisconsin?" I asked, holding on to normalcy with both hands.

"Elijah Kaplan did three years for breaking and entering." He stared at me, silent for a second, then: "And five for attempted murder. The boys in Texas think he might be a shooter."

"A—"

"A hired killer," he said.

4

A wedding is no way to begin a marriage.

—Lily Schultz, owner of the Warthog, who skipped out on her second wedding and went straight for the honeymoon

I FELT FOR A MOMENT like I was living in a vacuum. Nothing moved, nothing breathed. Will Swanson—excuse me, Elijah Kaplan—was a hired killer . . . who had been killed . . . in my yard.

Life is damned near hilarious.

The phone rang. I started, then stood up. The receiver felt blessedly solid in my hand.

"Hello?"

"Christina?"

"Yes."

"This is Holly."

"Holly . . . ?"

"Pete's girlfriend."

I wobbled into the nearest chair. "My brother Pete?"

She laughed a little. "Are you okay?"

Why did people keep asking me that? "Yeah." It was just another... What the hell day was it? What year? "Sure." I paused, waiting for my neurons to make some sort of sense of life. They failed. "Holly... how are you?"

"Fine. Good, actually. We're getting married, you know."

The neurons were scrambling now but still making no headway. "We?"

There was a pause. "Is something wrong?"

"No. You and Pete? You and Pete are..." I couldn't quite force out the words.

"June tenth. Here in Chicago. And I wanted to thank you. I mean, you're the reason I decided to go ahead with the wedding."

I winced. A guy had just been gunned down in my yard, now this. "Me?"

"I did what you suggested. You know, made some demands to see if Pete was willing to bend to get me back. And he did."

As I had heard it, she'd kicked him out of the house. Even knowing she was carrying his child, she'd slammed the door and changed the locks, which had subsequently caused him to return to the place of our births—i.e., our parents' house. Peter John, the middle of my three idiot brothers, may be a moron, but apparently he's not brain-dead enough to want to return home. I hadn't been sure until that instant.

Rivera disappeared from sight, and a moment later, Harlequin romped into the kitchen, happy as sunshine.

"Don't get me wrong," Holly said. "I'm crazy about him. I mean, he's a great guy. Funny. Easygoing."

Translation: lazy.

"But with the baby coming, I was worried he was... maybe... a little immature."

Translation: an idiot.

"A-huh," I said.

"But he's been great. Did everything I asked him to do. So I'm calling to ask if you'll be my maid of honor."

My mind went blank as a dozen images flashed through my mind. In each I was a bridesmaid. But my dress never changed. My hips looked wide enough to transport heavy equipment.

"Christina?"

I blinked.

"You sure everything's all right?" she asked.

"Listen, Holly, things are a little hectic right now." Hectic, that's what I call it when folks drop dead by my garage. When they're killed in my house, I call it messy. "I don't think I should commit to such a momentous occasion when—"

"Please." She always had a kindergarten voice, but now she almost seemed to lisp. My dim-witted brothers gravitate toward sugar-sweet women. Although I had to admit, Holly had done all right for herself. Although I didn't know a lot about her background, I knew she had a good-paying job as a legal secretary with Stock and Peterson. "Please, Christina, it wouldn't be the same without you."

"Well, I'll certainly try to be there, but—"

"Oh, thank you! Thank you! I don't have any sisters, you know. And this means so much to me."

"As I was saying—"

"Well, I have to go. I can't wait to tell Pete. Bye, now. See you soon," she said, and hung up the phone.

I did the same.

Rivera was scowling at me. "Bad news?"

"Holly's marrying Peter John."

He thought about that for a minute. "Peter John of dead-rat fame?"

Last time Pete had visited, he'd left a rodent in the freezer atop my favorite Häagen-Dazs. Rivera had seemed unsurprised by its presence. I wonder what that means.

"Dead rat, sheep droppings . . ." I paused, lost in age-old grievances. "If it's decaying, it's his friend."

"You're in the wedding?"

I gave a teetering nod. "Maid of honor."

"Isn't she just about due?"

I had told him about the impending birth of the little troglodyte-to-be, perhaps with some misgivings. I mean, as idiotic as my brothers are, they'd never been stupid enough to procreate before now.

"Wedding's next month," I said.

"Slipping under the wire."

"Hope she can limbo."

He was watching me. "Maybe this is good timing."

I still felt hazy. "If they wait any longer, the kid could be their ring-bearer."

"I mean, maybe it wouldn't be a bad idea for you to get out of L.A. for a while."

I scowled. "Get out of—"

"Listen." He toed a chair up beside mine. "I don't like you living alone. If you were at your parents' house—"

I snapped to my feet, panic brewing like Starbucks's finest. "What about my parents' house?"

"Sit down."

I tried, but sheer terror kept me rigid. "What about Mom's house?"

"Oh, for God's sake, sit down," he ordered, and yanked me down by my waistband. It was the color of pomegranates . . . and Prada. I think there's some kind of rule that one cannot be yanked around by their pomegranate Prada waistband. But maybe there's a loophole if it's already been slept in. "I'm just saying, you're going to have to go home for fittings or whatever, so maybe you should just plan to stay a while."

"I knew you were mean, Rivera, but I didn't think you were vindictive." I thought about it a moment, then, "Well, I knew you were vindictive, but I didn't think you were truly evil." Pause. "Well—"

"What the hell's wrong with you?" he asked.

I gave that some thought, mouth open.

"You could have been killed! Last night. Just like that." He snapped his fingers. I tried not to jump. Failed. "One minute you're alive, the next you're not. You think it can't happen but—"

I popped to my feet and stormed into the living room. "I think that can't happen? *I* think that can't . . ." I jerked around, cackled. "I was there, Rivera, two feet away when he died, when he was—" My voice broke.

"Then, think, God damn it!" He was standing close, eyes intense, expression madder than hell. "Why was he here?"

"To kill me?" The words hurt my throat.

His brows lowered a notch. "Who wants you dead, McMullen?"

"Nobody. Why would they? I'm a good person. Well, I'm an okay—"

"Fucking hell, woman, think!" he said, and grabbed my arms. "Who have you pissed off recently?"

I winced. "Besides you?"

For a second he almost smiled. His grip loosened the slightest degree. "Yeah," he said, "besides me."

"I didn't tip my waitress very well last weekend."

"Come on, you probably annoyed a dozen people since breakfast."

There was a noise in the kitchen.

"I think the dog ate mine," I said. "Breakfast." Another noise. "Probably yours, too." Something clattered to the floor. "Maybe the silverware."

"Who else?" he asked, and sliding his hands down my arms, took my fingers in his. "An unhappy client? A disgruntled commuter?"

His hands were warm and callused. He swept his thumb across my knuckles, reminding me that I was still alive.

"This is L.A., Rivera, if I worried about every disgruntled commuter I'd have fifteen different kinds of ulcers."

He blew out a breath. "I didn't even know there were fifteen different kinds."

"I'm practically a doctor."

He nodded. "Yeah. Smart *and* sexy," he said, and moved in closer. His chest felt hard against mine, and when he kissed me, I remembered I didn't really want to be dead. "Go to your mother's house, McMullen," he murmured.

"Not on your life." My voice sounded kind of iffy.

"If I beg?" he asked, and kissed me again, a little tongue this time. It had been—and I kid you not—seven hundred and two days since I'd shared my bed with a man. Wait. No, that's not true. It had been seven hundred and two days since I had shared my bed with a *straight* man. I sighed.

"No," I said.

"How about if I promise to sleep with you?"

That gave me pause. "You'd prostitute yourself for me?"

"I'm a giver." His dick was hard. "What do you say?"

"No," I said, but it was more difficult to make my lips function properly this time. Seems they had other things in mind.

He kissed the corner of my mouth. "I'm fantastic in the sack."

"So I've heard."

"Yeah?" He kissed my neck. "From who?"

"Whom." My breathing was getting a little shaky. "The correct pronoun is 'whom.'"

"Good thing you told me. Wouldn't want to screw up the grammar while we're screwing."

My breath stopped completely. "Are we going to . . ." I drew back a little. "You know."

He had backed me up against the living-room wall. I seemed to be straddling one of his thighs, or some other hard part of his anatomy.

"The dog's busy," he said, touching my face again, "and life's short."

I tried to nod, but there was a lump in my throat.

"You're not going to cry, are you?" he asked.

"Crying's for wimps. And hormonal teenagers."

His fingers felt warm and soothing against my face. "When I drove around the corner and saw you . . ." The muscles in his jaw jumped. ". . . on the ground . . ."

"You're not going to cry, are you?" I whispered.

"Maybe a little," he said, and placed both hands on the wall behind me, locking me in.

"That dog's not going to eat forever," I said.

He grinned, kissed me hard, and led me toward the bedroom.

Then his cell phone rang. We froze. His brows lowered.

"If it's another fiancée, I'm never sleeping with you again," I said. We have something of a history. Not much of it is good.

"After today?"

"After today."

He grinned, then reached into his pocket (I wished I had thought of that) and pulled out his phone. Flipping it open, he glanced at the screen, gritted his teeth, and held my gaze just an instant before pressing the TALK button.

"Yeah." There was a murmur from the other end, a moment's hesitation as he stared at my lips, then, "Okay," he said, and shut the phone. "They've got a witness."

"A witness?"

"Someone saw a man running down Hillrose Street about the time of the shooting."

I felt a little desperate. And kind of hormonal. And sort of like a teenager. "Won't he still be a witness after we . . . ?" I nodded toward the bedroom.

He kissed me again, pushing me back against the wall,

ravaging my mouth. My ovaries squeaked. "I don't just want a quick fuck here, McMullen," he growled.

My throat felt stretched tight. "What do you want?"

His cell rang again. Irritation ticked in his jaw. "Rest up. Get naked, then clear a week," he said, and searing my lips one more time, turned away, already snarling into his phone as he stalked off.

5

When men age they're called sophisticated. When women age they ain't called at all.

—Doris Blanchard, quick-draw and philosopher

OKAY, I'LL ADMIT IT; my body wanted sex . . . long, hard, ludicrous, weeklong sex. But my mind . . . What did *I* want? Shouldn't I want more? Shouldn't I *demand* more? Intimacy. Honesty. Security.

From Rivera?

The idea was almost laughable. The dark lieutenant was one bone-through-the-nose short of being a club-carrying Neanderthal. And yet, sometimes I couldn't help but wonder what it would be like to watch him sleep beside me at night. To wake up with him on Sunday morning. To discuss politics and history and why small dogs make twice as much noise as big dogs.

It was stupid, of course. Because Rivera wasn't that

kind of guy. I'd known it even before he'd made my endocrine system sizzle, had seen it on his face a hundred times. The most I could hope for from him was a seven-day orgy.

Holy shit.

I thought about that and squirmed on the Porsche's leather seat as I merged onto the 2, heading south. I hadn't planned on going to work, but as it turned out, the Magnificent Mandy hadn't actually canceled all my appointments. In fact, she'd only called one client before becoming distracted, possibly by a laser pen or a ball of string.

Micky Goldenstone was a couple of minutes late when he stepped into my office nearly an hour later. I'd been counseling him for fewer than six months, and I admit that the first time I saw him I was a little taken aback. He stood just over five-nine in his Nikes, was as black as an eight ball, with short cropped hair and eyes that spoke of a darkness I could only just imagine. Upon first impression, I thought he might be one of the Hell's Angels' brightest, but as it turned out, he taught fifth grade at Plainview Elementary in Tujunga.

It had taken me two weeks to learn he had also been a prison guard at Folsom. It had taken me eight to find out he'd been neglected by his mother and abused by her boyfriend. He'd left D.C. long ago and had kept the past hidden away for most of a lifetime. There's some sort of ungodly guilt associated with domestic abuse. Some kind of guilt that is harder than hell to purge. He had seen a psychiatrist in the past, but only for a short time, maybe because he hadn't been ready.

But he seemed ready now. In fact, we had become

friends of sorts. He'd even offered to slip me cigarettes if I was ever a guest of the California penal system. Apparently, he had some clout. The way things were going, it was good to know, but today he seemed a little tense, a little sad. I prodded gently.

"How is work going? Last time we spoke you indicated you were concerned about anger issues where your students were concerned."

He sighed. Leaned back against the couch cushions. "Fifth-graders." He looked introspective, inhaled deeply, flaring his nostrils. "Makes me wonder why Grams let me live past middle school."

The way he'd explained it, Grams was the reason he *had* survived. She'd taken him in after his mother had overdosed for the third time. Taken him despite a myriad of protests, governmental and familial. "Do you have reason to believe she resented your presence in her life?"

He stared at me a moment, then laughed, but the sound was coarse. He glanced out the window. "I threatened her with a switchblade once. Did I tell you that?"

I didn't answer. It wasn't unusual for him to leap right into the fray, to slap my sensibilities aside and leave me mentally gasping.

"I wanted to shoot hoops with the boys . . ." He paused. " 'The hoodlums,' as she called them." A glimmer of a smile appeared. I watched. He looked a little like Don Cheadle to me, but had a dark, damaged demeanor I couldn't quite explain or condone.

"*Were* they hoodlums?"

"We were all hoodlums. Hoodlums or worse." There

was sorrow again in his soul-tortured eyes. Another careful breath. "They called me 'Pit Bull.' Or 'Bull.' "

"They?"

He looked as if he hadn't heard me. "Shi's dead now. Terrence is doing life. And Cole . . . Haven't heard from him in years. Could be he made it," he said, but he shook his head, doubting.

"You still wanted to be with them, though."

"They were my niggers. My dogs. They got me."

"What did they get that your grandmother didn't?"

He caught me with his eyes, panther black, startling in their intensity. "That I was damned. Worthless. Like the fuckin' . . ." He jerked to his feet, paced, angry and quick.

I gave him a moment, then: "So your grandmother didn't think you were worthless."

"She fed me spinach. Slimy shit from a can. Said it'd make me strong. Kept praying for me. Always praying till I wanted to . . ." His hands were curled around nothing. "So I pulled a knife. When I was fourteen. Said I was running my own life from there on out and there wasn't nothing she could do about it."

"Were you right?"

He glanced at me, cords pulled tight in his throat.

"Was there nothing she could do about it?"

He watched me for several seconds, then laughed a little. "The woman was built like a nose tackle. Backhanded me so hard I couldn't walk straight for a week. Took my knife. You got any idea how embarrassing it is to tell your gang your grandmother took your blade?"

I steepled my fingers and tried to imagine the terror and guilt of his childhood, but I couldn't. By comparison, my own background looked pristine, a glittering mirage of normalcy.

"Cole laughed at me. Called me a pussy." He lowered his head, laughter eerily gone, looking past his brows, eyes gleaming with an emotion I couldn't quite read. My breath clogged in my throat. "I coulda beat the shit outta him. But it wouldn't a mattered." He was slipping into a different dialect, a different place in his mind. "Made 'im pay, though." His tone was throaty now, chilling the back of my neck, lifting the hair on my forearms, making it difficult to speak.

"How so?"

"He had him a sister." The words were almost whispered. "Twelve, maybe thirteen." He paused.

I was gripping the arms of my chair and forced myself to ease up a little.

"Met up with her in the alley between a crack house and the porn shop. She was with her friends. Her peeps. But she had a thing for me. I knowed it. Even then I knowed it. Told them to go on ahead."

I was holding my breath.

"Biggest fuckin' eyes I ever seen. Flirted with me like a..." He closed his eyes, swallowed, seemed to come back to himself. "She begged me not to." His fists tightened, loosened. He wouldn't look at me. "But I was a man. Had to prove myself."

Oh God.

"Afterward..." His face was drained of emotion. "She never cried. Never..." He cleared his throat. "There was talk... later... that she got an abortion."

At thirteen. I felt like barfing. "Did Cole know?"

He drew a careful breath, lifted his chin slightly, found

my gaze. "She never told. And I was too much of a . . ." He glanced toward the door. "I told myself it would just cause trouble if her brother found out. I felt bad. And that was enough, wasn't it? Guilt." Anger flared in his eyes. "I prayed for forgiveness, just like Grams taught me."

"But you don't believe you're forgiven."

"I'm not," he said, and I knew what he meant.

"How about the girl?"

"Kaneasha." His voice was soft, mourning. I braced myself, fearing the worst. "She left. Went to live with her aunt."

"You haven't spoken to her?"

He tensed as if waiting for a blow. As if almost welcoming it. "Should I?"

"Do you think you could be forgiven?" I asked.

"I raped her." He said the words through his teeth. "A child. A kid with eyes so big they could swallow you whole." He turned toward me, his own eyes haunted, pleading. "Would you forgive?"

No. "I meant *you*," I said. "If you spoke to her, do you think maybe you could forgive yourself?"

It was nearly two hours later that I stood up to retreat for lunch. But the doorbell rang again. I could hear Mandy's hushed voice and then my intercom line lit up. I'd never been more proud than the day she'd figured out how to use it.

"Yes," I said, using the professional tone I keep for such occasions.

"Yeah, Chrissy." She sounded a little breathless. "There's

a guy here wants to see you. Got a face like one of them poet fellows and an ass like a frickin'—"

I rubbed my forehead rhythmically. "He can hear you."

"What?"

I felt old and pretty damn tired. "You know he can hear you, don't you?"

There was a moment of silence, then, "Even if I'm talking on the intercom?"

I sat back and thought for a moment. "I miss Elaine," I said.

She sighed. "Yeah, she seemed like a good egg. You want I should send this guy in?"

"That would probably be best."

I'm not sure whom I was expecting, but when the door opened I was surprised and temporarily uncertain.

"Mr. Manderos?" I asked. I know my hesitation seems strange, especially since he's one of the guys about whom I habitually fantasize, but Julio Manderos bears an unnerving resemblance to Senator Rivera, Lieutenant Rivera's father. In fact, he's been known to impersonate the good senator, but only at the other's request . . . at least as far as I know.

"Christina . . ." He was dressed well but casually and carried a leather satchel in his left hand. Setting it aside, he reached for my fingers and kissed my knuckles. His eyes were as dark and sexy as Belgian chocolate. "It makes me glad to see you."

The touch of his hand against mine was strangely erotic, dredging up feelings still simmering from hours before. And even though he was doing nothing more scandalous than holding my fingers, he was doing it with Latino intensity.

Maybe it was that intensity that had helped him survive his early years in a backwater town in Mexico. He had, in his fifty-some years, been an orphan, a stripper, a businessman, and . . . well, the gigolo I mentioned earlier.

We had met under rather unorthodox circumstances. Circumstances during which I had learned he had occasionally doubled as Rivera's politically affluent father. By the time I realized there was a possibility that Manderos was also a murderer, I had gazed into his Puss 'n Boots eyes and heard his childhood story. Hence, I had kept his involvement to myself and seemingly gained his undying devotion. A devotion the junior Rivera didn't particularly appreciate. But Rivera and I weren't exactly picking out china patterns and I doubted we'd find time during that brain-melting week he'd mentioned.

I cleared my throat and remembered to take back my hand. "It's good to see you, too. Please, sit down," I said, and waved the still tingling digits in the general direction of the couch.

He sat with an easy, masculine grace. His camel-colored dress pants sported a crease down the exact center of each leg. They were cuffed, accented with smooth leather loafers, and topped with a lime green dress shirt of some wrinkle-free fabric that looked moleskin soft. On another man the ensemble might have seemed effeminate. On him it looked good enough to snack on. Or maybe that was just my celibacy stretching behind me like a sex-deprived haze.

"Christina . . ." He watched me for a moment. I watched him back, reminding myself of several things. One: He'd been known to charge money for sex. Two: He was closely connected to Miguel Rivera, whom the younger Rivera detested. Three: He was old enough to be my father.

But technically, so is Pierce Brosnan. Makes you think, doesn't it?

"You are doing well?" Julio asked.

"Yes. Certainly," I said, but he was still watching me with those ever-earnest eyes.

"Something is wrong."

"No," I said, but I remembered the dead guy on my sidewalk and may have cringed a little.

"What is it?" he asked, leaning forward.

"Nothing." I picked off some imaginary lint from my ivory slacks. "So how are *you* doing?"

He sat back a little. "I am well," he said.

"Business is thriving?"

He owned a place called the Strip Please, where fantastically good-looking men with slicked-up muscles and million dollar smiles took off their clothes to music. If I owned the Strip Please I would be well, too.

"There has been trouble," he said.

"What kind of trouble?" I asked, and hoped to hell he wasn't expecting help from me. But why else would he have come?

"I mean to say . . ." His voice was slow and melodious, his smile tender enough to make me want to cry. ". . . there is trouble with you. I can see it in your eyes. Little matter how you try to hide it."

"Oh." I cleared my throat again, played with a snap on my tailored black blouse, and failed to meet his gaze. "Well, okay, yes, there's been a little . . ." Will's sightless eyes stared at me from my memories. Who had he been and why had he pursued me? "... maybe a little bit of trouble," I admitted, glancing up.

Manderos had the smooth, tan features of an Aztec warrior, with all the cares and hardships of his people laid across his capable shoulders.

"What is it?" he asked, and sliding off the couch, knelt by my feet to take my hand. "What is it that troubles you?"

I felt my tears well up at the feel of skin against skin, and though I tried to be tough, the words slipped out. "I met a man yesterday." I swallowed, trying to be all grown up. "He seemed really nice."

"Good. That is good." He stroked my knuckles. "You deserve nice, Christina. Indeed, I believe—"

"I think he might have been planning to kill me."

The stroking stopped. His brows lowered. "I do not understand."

I shook my head, thinking. "Me, either."

"Surely no one would wish you harm."

I laughed. There was a little hiccup at the end.

"Except Mr. Peachtree," he amended.

Robert Peachtree had been a friend of Senator Miguel Rivera. He'd tried to kill me with a poker. Actually, he'd tried to kill me by several different, and rather ingenious, methods. I cleared my throat and refrained from telling Julio about others who had been similarly inclined. "They think he might have been a hit man."

He canted his head a little. "They?"

"Rivera. Lieutenant Rivera."

He thought about that for a second. "And you think this man meant to..." He shook his head. "... to kill you?"

I shrugged. "I don't know. I'll probably never know. Because he's dead."

Manderos's eyes went wide. "Not the lieutenant."

"No. The hit man. Someone shot him by my garage."

For a moment there was absolute astonishment on Julio's face, but I was still kind of surprised, too.

"Dios mio!"

I nodded, having no idea what he'd said. The King's English is almost more than I can handle.

"You have suffered a great shock. Yet you are here at work, laboring to help those who are troubled."

"Yeah, well . . ." I sniffled a little. ". . . they'd probably do better just watching Dr. Phil."

He smiled gently. "I was correct," he said, "you are the most brave of women."

I remembered myself sniveling and cursing and crying as I crawled on bloody knees toward the house after the shooting.

"I hate to argue," I said, "but I think you might be wrong."

"One moment, please," he said. Rising to his feet, he stepped into the hall and closed the door behind him. But in a moment he was back.

"Christina," he said, gazing at me. "You must not be here this day.

"I—" I began, but he raised a peaceful hand.

"It is good for neither you nor your patients. I spoke with your Ms. Amanda. She has agreed to reschedule everything. I shall take you to dine, then see you safely home."

"I can't," I said. Partly because he was right, I was in no condition to see anyone, including him. But mostly because there was just a shitload of baggage tied up with this guy, and jumping his bones wasn't going to simplify matters. Not that I would do any such thing, of course. I mean, I'm a classy, well-educated woman with a Ph.D. and everything, but sometimes, when guys kiss me, then die on my property with a bullet in their brains, I feel a little needy.

"Christina . . ." Julio held me with his eyes. ". . . you are a strong, capable woman, yes. But even so, you must care for yourself. Eat . . ."

"I eat enough."

"Please don't tell me you think yourself too plump."

"Okay."

He smiled and took my hand. "You are a beautiful woman."

I felt my defenses topple like trailer houses in a windstorm. "That's what Will said."

He studied my face with solemn, sympathetic eyes. "The man who died."

I cleared my throat and glanced out my window toward Sunset Coffee. My hand trembled a little in his. "Yes."

"Amanda." He barely said the name above a whisper, but my secretary popped in as if on springs.

"Yeah?"

"I will be taking Ms. McMullen home. Notate any messages she receives but do not call her. She needs some time for rest and meditation. Do you understand?"

"Sure."

If she did it would be the first time, I thought, but somehow I didn't care, and let Julio lead me out of my office.

"If you like, I can drive your automobile so that you need not bother retrieving it," he said.

"Okay," I said, and numbly pointed to the Porsche. For one crackling, paranoid moment, I considered insisting on driving, but taking a nap on the express lane seemed safer in my present condition, so I handed over my keys.

"A handsome automobile," he said.

"It's a friend's." I got in. He did the same, put his satchel between us, and started the engine. I dropped my head against the cushion as he pulled smoothly out of the parking lot. But in a moment, a realization struck me; he hadn't asked for directions. I jerked upright. "How do you know where I live?"

He scowled, eyes concerned. "What?"

"How do you know how to get to my house?"

"I fear there has been a misunderstanding. I meant to take you to my home."

"Your house! Your— No!" My heart was humping like an unneutered poodle. Yeah, sure, a minute ago I was afraid I wouldn't be able to keep my pants on if he gave me a glance from the corner of his Latino eyes, but now I was pretty sure he was going to kill me. Eventually most people give it a shot. I don't know why.

"Christina, there is no need for you to fear me," he said, and reached across the seat. Maybe he meant to reassure me, but in that second his bag toppled toward me, spilling a gun into my lap.

If you don't scare the neighbors while copulating, I'm afraid you're doing something terribly wrong.

—*Eddie Friar, Chrissy's favorite gay ex-boyfriend*

"HOLY CRAP!" I SAID, and plastered myself against the passenger door.

Reaching out, Julio retrieved the gun, then wheeled to the right and brought the Porsche to an abrupt halt.

But all I could think of was the weapon. It looked cold and black and deadly in his ultra-steady hand. Our eyes clashed.

"I am sorry, Christina. Truly I am," he said.

I could barely breathe, but my mind was scrambling in circles, trying to make sense of things. To understand why. "Sorry for what?" My voice was breathy. His gaze held mine, firm and steady, just like his hand on the pistol.

"For frightening you," he said, and after a moment, wrapped his fingers around the muzzle and handed it to me.

I scrunched more firmly against the door. "What are you doing?"

"Christina . . ." His tone was melodious, his eyes sad, but he could have been Mother Teresa and my heart would have still been thundering along like a runaway freight train. "You have been good to me. Kind when you could have caused me grave trouble. You are brave and noble. I may not possess a bold soul such as your own, but I do not harm my friends." Picking up my hand, he pressed the pistol into it. The metal was cool, smooth, and heavy. I swallowed, as afraid of the weapon as I had been of him only moments before. "Do you know how to use it?"

I shook my head.

"It is not complicated. One does not need a fine education to take a life."

"Uh-huh. What the hell am I doing with this gun?"

"You are protecting yourself."

"From . . . ?"

"Me. And every man who might wish to take advantage of a beautiful woman. Do you feel safe traveling to my house with me now?"

I blinked, but the gun remained, real and heavy and earnest. "Maybe . . ." I swallowed and tried not to pee in my pants. ". . . maybe I should just go home."

He stared at me for a second, then nodded solemnly and shifted back into drive. "How shall I get there?"

He didn't know my address after all. I thought that was refreshing and kind of a good sign. I believe everyone who'd tried to kill me thus far had had my address locked into their GPS systems.

I told him the directions, then stared down at the gun, turning it in my hand. "What kind is it?" It seemed like it should say on the product, like Doritos or Virginia Slims or other things that are likely to kill you.

"It is a Glock."

"Is that good?"

He shrugged. "It will discharge a bullet. That is very nearly all I know. That and the fact that you must have protection."

"Why do you think that is?"

He glanced at me, eyes fuck-me sober. "So that you remain safe."

"I mean . . ." I pried my gaze from his, feeling a little bit sorry for myself. People kept trying to kill me, and I still couldn't have sex with this guy. "Why me? Why do you think these things keep happening to me?"

He thought about that for a moment. Maybe he was afraid that if he gave the wrong answer I might toss myself out of the car, but it was unlikely. The gun looked so much more expedient.

"I believe it is because you are too good," he said finally.

Here was a theory I hadn't previously considered.

"You spend your days helping those who are deeply troubled. Do you not think it likely that these same troubles would come to rest on your own weary head now and again?"

I blinked, then thought about his theory as we rolled along the 210. Maybe the interstate was as hair-tearingly horrible as usual, but I didn't notice. "David Hawkins was my mentor," I said. "And my friend. I trusted him. Told him things. . . ." My voice faded off. I pointed to my exit. He took it without question.

"I do not know this David Hawkins."

"He was—*is* . . ." I cleared my throat, then gave him a few directions, until he finally pulled the Porsche onto the side of the little street I called home. ". . . a world renowned psychiatrist. And the first man who tried to kill me."

He stared at me an instant, then got out of the car and came around to my side. Pulling open my door, he reached for my hand.

"Come," he said. "We shall speak of these things inside." Perhaps I hesitated a moment, because he added, "You may bring the gun."

Harlequin met us at the door, bounding and panting. He seemed to have gotten over Swanson's untimely death pretty well. Julio stroked the dog's ears and said something sexy in Spanish. Harlequin grinned like a clown. Better him than me.

"I did not know you had a dog."

I nodded numbly. "Can I get you something to drink?"

"No," he said, and taking my arm led me firmly into the family room. Turning me at the couch, he pushed me gently down. "Today, you think of none but yourself. Consider me your servant," he said, and raised his arms slightly. "What is your command?"

I stared at the width of his shoulders, his lover's eyes, and cleared my throat.

"You must be hungry," he said.

"A little," I admitted, and set the gun on the cushion beside me.

"Good. Unfortunately, I am a terrible cook. I am not so bad at the ordering, however."

I kept my gaze firmly on his. I wasn't some oversexed, tuba-playing, cocktail waitress. "A valuable skill."

"I think I will place a call to Melisse if that is satisfactory to you. Then I shall mix you a drink."

I gave him the okay and told him where to find my unspectacular liquor cabinet. He turned away. The view was very nice from behind.

In a few minutes, he returned. The view wasn't bad in that direction, either, especially now that I knew he wasn't going to shoot me. I took the drink he offered. It was amber-colored.

"What is it?"

"Taste it."

I did. As you know, I can't even hold my Nyquil, so I generally avoid liquor, but this was good stuff. Sweet and rich and strangely satisfying. "How'd you make it?"

He shrugged and sat beside me on the couch. "I am good at only a few things. That is one of them."

I drank again, impressed. "What are the others?"

He smiled.

"Oh," I said, and he laughed. The sound was rich and sexy, a bit like the drink.

"Put your feet here." He patted his thigh. "And I will show you."

"I don't think—"

"Christina, please, let me pamper you this once," he said, and stared at me with those sexy, soulful eyes.

I turned slowly about and settled my feet cautiously onto the couch.

"Perhaps I should tell you—" I began, but in that moment he took my left foot in his hands. Now, here's the thing, I'm an American. A Midwesterner by birth, in fact, and Midwesterners don't touch except to copulate and give purple nerples. Hell, they barely talk. So the feel of his hands against my arch was shocking. His smile, on the other hand, was just short of celestial, and when he pressed his thumb up the middle of my sole, I felt myself go into a full-body swoon.

"What were you about to say?" he asked, and massaged again.

"Ummm. Oh, yes." I'm sure I wasn't panting. Damn noisy dog. "Rivera and I . . . *Jack* Rivera . . . we're—"

He massaged my little toe. Holy fuck, who knew the little piglet was the center of all things erotic? "You are what?"

My neck had gone rubbery and my mind was about to follow suit.

"We're . . . friends."

He smiled and moved on to the next toe. Lightning zinged straight from my digit to every sex organ in my body. "It is good to have friends."

"Of course, that doesn't mean that *we* can't be . . ." He pressed his thumb slowly up my sole again. I stifled a moan. "Friends," I added.

"That is good, Christina, for I wish to make you happy." His thigh felt hard beneath my heel. It made me wonder about other parts of his anatomy. "I believe you will enjoy the lobster."

"The . . ." My gaze zipped nervously to his crotch.

"Melisse is renowned for its bolognese."

"Oh." I snapped my hot attention back to his eyes. "The . . . the . . . restaurant."

"Yes."

I couldn't decide if he looked amused or bemused.

I nodded spastically and took a drink. "Where . . . ummm . . . where is this Melisse exactly?"

"On Wilshire. In Santa Monica."

I stared. "Are you kidding? That's half a state from here."

He laughed. "I have friends, too, Christina."

"Did you give them foot massages or something?"

He laughed. "Or something," he said, and sobered. "Tell me of this David Hawkins."

I scowled. I was just beginning to relax and didn't want to think about anything but the sunshiny feel of his hands against my skin. Besides, it was kind of embarrassing to admit that the man who'd been my hero was now doing life in a California state pen.

"It may help you to talk about it," he said.

I scowled, drank, took a deep breath. "David helped me out when I first arrived in L.A."

"Arrived from where?" he asked, and flexed my toes with the palm of his hand. I let my eyes drift closed for a second.

"Chicago. That's where I grew up."

"I bet you were a beautiful child."

"You kidding?" Was my diction slipping a little? "They barely made a tuba big enough for me."

He smiled. "Well, you are just the right size now."

"For a tuba?"

He laughed. "For a man."

I felt myself blush down to my freshly massaged toes.

"I did not mean to embarrass you, Christina," he said, watching me. "Tell me more of your childhood."

I considered refusing, even thought about pulling my feet from his lap, but just then he slipped his hand under my pant leg and massaged my calf. I thanked God I had shaved just that morning.

Happy feelings shimmied up my leg to my groin. I stifled a moan.

"Do you have siblings?" he asked.

"Not unless you count brothers," I said.

"Boys can be cruel," he said, voice soft.

I shrugged.

"So this is why you became a therapist."

"Cocktail waitresses are on their feet too much."

"And such lovely feet they are," he said, sketching a circle in my sole. "You are tense, Christina. You should hire a masseuse to help you relax."

"Yeah? What do you charge?"

He had a laugh sexy enough to make a lesser woman cry. I just sniffled a little and felt my inhibitions waver.

"For you it is free," he said.

Good God, he was pretty.

I cleared my throat. "And what if I wanted more?"

He frowned, stared at me, absolutely still. "I beg your pardon?"

Holy shit! I'd read him entirely wrong. "I'll have more," I sputtered, and lifted my empty glass, covering for my smutty mouth. If I had still been thinking, I would have crawled under the couch at that point, but I'm pretty much toast after one drink. Add a foot massage and you might just as well use me for plant food. "If . . . if you don't mind."

"Of course not." He set my legs carefully aside, rose to

his feet, and took my glass with a slight bow. "It is an honor to service you."

My mouth dropped open, but he had already turned away. Oh, crap! Service me? Service . . .

But he had returned before I could figure out if "service" meant the same thing in his native language that it meant in mine.

I took the new drink and considered dumping it into my lap. "Thank you." He sat back down and pulled my feet onto his thigh once again. "Is this your specialty . . ."

He slid his hand up my shin, massaging gently. I barely retained consciousness.

". . . drink?" I finished, flushed and stupid and so damned horny I thought I might burst into spontaneous flames.

"Specially for you," he said.

Was he trying to seduce me? I wondered hazily. But that was ridiculous. If he'd been trying, he'd already be calling a cab and I'd be lighting up a cigarette.

"So you . . . just guessed what I would like?" I asked.

"I understand women quite well, Christina. It is my job."

I remembered back to the first time I'd met him. He had had close ties to Salina Martinez, Rivera's ex-fiancée. *Really* close ties, maybe literally. "How well do you know men?"

He shook his head and kneaded my arch. I held the orgasm at bay. "Men are animals."

"Yeah." I nodded. "But why do you suppose they keep trying to kill me?"

His expression was sad as he smoothed his hand up my

heel and along my ankle. Yikes. "How are you certain that this Will Swanson wanted you dead?"

"He was a hired killer. Rivera said so."

"But is there any reason to believe he wished to kill *you*?"

"He was here."

"As am I?"

Was that a warning? A come-on? A threat? The gun felt hard and cool against my thigh. "He didn't give me a foot massage," I said.

His smile was slow and sweet. "Maybe he hoped to."

I blinked.

"I said men are animals, Christina," he said. "Not all animals kill. But they all survive on their instincts."

Should it worry me that a male stripper/prostitute was stretching my philosophical sensibilities? "What?"

"Perhaps . . ." He rolled my calf between both his palms. ". . . perhaps this Will Swanson wanted nothing more than to spend a bit of time with a beautiful woman."

"Beautiful— Oh." I forced my gaze from his dark, magical hands. "You mean me."

He laughed and slid closer, pulling my legs across his lap. My knee bumped his chest. My heart did a funny little flopping motion. His lips were mere inches from mine, but just then my front door opened and Lieutenant Jack Rivera stalked into view.

7

Apparently it takes, like, forty-seven muscles to frown. Flippin' the bird's a hell of a lot easier.

—*Amanda May Newton,*
aka the Magnificent Mandy

"DON'T YOU EVER LOCK your damn—" Rivera's words jerked to a halt.

I'm not sure why I felt the need to snap my legs off Mr. Manderos's lap. It wasn't as if I was doing anything wrong. Nevertheless, I yanked away like a puppet on crack.

"Rivera!" I said. My voice sounded kind of sandpapery. I cleared my throat, reprimanded myself for my childish demeanor, and tried again, setting my feet primly on the floor and smoothing my slacks around my thighs. Classy as hell. "Rivera," I said, tone sophisticated, mind screaming bloody hell, "you remember Mr. Manderos."

The lieutenant remained silent. Something ticked in his jaw as he shifted his dynamite glare from Julio to me.

I cleared my throat again, then cursed myself for the weak-assed gesture. Rivera had no claim on me, hadn't even said he *wanted* a claim.

Julio rose to his feet with a dancer's grace and extended his hand, Spanish gaze earnest and level. "I have not had the pleasure of making your acquaintance," he said, "but I would know the good senator's son by reputation alone."

For a moment I thought Rivera might drop the flimsy veneer of propriety and pop him in the face just for spite, but he took a step forward and shook the other's hand, almost as if he were civilized. "You own the strip club," he said. There was a buttload of feeling in that statement, but I wasn't sure exactly how to interpret it.

"*Sí,*" Julio said. "The Strip Please. And you are a lieutenant for the Los Angeles Police Department. Your father is very proud."

The corner of Rivera's mouth jerked, then, "Impersonating the senator doesn't mean you know him, I see," he said.

The two measured each other in silence. There was an odd history between them even though they'd never met. As I've said, Julio had, on occasion, spent time with Rivera's ex-fiancée, who was, for a spell, Rivera's father's *current* fiancée.

This is L.A. We couldn't recognize normal if it bit us on the ass. But then, why would normal bite you on the ass? Unless . . . Shit, was I drunk?

"You are correct," Julio said. "I am being . . . pretentious. I do not know your father well."

Rivera was still scowling. No surprise there.

"And yet I am certain he has great pride in you." Julio nodded once, eyes narrowed. "Though he may not know how best to show it. It is the same with many great men."

Rivera puffed an almost silent snort. "You think my father's great?"

Julio was silent for a moment, studying him, then: "He has been that and more to me, Lieutenant. But in truth . . ." He canted his head, thinking. ". . . I was speaking of you."

A flicker of uncertainty raced across Rivera's hard-ass features. I soaked it in. Rivera is rarely uncertain. He's often wrong. But he's usually emphatically wrong.

"I didn't see a car outside," he said finally. "You take a cab here, Manderos?"

I tensed, but Julio didn't seem the least concerned. Maybe he spent every day giving women foot rubs and nobody had taken umbrage so far. Maybe he'd never met a man like Rivera, who took umbrage at sunshine.

"No. I felt Christina should not drive, thus I took the liberty of escorting her home."

I could feel my pulse beating in my left eyeball. I could *see* Rivera's in his.

"From where?" he asked.

"I stopped at her office. She seemed . . . distraught. Thus I thought it best that she have some time to relax rather than seeing to others' problems."

There was a two-beat silence, during which I fortified my defenses before Rivera inevitably turned on me. "You went to work?" he asked finally.

"I do serious work at my office, Lieutenant Rivera," I said. It was sort of a preemptive excuse.

"Yeah?" His tone was stiff. "Lepinski still can't decide about luncheon options?"

"Listen—" I said, but Julio interrupted.

"She is a very brave woman, Lieutenant."

Rivera shifted his thunderbolt gaze back to his father's look-alike. Gone was that moment of tender anger. Now all-out rage flashed across his features. "Are you aware that someone tried to kill her last night, Manderos?"

Julio hesitated an instant, then, "I was told that a man named Will died while visiting her."

"Shot between the eyes," Rivera said, "while, or shortly after, she was standing directly in front of him."

Julio shook his head, his expression troubled. "This is a terrible thing indeed, but surely no one would wish our Christina harm."

Rivera snarled a smile. "Hit men are funny."

Manderos considered that a moment, then shook his head. "I do not believe that was his intent."

"Really?" The lieutenant's eyes were narrow. "Maybe you were a friend of Mr. Swanson's?"

If Julio was getting tired of Rivera's shitty attitude, he didn't show it. "No, I knew no one by that name, but look at her," he said. His tone almost seemed reverent. "Is she not beauty itself?"

My gaze skipped from one to the other. Julio's eyes were soft and earnest. Rivera's looked like they could scorch your shorts. "What the hell are you getting at?" he asked, shifting his glare to Julio.

Manderos shook his head sadly. "Surely you have not walked so long amidst evil that you cannot think of an innocent reason a man might wish to spend an evening with a lady of Christina's caliber."

Rivera turned his black eyes back toward me. His nostrils actually flared. I considered scrambling over the coffee table and out the front door like a shrieking virgin. "Nothing too innocent," he said, then looked back at Julio, expression closed, eyes flinty. "Where were *you* last night, Manderos?"

For a moment Julio's eyes widened, and then he smiled the smallest degree. "I was in the company of a friend, Lieutenant."

"A friend who'll corroborate your story?"

Julio paused, sighed. "A friend who is married."

Rivera took a step forward. "So you have no alibi. Tell me, what made you decide to visit Ms. McMullen's office this afternoon?"

"I wished to make certain all was well."

"Why today? Do you stop by often?" He was starting to crowd.

"I fear my duties at the club keep me too busy to do as much socializing as I would—"

"Then why did you—"

"Oh, for God's sake," I said, and stepped between the two. I should have done it sooner, but all this talk about beauty and innocence and the dark looks and the flared nostrils had pretty much unhinged my jaw. Still, enough was enough. "Julio . . ." I turned toward him, showing Rivera my back. ". . . thank you for bringing me home."

His eyes were gleaming, but with anger or humor or some other emotion, I couldn't tell. "It was an honor, Ms. Christina," he said, and lifting my hand, kissed my knuckles with slow deliberation. His lips felt firm and shivery hot against my skin. "You will call me if ever you are in need, will you not?"

I cleared my throat and refrained from giggling like a nervous majorette. "Certainly."

He nodded and turned toward the door. I followed him.

"Wait. You don't have your car," I said, but he smiled and turned in my mini-vestibule.

"I've no wish to intrude on your day any longer." He glanced at Rivera. I could only imagine the lieutenant didn't look any happier than he had during the first few months of our acquaintance. "I believe the two of you have much to discuss. There is a bus stop just around the corner. I have not been so long from my humble roots that I do not remember the value of public transport."

He kissed my cheek. I didn't turn to see Rivera's reaction.

"I'm sorry," I said instead, but Julio laughed and leaned close, lips nearly touching my ear.

"You need not apologize for a man in love," he said quietly, and bidding Rivera adieu, stepped onto my stoop and shut the door.

I gaped after him. A man in . . . What?

"What the hell's wrong with you?" Rivera snarled.

I turned on him in a haze. *A man in . . . where?*

"Fuck it! Why don't you just put a gun to your damn head?"

I felt a little dizzy. "What are you talking about?"

"Shit!" He paced, jaw flexing. "He come to check out your garage, too?"

My brain shifted, ground gears, started spinning. "He's a friend."

"A friend!" He barked a laugh, jabbed a finger toward the door. "He's a fucking gigolo."

I felt my temper start to fume. "What other kind would there be?"

"You so desperate you're willing to pay for it now, McMullen?"

I stopped the words about to spill from my mouth and took a cleansing breath. "Why are you here?"

"Why the hell was *he* here?"

"I told you. He's a—"

"He's a damn murder suspect!"

My hands went numb. "What?"

He glared at me. "He was at Salina's house the night she died."

I blinked, paused. Feeling was already tinkling back to my extremities. "So were you. So was I, for that matter."

He held my gaze for another second, then jerked it away, pacing again. "He's a damn whore," he said, but he sounded sullen now, seething.

"He's a—"

"And my old man's gopher," he snarled. I couldn't tell which term he found more distasteful.

"What does that have to do with—"

"What was he doing here? What does he want? Maybe the good senator *was* innocent of Salina's death, but that doesn't mean you're safe from him."

"What the hell are you talking about?"

"Murder!" he growled, and stormed across the room toward me. "Death. Stupid-ass gigolos who think my father's a fucking saint. Why was he here?"

"Is it so hard to believe a man would be interested in me just for me?"

"Damn right, it is," he growled. "You know things. About my father. The real him. The shitty him."

I felt strangely relaxed now, cool under fire. "So you think Julio Manderos came to my business, gave me a ride home, fixed me a drink, and planned to kill me so that I wouldn't reveal the fact that he has doubled as your father."

Rivera shifted his gaze away and back. "It's possible."

"Really?"

He fisted his hands and gritted his teeth, steadying himself. "Maybe you think his eyes are too fucking soulful for him to be dangerous."

"You noticed."

Control was seeping in by careful measures. "Oh, yeah. He's dreamy."

"Isn't he just?"

"So tell me, McMullen, do you become fast friends with everyone who gives you a foot massage, or is it just men who look like my old man?"

"He's not as old as—" I began, but stopped abruptly. "How the hell did you know about the massage?"

The room went silent, his jaw flexed. "It looked like he'd found your G spot. I assumed it was a massage. You want to enlighten me?"

I searched for one of those witty zingers I had contemplated moments before and snatched up the best one. "You're an idiot," I said.

The doorbell rang simultaneously. I jerked. "Who's that?"

"Could be Charles Manson," Rivera said. "Should I let him in?"

I gave him a glare and headed for the vestibule, but not too fast. With my luck, Manson would have been a pleasant surprise. "Who is it?" I called.

"Sophie," came the response.

The voice was trilling and feminine with a lilting foreign accent, but my pulse was still racing. Just because no woman had tried to kill me lately didn't mean one wouldn't soon. Maybe it just meant that my good luck was coming to a screaming halt.

Rivera eased up beside me, nudged me away from the door. Maybe I let him do so because I'm a perfectly secure woman with a Ph.D. and a mortgage, but maybe I was scared out of my mind. He opened the door. The woman on the other side was French—pretty, long hair blue-black and caught up at the back of her head, dark eyes expressive enough to make a weaker woman cry. Curvy enough to make anyone cry.

"Can I help you?" Rivera's voice had softened toward human. What kind of freaky magic do these foreign women possess anyway? Besides the curves. And the hair. And the damn accent. I'm going to get me an accent.

"Yes. I hope so." She gave him a smile from full, recently glossed lips. She wore a white blouse with a little ruffle down the front, and a red knit skirt secured around a ridiculously small waist with a fat belt. "Is this . . . ?" She glanced at the scrap of paper in her hand and read off my address.

"Yes," I said, elbowing forward. Move over, secure women with Ph.D.s, Christina McMullen was in town. "What can I do for you?"

She glanced past me. "Is, perhaps, Julio Manderos present?"

"Julio . . . Oh," I said, noticing the paper bag that dangled from her hand for the first time. It was large and white and smelled like Shangri-La on steroids. "You're from Melisse."

"Melisse," she said, correcting my pronunciation congenially. "*Oui*. He ordered lobster bolognese." She glanced at Rivera.

"I'm sorry," I said. My voice sounded like a jackhammer after hers. "He had to leave unexpectedly."

"Oh." She scowled. "That is too bad."

A heavenly scent was wafting up from the open edges of the bag, firing up my taste buds. "But I'll pay for the meal."

"Pay!" She looked aghast, black eyes going dinner-plate wide. "Oh, no. Julio Manderos does not pay for his meals from Melisse. Not so long as I am present." She handed over the bag with something of a flourish. "Enjoy," she said, and narrowing her French fantasy eyes, slid her gaze up Rivera's jean-clad body to his face. "You, too, Officer," she said, and turned away.

8

Women have to be in the mood for sex. Men have to be breathing.

—Hippolyta, Queen of the Amazons and Brainy Laney's alter ego

"WHAT THE HELL was that about?" Rivera asked, but his voice sounded kind of hazy, his gaze still locked on Frenchie's retreating form. "Form" being another word for ass.

I considered kicking him in the shins . . . "shins" being another word for balls. "Don't ask me," I said, scowling. "Do you know her?"

"No."

"You sure?" It wasn't like I was jealous or anything. But damn it, foreign women always make me feel kind of . . . lumpy.

She was still walking away, scarlet skirt snug across her bottom, then flaring to swish flirtatiously against the backs of her thighs.

"I'd remember," he said.

Maybe it was hunger that made me want to drop-kick him into my dusty yard and lock the door behind him. "You sure you weren't engaged to her or something?" I asked, tone sweet, lashes fluttering like discombobulated butterflies.

He glanced at me, snorted, and closed the door. "Still jealous, McMullen?"

I headed for the kitchen, put the bag on the table, and realized that if I killed him I could have all the . . . whatever the hell it was . . . for myself. "So that Julio Manderos," I crooned, "isn't he the dreamiest?"

A muscle jumped in Rivera's jaw, but he turned away without strangling me, opened the appropriate drawer, and pulled out what I generously refer to as silverware.

I put plates on the table, added a mismatched pair of glasses, and opened the bag. After that it was all kind of a haze. I considered telling Rivera he wasn't invited to share my meal, but in actuality there looked like there was enough for Genghis's army—or me, so I put on my game face and dug in.

There were juicy tomato slices topped with cheese, and a lobster dish served in a sauce that made me glad to be alive.

By the time I was slurping up the last bite, Rivera was staring at me. I classily wiped my mouth with a napkin and refrained from belching.

"Does he come by often?" he asked.

It took me a moment to figure out what he was talking about. But then I remembered the foot massage. Which had been very nice, but juxtaposed beside Melisse's lobster stuff . . .

I leaned back in my chair. "Manderos is a nice guy," I said, wanting quite desperately to pop open my waistband and recline somewhere inconspicuous. "And maybe he was right. Maybe Swanson's death didn't have anything to do with me," I said, and began clearing the table.

"You believe in the Easter Bunny, too?"

"I saw him at the mall. Just a couple months ago."

"I'm staying," he said, and tossed the empty cartons in the trash.

"Over my dead body."

"I was hoping it wouldn't come to that." The tic again. His eyes spoke volumes. None of it was polite. "Listen, McMullen . . ." He glanced out the window, body tense. "Manderos was right."

I scowled at him, waiting.

"You're as sexy as hell."

Swear to God, if he had morphed into a monarch butterfly and flown to Pacific Grove I couldn't have been more surprised. I mean, yes, I knew at times that he was attracted to me, but . . . weren't we fighting?

"Shut your mouth," he suggested.

I did.

"You and me . . ." He glanced toward the window again, exhaled sharply. "Shit!" He looked back, shoved his hands into the pockets of his jeans. "Don't you wonder why we haven't done it yet?"

"I thought it was because of your phone."

"Fuck the phone!" he snapped. "I could take you right now. Thirty seconds. Just . . ." He closed his eyes, gritted his teeth. "Maybe I want more than that."

"More . . ." I shook my head. "Like a week?"

"Like a fucking lifetime," he said, and paced the length of my kitchen.

I felt the blood drain from my face. "What?"

"Why Manderos? Why him?" He had stopped abruptly, eyes sizzling with dark intensity. "Did you sleep with him?"

Something in me wanted to tell him the truth, but the rest of me was kind of spiteful and a little nuts. "Is that any of your business, Rivera?"

His brows dipped toward his ever-dark eyes. "Maybe I'd like it to be."

My heart did a fish-flop. "Maybe?"

He blew out a breath. "You make me crazy."

"I don't think I can take all the credit."

"Half the time I want to strangle you and the other half . . ."

My heart was beating a slow tango in my chest. "Does the other half last about a week?"

He chuckled and stepped forward. I stepped back, but not fast enough. He caught me, pinning my arms to my sides with his. "Maybe a month," he rumbled.

I tilted my head back to watch him. "But you're gay?" He pressed against me a little. "My next guess was that you were injured in the line of duty," I said, "but I guess not."

"Have you got a thing for him?"

I scowled.

"Manderos," he said.

I shook my head. "He's a nice guy, Rivera. I—"

"How 'bout my old man," he asked.

"I don't know if he's nice or—"

"You got a thing for *him*?"

I didn't answer right away. So this was jealousy. Who would have thought?

"You can tell me," he said. "You wouldn't be the first to fall for his shitty lines."

So he was still hurting over Salina's betrayal.

"One Rivera in *my* life is plenty," I said.

He looked as if he might continue in the same vein, then changed directions, face tense. "I never said my family was normal. Not like the sainted McMullen clan."

"Screw you," I said, but the words were kind of breathy.

He moved a little closer. "You got a week?"

I swallowed and remained very still, lest the slightest motion tilt me over the horny line and into the humping-his-thigh region. "I was speaking metaphorically."

"Uh-huh," he said, and kissed me. My hormones fired up like cherry bombs. I kissed him back. I knew it wasn't a good idea. But . . . some guy had died in my yard. And . . . well, hell, he's got an ass tight as a cement mixer. I was panting like a racehorse when I reached for it, and that's when his phone rang.

I broke off the kiss and said something nasty.

"What'd you say?" he asked, words a caress against my cheek.

Good God, I could still feel his erection against my thigh. Just sitting there, not doing anything constructive. "Nothing."

He chuckled, delayed a second, then pulled his cell from his pocket. Flipping it open, he stared at the screen. "This could be important," he said.

And twenty-one months of celibacy wasn't? "Of course," I said.

His eyes scorched me for a second, and then he pushed a button. "Mama," he said.

I refused to let my jaw drop at the idea that he would choose a conversation with his mother over mind-imploding sex. If the world was fair, that alone would force him to give up rights to his Latin heritage.

"I'm not home right now," he said, and watched me with smoldering intensity. I resisted squirming. And then it hit me. Maybe it wasn't his mother at all. Maybe he called all his girls "Mama." Except me, of course. "No." There was another pause, a quirk of the lips. "I'm at McMullen's."

"Christina's?" It was the first clear word I heard from the other end of the line. It *did* sound kind of like his mother. And her tone was thrilled. Mrs. Rivera and I had once bonded over a trough of liquor and talk about men having descended from the porcine species.

"I'll tell her," he said. "Tomorrow night?" There was more mumbling, then, "Okay. Everything all right?"

There was a muted answer.

"You sure?" he asked.

She must have assured him all was well, because he didn't torpedo through the door to her rescue. Instead, he slipped the phone back into his pocket and glared at me.

I fidgeted a little, wondering if she'd told him something about our exploits from a couple months before. Maybe something I myself couldn't remember. I'd been as drunk as a carny.

"Nothing's wrong, I hope," I said.

He narrowed his eyes. "She likes you."

"That a crime or just a rarity?"

His lips twitched. "I don't want to disappoint her."

I wasn't sure where he was going. "Okay."

"So I figure we've got two options. We could do it right now before my phone rings again."

I was holding my breath. "Do what ex-exactly?"

"Make her a grandchild."

I stumbled back a step. "Holy crap! What? What's wrong with you?"

There was a devil in his eyes as he stepped forward and pinned me against the wall again. His thigh settled with smug intimacy against my core. His lips slanted across mine. I felt my brain go numb, taken hostage by my ovaries.

"Was there a second option?" I rasped.

"No."

"Oh." I think I nodded. "Okay."

He leaned in, eyes dark, hands hard and hot against my wrists. That's when his phone rang again. He snarled, but a second later he released me, pulled out his cell, and flipped it open. "Yeah!"

Someone muttered something.

"You're kidding, right?"

Another mumble.

"You've got the wrong damned number," he said, and hung up.

Wrong number! Thank Jesus! It was a wrong number, I thought, but suddenly memories fired up, flashing suspicions in every inconceivable direction. "Who was that?" I asked.

He eyed me. He was still cradled between my thighs, still feeling like a million bucks against my needy stuff, but they say once burned twice shy. I'd been burned about seventy-seven times. The last pyro had been a paid assassin. Maybe. "You think it was a woman?" he asked, and flexed his thigh a little.

I swallowed. "Was it?"

"You still don't trust me."

I didn't respond. His thigh was doing stuff again, but he took a deep breath through his nostrils and said, "Maybe we should go with option B."

"Which is?" I didn't really want to know, but it seemed polite to ask.

"Start at the beginning," he said. "Get to know each other."

"In a biblical sense or—"

"Talking. Maybe holding hands," he said, and slipped his nails across my cheek. I shivered down to my psyche. "Did I tell you you're driving me crazy?"

"You might have made mention."

He exhaled carefully, not moving. "Maybe it's time we figure out if we like each other, McMullen."

"While we were doing that would we be—"

"No naked."

"Ever?" Maybe I sounded a little like I was going to cry. Maybe I was.

He touched my cheek again. "Not until you trust me."

"I . . . do trust you," I said, but I didn't sound very convincing, not even to myself.

"Last time I got an anonymous phone call you tailed me."

"That's 'cuz it was your fiancée."

"*Ex*-fiancée."

"Who you galloped off to at the first sign of—"

He was staring at me. I cleared my throat and looked away. "Okay. I see your point, but maybe you're not so normal, either. I mean . . ." I nodded toward the front door where Manderos had exited. ". . . it was only a foot massage."

The muscle again. "From a man my father hired to satisfy his girlfriends."

"Is it his profession or the fact that he looks like your father that bothers you?"

His eyes fired up, but his tone was level. "Doesn't matter how mad you try to make me, McMullen. I'm still going to get to know you . . . first."

"You're going to have to address your paternal problems if you're ever going to move beyond your adolescent disappointments and heal the wounds that—"

"I'm going to get to know you even if you keep saying stupid-ass things like that."

I scowled, drew a deep breath, exhaled. "Okay," I said. "We'll start slow."

"Great. You don't mind if I sleep in the nude, do you?"

I shoved him. He rocked back half an inch and laughed, but I gritted my teeth at him. "You're not staying."

"We're never going to get to know each other if we don't spend time together."

My crotch was burning up. There were about thirty-four seconds remaining until I tossed him on the ground and had my way with him. "Now's not a great time."

"I'll sleep on the couch."

And suddenly I remembered the Glock. It lay nestled beneath a couch pillow. I opened my mouth, but he beat me to the punch.

"Platonic," he said, but his thigh moved just a little, making me teeter on the edge of stupid. "Like in fifth grade."

"I kissed my first boy in fourth," I rasped.

"Really?" He kissed the corner of my mouth. "Tell me about it."

"You want platonic tonight, go see your mom."

"I think I can fight you off."

I gave him a look through my lashes then reached up and popped open the snaps on my slinky, tailored blouse. His gaze lowered. The smile fell from his face like a shit-load of bricks.

"Maybe I'd better go," he gritted.

"You bet your ass," I said.

9

Love is like skydiving without a parachute.

—*J. D. Solberg*

I LET HARLEQUIN SLEEP on my bed that night. Okay, he sleeps on my bed every night, but sometimes he has the decency to wait until I'm asleep before sneaking onto the mattress and draping himself over my legs. Sometimes I resent it. Usually about the time the lower half of my body goes numb. But this time I was kind of grateful for his company.

It was still early when he dropped a paw over my face, inadvertently waking me up. I pushed out from under his sandpaper pad and glanced at the clock. Five forty-two. Dragging myself out of bed, I made use of the toilet while simultaneously blowing my nose, then I stumbled into the kitchen for a drink of water. I glanced out the window as I guzzled. The world was softening a little around the edges, turning a lighter shade of black. All seemed well. Traffic is nonexistent at this time of day. A cat of nondescript lineage ambled saucily down Owens Avenue, past the Sheridans' giant jade and the dark car parked—

My mind screeched to a halt and rewound at top speed as I jerked my attention to the vehicle across the street. Whose was it? How long had it been there? Did— But recognition erupted like firecrackers in my head. It was Rivera's Jeep. Maybe. But why? He'd left my house hours ago. Had he stayed to make sure I was safe or . . .

Will Swanson's blank eyes stared at me from death. I swallowed and stared at the fuzzy shape of the Jeep until my eyes watered. Nothing changed. If he was safely locked inside, I couldn't see him. Finally, when I felt as nutty as a Snickers bar, I pattered back into the bedroom to stare at myself in the mirror. Not good. If Rivera was alive and well, I didn't want to scare him to death.

Five minutes later, legs freshly shaven, I considered retrieving the Glock, but if Rivera knew I had it, he'd probably throw me in jail for a couple lifetimes, so I stepped out my front door armed with nothing but Mace and a buttload of psychoses. There was still no traffic. The concrete felt rough and cool against my bare feet. The Jeep did look like his. I rounded his bumper, heart beating like a metronome, and glanced in his window.

That was when something flew at me from inside. I jerked back with a shriek and realized belatedly that Rivera had put a hand through his open window while sitting up. I also realized, with something of a shock, that I was pointing the Mace directly at his left eyeball.

He stared at me point-blank. "What the hell are you doing?" he asked, tone rough-night gritty.

"*Me?* Me?" I managed to lower the Mace and my voice as I glanced toward my house, wishing like hell I'd never left it. "What are *you* doing?"

"I *was* sleeping."

"Well . . ." I felt stupid and fidgety and wished quite desperately I was wearing clothes. "I noticed a vehicle out here and . . . you've always said I should be more aware of my surroundings, so when I saw an unknown car—"

"You didn't recognize my Jeep?"

I realized, albeit belatedly, that perhaps it would be a bad idea to be out there half-naked if he were a complete, and possibly felonious, stranger. "I was pretty sure it was you, but I thought you might be . . . dead."

"Dead?"

"Well . . ." I waved the Mace a little. ". . . I didn't know. I mean . . ." My eyes were beginning to tear up though I didn't really know why. Nerves stretched a little tight maybe. Or it might be that psychosis problem again. ". . . things have been kind of dicey lately. You know. With the dead guy and all."

"So you came to save me?" The corner of his mouth flicked up.

Was he laughing at me? I raised the Mace a little. "Maybe I just wanted to see you barfing up your guts."

He chuckled and got out of the car. I saw then that he was holding a gun, a small, dark pistol which he shoved into the waistband of his jeans. I'd never wanted to be a gun so much in my life.

I stepped back a pace, but his smoky gaze had already caught me and skimmed like hot whiskey down my exposed . . . everything. If my T-shirt had been more than twelve inches long, I would have maybe tried to cover up.

"Or to screw me," he said, and gave me a look that somehow managed to make me horny and mad all at the same time.

"What the hell are you doing here?" I demanded. Mornings aren't my extra-special friends. "Am I in danger? What have you found out?"

"You treat your neighbors to this every day?" he asked, and putting a hand to the small of my back, steered me toward home.

The ball of my foot found a pointy stone. I swore and hopped a couple steps. "I thought you were dead," I repeated, but we'd already reached my door. He turned me toward him and kissed me with enough heat to weld me to the concrete.

"Not quite," he said.

"You were guarding my house." I breathed the words and he kissed me again.

"Lock up," he ordered, and giving me one last, smoldering glance, turned on his heel and stalked away.

I stepped inside and locked up, but I couldn't relax. He hadn't answered my questions. Did that mean he'd learned I was in danger, or hadn't learned anything? I'd been threatened half a dozen times in the past year; he'd never slept in his Jeep outside my house before.

The lack of information was driving me crazy. Who was Will Swanson? Why had he come? I paced and scowled and paced, thinking hard, and finally jumped online. But nothing came up under his name. Dredging up worrisome memories, I remembered two of the names Rivera had mentioned and tried those. I got lucky on the second one. Elijah Kaplan was born in Amarillo in 1971. His parents split when he was twelve. Ten years ago he'd been found guilty of breaking and entering and served three years at Apalachee Correctional Institution.

Pushing my chair back, I prowled around the house. He was a felon. And I had been attracted to him. Charmed by him, if I was going to be honest. What did that say about me? Our conversations played back in my mind. He'd seemed intelligent and gentle, used big words, implied that he was impressed that I was a psychologist, and . . .

I stopped in my tracks. "How did he know?" I whispered. Harlequin had followed me from my office. He cocked his head and lifted an inquisitive ear.

"How did he know I was a psychologist? I didn't tell him. Or maybe I did, but no one remembers. Everyone thinks I'm a psychiatrist. And how did he know I liked big words? That I was . . ." The conversation rolled back in my mind. ". . . that I was from the Midwest?"

Had he been spying on me? If so, why? And from where? I rushed back to my computer.

It took me almost three hours to learn he had spent five years in the California State Prison in Lancaster for attempted murder.

David Hawkins, my former mentor and would-be murderer, was currently an inmate at that same institution.

Numb and shaken, I reached for the phone.

Rivera picked up on the third ring. "Yeah?"

"Did you know Swanson did time at the Lancaster state pen?" I asked.

There was a silence that said too much. In the background I could hear two men conversing. "Listen," he said. "Things are crazy here right now. I'll call you back when—"

My stomach twisted. "When did you find out?" I asked.

"I don't want you anywhere near Lancaster. Do you hear me?"

"Hawkins is there," I said, though I knew he knew. "He put Swanson up to this, didn't he?"

I could feel him grind his teeth. "This is police business, Chrissy. Stay—"

"Police business! Are you out of your mind? This is my life. Or . . ." I laughed a little manically. ". . . my death."

"I'm looking into it."

"When were you going to tell me they knew each other?"

"We don't know they did."

"You say you want to talk? To get to know each other? And you don't even tell me *this*?"

"You're blowing this way out of proportion. We—"

I hung up on him.

The rest of the morning I pretended to be normal, showered, got dressed, saw clients.

It was early afternoon when Solberg bobbled into my office. He'd aged since I'd seen him three days before. He had abandoned his contact lenses for a pair of god-awful tortoiseshell glasses and there was a stain on his wrinkled tee. Apparently if Laney wasn't in his life there was no reason to confine food to his oral cavity. I sat down at my desk, hiding the spot I'd somehow managed to collect on my spiced orange sheath. It boasted an empire waist with a little buckle under the left breast, three-quarter sleeves, and a boatneck. I looked good for a psychotic murder victim.

"Thanks for the loan," I said, not all that thrilled to have the Porsche replaced with the Saturn.

"No problem." He only sounded half-alive as he stared out my postage-stamp window. He looked distracted and a little jittery. Laney's presence was the only thing that seemed to calm his frog-legged nerves. I took a deep breath and kept my toe from tapping impatiently. "You heard from Ang—" He stopped himself, knowing I found it creepy when he called her Angel. "Elaine?"

"Not for a couple days. You?"

"She called last night," he said, but he was scowling.

"What'd she say?" I wasn't jealous. Just because I'd shared Mom's homemade pudding with her in the fifth grade didn't mean she had to call me every day. I was a big girl. Big enough to have multiple men trying to kill me.

"Not much." He turned away. "Sounded tired."

"Well, they're shooting action scenes. I'm sure it's exhausting with—"

"Do you think she met someone?" he asked, jerking toward me.

"What?"

I realized suddenly that he didn't merely look nervous, he looked hunted—eyes bloodshot, hair standing on end. People were trying to kill me every time I turned a corner, but I was pretty sure I looked serene by comparison. Was that love?

"Angel." He said the word like a prayer. "She's met someone else, hasn't she?"

I shook my head and stood up, pulling myself from my own sloppy quagmire and surprising myself with my own kindness. I mean, I'm not evil or anything, but sometimes it's hard being nice to a guy who has repeatedly propositioned you while using fourteen derivatives of the word "babe." That, however, was pre-Laney. Post-Laney, I could have stripped naked, danced the hula, and sang "A Bushel and a Peck" with a Hungarian accent. He wouldn't have noticed. "She'll be back in a few weeks. Once she gets home, things will return to normal."

"You think so?" He blinked at me like a myopic puppy as I led him toward the reception area, but before I reached my door, the front bell rang.

"I'm back," Mandy yodeled. It was something of a high point for us. She was only twenty-five minutes late from her lunch break.

"Absolutely, and until then we have to support her," I told Solberg. And as I escorted him to the sidewalk, I wondered rather maniacally how to sabotage my best friend's career and regain my secretary.

At 7:12, two minutes after Mandy left for the night, I dialed the phone for the California State Prison. I was keyed up like a pendulum clock.

A recording answered, rambling on about career opportunities my frenetic mind refused to register, but finally I pressed 0 and a live person answered.

"Yes, hi," I said, "I'd like to . . ." I cleared my throat, closed my eyes, and gave myself a little pep talk that went something like this: Do you want to be murdered by your garage? No, you don't. Do you want to find out who tried to murder you by your garage? Yes, you do. "I'd like to talk to Dr. David Hawkins."

"Dr. Hawkins?" The woman on the other end of the line

sounded bored and maybe a little premenstrual. "Is he on staff here?"

"No. No. He's a . . . he's a murderer." My hand was shaking a little.

There was a pause. "Who is this?" Definitely premenstrual, and maybe a little homicidal. "Is this a prank call?"

"No! No. He's an inmate."

"Oh." She sounded dubious. A prank call would probably have been easier to deal with. "And you want to speak to him?"

No. Please, God, no. "Visit him," I said, and cleared my throat. "I'd like to visit him."

"Visitations are on Saturday and Sundays. Eight-thirty to three. Come to—"

"He tried to kill me," I said. The statement was greeted with dead silence . . . no pun intended.

"What's that?"

"I'm . . . umm, I'm the victim." I don't know why that made me feel guilty. But I'm not alone in this. Victims often take the blame.

"Oh." Pause. "Well then, you'll need to contact a facilitator. Hold on," she said, and clicked me over.

In a minute a woman with a smooth Spanish accent answered. I explained the situation to her, and she explained the situation to me. California State Prison, Lancaster, did not allow victims to meet with their assailants without the victim having gone through counseling with a mediator.

"That won't be necessary," I said, sick to my stomach, head starting to pound, even though I was medicated to the gills. "I'm a psychologist."

"I'm sorry, but that's our policy. Generally, however, the

victim is allowed to meet with the inmate a few months after applying."

"Months?" I might be dead five times by then.

"Unless he doesn't wish to speak to you, of course."

I blinked. "He can refuse?"

"Those are his rights."

"But . . . he tried to kill me."

"I'm sorry, ma'am. That's the law."

I hung up, paced, and wondered rather hazily if there wasn't some kind of law against guys trying to kill unsuspecting psychologists in their own living rooms.

By 7:23, I was as crazy as an Irishman. Crazy enough to pull Micky Goldenstone's file from my cabinet and pace around my office with it. Fraternizing with clients is strictly forbidden in the shrink profession. And if the board finds out, they can really put a damper on your business. But getting murdered isn't exactly a financial boon, either. My hand shook a little as I dialed the phone.

"Doc," Micky said. He must have had caller ID.

I cleared my throat. "Hello, Micky."

There was a pause, then, "You need to reschedule my appointment or something?"

"No," I said, and closed my eyes. "I need a favor."

My trip home afterward seemed endless. Had Hawkins known Swanson? Had he told him my preferences, my dreams? Had they chuckled over my picture? Had he hired Swanson to kill me?

Turning onto Sunland Boulevard, I glanced behind me and noticed a red Corvette doing the same. I turned left on Oro Vista. It turned left, too. My nerves were jumping and my mind dizzy. I pulled my purse up against my hip. It contained a cell phone and a lot of other stuff, including the Glock. I'd felt silly about putting it in there, but I didn't feel so silly now. I didn't know anyone who owned a red Corvette. But that didn't mean I couldn't shoot him.

I took a sharp right onto Hillrose but the Vette stayed with me. Panic was starting to bubble up and suddenly the little roadster gunned up beside me. I glanced to the left. The passenger window was open. My heart stuttered. He was going to shoot at me. He was going to—

"Where the hell are you going?" shouted the driver, and suddenly I recognized him.

It wasn't a coked-up psychopath with a split personality and anger issues after all. It was my soon-to-be-married brother, Pete.

And here I had thought things couldn't get any worse.

10

If you don't like your teeth, keep your mouth shut.

—*Glen McMullen,*
a practical man

"WHAT ARE YOU DOING HERE?" I might have sounded less than congenial as I climbed out of my Saturn. I hadn't stopped driving until I'd reached my house. Peter John had pulled up behind me, kissing my bumper a little as he did so, then grinning like a hyena as he twirled his keys and sauntered toward me.

"What do you think of the Vette?"

I glanced at the car. It was sleek and sexy and looked expensive as hell, but I was in a bad mood and would rather have suffered ice-cream deprivation and shave daily than share that opinion. "Whose is it?" I asked.

"A friend's. I'm thinking about buying it."

I held a snort in reserve. I'd need it later. "Aren't you expecting a baby or something?"

He shrugged, casual. "She can get her own Vette."

I considered a couple pithy remarks, opened the gate, and stepped into my yard. The picture of maturity. "What about Holly?"

"Holly?"

I turned back toward him as I jiggled my key in the front door. It had a tendency to stick. "Your fiancée?"

Twin dimples winked at me. My brother James got the sad Irish eyes, and Michael had inherited enough muscle to sink a battleship, but Peter John has a smile that can knock a woman brain-dead at fifty yards. This has been proven by four unsuccessful marriages and a string of other relationships with even less longevity. Which, perhaps, suggests the brain-dead condition is reversible.

"I remember who she is," he said. "But she didn't wanna come. She hates California."

I won the battle with the door and stepped inside. Harlequin thundered up, nails clicking. I gave his ear a tug before he galloped a loop around us, then scrambled down the outside steps. I closed the door behind him and turned toward Peter.

"Then I repeat," I said, "why are you here?"

Pete sauntered into my kitchen and began rummaging through my refrigerator. "If I didn't know better, sis, I'd say you're not very happy to see me."

I scowled at his rear end. Why didn't McMullen men get fat? "I'm pretty well stocked on dead rats right now," I said.

He chuckled, gave me a glance over his shoulder, then

gazed back into my fridge again. "So you found that, huh? Christ, don't you keep any food in this place?"

"Peter, why are you here?" I asked. "It's, like, what, three seconds before your wedding?"

"Jesus, Christopher!" He straightened. "Can't a guy visit his little sister a couple weeks before his wedding?"

I stared at him, remembered the rat and a dozen other decaying rodents, and said, "No," with some feeling.

He laughed again. "I'm starving." Harlequin whined at the door. Pete let him in, grabbing at his tail as he entered, and Harley, always ready for a romp with the boys, made a lunge and galloped past, doing a mad loop through the family room and back into the kitchen. Pete snagged him on the way through and flopped to the floor, dog on his lap, both panting happily. "Harley's hungry, too." He glanced up. "Let's eat."

I opened the cupboard where the dog food should have been. It was, quite literally, bare. I swore under my breath.

"What's wrong?"

"Nothing."

"You're out of dog food, aren't you?"

I didn't answer, but he was already crooning to Harlequin as he wrestled him onto his back. "Mommy's out of dog food. She's not a very good mommy, is she?"

I refrained from cracking him over the head with a frying pan so as not to give the impression that I wasn't a very good sister, either.

Popping to his feet, Pete make a feint to the right. Harlequin lunged after, then seeing the fake, dashed off into the family room again, ears flying, paws scrambling madly. Pete dashed after. If I hadn't had the misfortune of knowing him since my birth, I would have thought he was on drugs. But it was just his normal behavior. Had ADHD been discovered earlier, the whole damn McMullen clan would have been high on Ritalin and self-pity years ago.

"Hey." He was back in a second. "Let's go get some groceries."

"Why are you—"

"I'll cook," he said.

My mouth remained open for a second, prepared for the genius to come. "You cook?" The idea was both ludicrous and intriguing.

"I'm not a kid anymore," he said, and handed me my purse. I reached for it, but he had already snatched it back.

Still I didn't kill him. Instead, I left Harlequin with a promise of goodies and was soon sliding behind my Saturn's little steering wheel. Pete plopped in beside me.

"Shouldn't a classy psychiatrist like you have a flashier car?" he asked.

"Psychologist, Pete," I said. I felt tired.

"What?"

"I'm a psychologist," I said.

"Yeah?" He was staring at me. "Since when?"

I gritted my teeth. A blue Pontiac zipped past on the shoulder. This is a relatively common occurrence in the City of Angels, and not exactly an anomaly in Chi-town, but Pete jerked away from his door, and I turned toward him, curious. "Something wrong?"

"No. Why?"

"You seem nervous," I said, and refrained from grinning even as I thought of a thousand times he'd scared the living bejeezus out of me. My mood was improving.

He snorted, glanced out the window once more, and settled back against the seat cushion. "Why should I be nervous?"

I studied him. In the dimming light of evening I could see that he had aged a little. Still lean, still irritating as a premedicated kindergartener, but older. "You chickening out?" I asked.

"What're you talking about?"

"Matrimony. Diapers. Orthodontist bills. Huge responsibilities." The McMullen Neanderthals have never been big on responsibility. Giants in the belching arena, and pretty damn handy in a drinking contest of any sort, but responsibility? Not so much.

"No big deal," he said. "I've been married before, you know."

"Several times, I believe."

He didn't acknowledge the insult. Or maybe he didn't recognize it.

"I just needed a little downtime. Nothing wrong with that, is there?"

I studied him. There was something different about him. A tension maybe. "How's it going with Holly?"

He inched up one shoulder and gazed out his window. "Great."

"No problems?"

"No." He tapped a rhythmless tune on his blue-jeaned thigh. "Why would there be?"

'Cuz he was an imbecile? "Wedding going ahead as planned?"

"Of course. You're coming, right?"

I scowled, mind rushing along another path. "I've been meaning to talk to you about that," I said, and glanced out my own window. Yes, he was a first-class nincompoop, but that didn't mean I didn't feel guilty at the thought of ditching his wedding. "I'm really terribly busy and—"

"Wearing the big pink ass-bow?"

"—with Laney gone—" I continued, then snapped my gaze toward him. "What?"

He grinned like a lower primate. "Hey, you're maid of honor. Gotta wear the dress."

I felt my insides go sour. "Holly picked out my dress?"

"Sure. She's the bride. It's what brides do."

"You'd better be kidding me."

"Pretty in pink," he said, and grinning, put one foot up on the dashboard.

Shades of weddings past snaked through my mind. "It's pink?"

"With a bow the size of a frickin' tank," he said, spreading his hands to show the immensity.

"Are you lying?"

"Hey, I know it's tough. But you gotta be nice to her. She's pregnant. Did you know them hormones make your feet swell up like buffalo bladders?"

"Listen, Pete." My familial emotions were firing up. "I'm sorry she's got fat feet, but I've put up with a load of crap from you already and—"

"What are you talking about?"

His innocent tone made me angry, and maybe a little insane. I gripped the steering wheel like a road mender on a jackhammer. "The sheep droppings?"

He stared at me, then laughed. "Hell, that was centuries ago."

"The underwear." I glared at him. He'd once given a pair of size 22 panties to Stevie Cromwell, my boyfriend at the time, saying they were mine. Needless to say, Stevie and I didn't quite make it to the altar after that little prank. Not that the breakup was any terrible loss. I believe Stevie's current girl is inflatable.

"Oh, yeah, them gigantic bloomers." He was still chuckling. "That was a good one."

I refrained from planting my feet against his thigh and thumping him onto the highway, but I couldn't control the voice. "Listen," I snarled, "I will not wear some Pepto-Bismol pink monstrosity to another one of your godforsaken—"

"Jesus, calm down."

"I will not calm—"

"I was just kidding."

I sucked in a breath and narrowed my eyes. "What?"

"I was joking. Shit! You always take things so serious. I'm just glad you're going to be there. It wouldn't be the same without you." He straightened as I took a right into Vons parking lot. "This it?"

Two cars followed me in, but I failed to remember to be paranoid. Had Peter John just said something marginally nice? Might there be a Santa Claus? Was the world coming to an end? I killed the engine, staring at him, but he was already hoisting himself out of the car.

"Come on, Pork Chop, let's get a move on. I'm starving."

Oh, good. Everything was normal.

The grocery store was busy. Pete grabbed a cart and wheeled it around the corner into the produce department. A woman with sleek blond hair caught back in an incomprehensible updo gave him a look over the top of the weird-fruit stand.

"Hey," he said. Glancing at her trim, silk-sheathed form, he came to a halt in front of some bumpy vegetation that didn't look real, much less edible. Picking up a yellow something or other, he kept his gaze glued on the classy chick, his patented grin in place. "My sister needs more vegetables in her diet. You like these?"

I waited for her to slap him down like the sheep-dropping dealer he was, but she smiled instead. "They're quite good in curry sauce."

"Really?" He put the little extraterrestrial down and leaned a palm against the stand. "Don't tell me you cook."

She tilted her head, oozing class from every minuscule pore. "I'm afraid I don't get much time with my law practice."

"You're a lawyer?"

"Corporate," she said. "How about you?"

"I'm an agent for the government." Translation: firefighter. "But I've been considering taking my bar exam just to see—"

I rolled my eyes toward the kiwi fruit and confiscated the cart. I'd been watching the McMullen Maniacs do their dirty deeds since birth and really didn't think I could stomach much more at the august age of... thirty-something.

Skirting the math, I picked out a pineapple, three oranges, and a lime. I had no idea what I was going to do with them. Mostly, dining-in means a bag of Cheetos and a jug of milk. But slick-haired ladies conversing with my lamebrain brother as if he were lucid had thrown me off track.

Turning the corner of the produce section, I examined

the strawberries and had a virtual encounter with chocolate fondue.

"The berries look good, huh?"

I glanced up. A man stood on the far side of a melon stand, holding a plastic box of strawberries in his left hand, which looked like it had just been manicured. He wore dress pants with cuffs, a wrinkle-free linen shirt, and perfectly polished penny loafers with tassels. He had a square, average face and a rockin' body. But Will Swanson had had a nice body, too. Now he was in the morgue.

"I don't know, though," he continued, musing. "The grapes are from Colorado, and Mom says all the best fruit comes from the Denver area. Something about the climate."

I felt restless and mean, but resisted pulling out my Glock; the man had a mother. Still, I wasn't as trusting as I used to be. There's something about a dead guy on your lawn that makes life more complicated.

"You getting the berries?" he asked, glancing up.

"I'm not sure."

He smiled. It didn't make my heart go pitty-pat, but it didn't make me duck and cover, either, which was pretty good at this stage of the game. "That your brother?" he asked, tilting his head toward Pete.

I glanced at the idiot. He was still busy flirting. Or, as they would call it in the real world, lying. But a thought struck me. I tensed and turned back toward the stranger. He was blond and very fair. "How did you know?"

He raised his brows, startled by my tone. "Know what?"

I cleared my throat, added an uncertain smile, and tried for normal, but I'd left that blessed state about three corpses back. "How'd you know he was my brother?"

"Oh." He chuckled, relaxing a little. There was a store full of witnesses after all. He probably thought he was safe from L.A.'s crazies. "Well, he's obviously not a boyfriend. And he better not be your husband."

I'd lost the battle with my smile.

"The way he's hitting on that young lady in the silk dress," he explained. "You don't look like the sort to put up with that kind of behavior. Well . . ." He put the strawberries in his neatly arranged tote and moved on. "Been nice meeting you."

I didn't have the wherewithal to come up with any clever parting rejoinders and wheeled my cart around the corner.

"Who was that?" Pete asked, strolling up behind and dropping a pound of hamburger into my cart.

I eyed the T-bones in the coolers. "Don't know."

"Don't tell me my little sister lets strangers hit on her in the fruit department."

"Shut up," I said. And here I thought I was out of clever comebacks.

"Maybe I should ask him about his intentions," said Pete, trailing along.

"Maybe you should grow up."

He turned as if searching the store. "It's my duty as your big brother."

"Seriously," I said, coming to a halt and belligerently staring him in the eye. "What is wrong with you?"

He stared back, face suddenly earnest. "I need a loan."

I paused, waited, stared some more. "What?"

He drew a long slow breath, stuck his hands in the front pockets of his jeans, and hunched his shoulders. "Listen, Chris, I didn't want to just spring this on you out of the blue, but here's the deal . . ." He rocked back on the heels of his threadbare sneakers and blew out a breath as if bracing himself. "I really want to make this marriage work."

I waited. Nothing. "And?"

"I'm thinking of going back to school."

"Back to . . ." I shook my head. "Elementary—"

"Okay!" he interrupted, and shooting me a peeved look, glanced away and scowled. "Okay. I'm thinking of going *to* school. College. Well, tech school."

Had the world gone mad? "For what?"

"I think I'd make a helluva electrician."

I shook my head, mind spinning. "What about firefighting?"

"I don't know." He shrugged. "I mean . . . doesn't it seem like, you know, kind of like a kid's job?"

But he was a kid. A kid in wolves' clothing.

"Holly's ex was a CPA."

I stopped short. "Holly has an ex?"

He shrugged. "Old boyfriend. A live-in. Long time ago. She don't talk about it much. Guess he was kind of an ass. A control freak."

"And now she's marrying you. Someone with no control at all," I said, and rolled slowly into baked goods.

"Yeah," he said, missing my mean-spiritedness again. "I mean . . . shit . . ." He exhaled. "I'm going to be a daddy. A father." He said it kind of like someone else might say he was going to morph into Daffy Duck. Which, knowing Pete, may yet happen. "Like you said, that's a big responsibility."

"What school?"

He glanced behind us again. I did the same.

"Looking for an attorney, Pete?" I asked.

"What? No. School? Oh. Lakewood Tech. If I was an electrician, I could work regular hours. Spend evenings with my girls."

"Girls?" My mind was spinning. Peter John in a grown-up job? It boggled the mind. Maybe that's why I added tofu to the cart.

"Holly," he explained. "And my daughter. Did you know it's a girl? Holly's pretty pumped. Doesn't have no family in the area. Hardly has no family at all. Her old man split when she was little. Maybe that's why she wound up with what's-his-face."

"Who's his face?"

"Her ex." He drew a deep breath. "But I'm going to make it all up to her."

He looked unusually sincere, and suddenly I thought maybe I'd misjudged him. Maybe he was growing up after all. Getting ready to take on life. *Miracles happen every day,* I thought, and wrestled an eight-hundred-pound bag of dog food into the cart.

"How long would it take you?" I was only puffing a little.

We'd made it to the dairy department without adding more than ten thousand grams of carbs to the cart. He picked up a gallon of milk, but didn't pop the top and slug it down like Gatorade. Impressive. Instead, he put it in the cart, grabbed another, and then an orange juice.

"Depends," he said, placing it with our purchases and glancing toward the cheese products behind us. "If I had to keep my job and just study evenings or if I went full-time."

I nodded, stunned; he'd actually thought things through. A few minutes later, we had checked out. Peter John had insisted on paying. My mind was still reeling when I started the Saturn and pulled out of the lot.

"So that's why you came here," I said, "to ask for a loan."

"Well . . ." He shifted in his seat, drawing his knee up and half facing me as he grinned. His upper incisors were a little crooked. Our father would rather have bitten off his own tongue than pay an orthodontist one red cent. ". . . that and to put a snake in your underwear drawer," he said.

"You touch my underwear and I'll tell Mom you cheated on your algebra test."

He laughed and leaned his head against the door behind him. "You know, I kind of miss you, sis."

Okay, he was an ass, and a liar, but he was still my brother. And family was forever. Damn it! I took a deep breath. I was hardly flush, but. . . "How big a loan would you need?"

"Twenty thousand."

"*What?*"

He straightened, expression earnest. "I know it's a lot of money, but—"

"A lot of money!" I was floored and may have been spitting a little. "Fifty bucks is a lot of money. Twenty thousand is an inheritance."

"I know." He raked his fingers through his hair. "I got no right to ask, but with the baby coming and . . ." His voice trailed off.

I glared at the road. I would not think about that baby.

"You must have some savings," I said, but my voice had lost its enraged edge.

He was silent as he glanced out the window. In the past, prolonged silences had generally been followed by the culmination of some asinine practical joke. "Maybe I haven't been real smart about money."

I thought of a couple nasty things to say . . . but that damned baby! "Can't you take out a loan?"

"God, no!" he said, and glanced out the back window.

I looked in the rearview. Traffic was rolling along behind us at its usual Humpty Dumpty rate. "Why not?"

" 'Cuz I . . . Well, I just can't. I mean, that's no way to start a marriage. Holly don't always think real high of men, and I don't want to be one of them guys who lets her down. Not anymore."

I turned onto Owens and pulled up to my curb. It was dark now even though I'd finally gotten the outside lamp fixed.

"I'd like to help you, Pete. Really I would," I said. Getting out of the car, I opened the rear door and grabbed a paper bag by the handles. I prefer plastic, but Laney had threatened me with deterioration of my soul if I didn't reduce my ethylene/oil consumption.

Pete snatched up another two bags. The front door was tricky, what with the groceries and my purse and the stupid sticky lock. But I managed. Harlequin torpedoed at me from the kitchen, reared in happy greeting, and thundered out the door toward my brother. "It's not that I don't understand what you're going through, Pete. Really," I said. "But I have some problems of my own." I paused, soul-searching, tone weakening. "I didn't tell you this, but . . ."

And suddenly Harlequin was back. He sprinted through the door, ears crushed against his bony head as he scooted beneath the leggy console that stood beside my front door. "What's wrong with—" I began, and glanced behind me. The yard was empty, the car door open. "Pete?"

No answer. I set the groceries beside my door and hugged my purse to my chest. Everything looked quiet. I stepped onto my walkway.

Then someone yelled. There was a guttural grunt. And suddenly a black form was streaking along my fence line.

"The keys!" someone rasped.

A gunshot zinged through the night. I squawked something indiscernible.

"For God's sake, Chrissy, give me the keys!" yelled Peter, and dove into the backseat of the Saturn.

A bullet pinged between me and the house. I was galloping toward the car before a coherent thought cleared my cranium, but Harlequin whizzed past and leapt onto Pete. The driver's door stuck for a moment, but finally I wrenched it open and dove inside, temporarily stunned.

"Jesus Christ!" Pete was clawing his way out from under the dog and looking behind. Three forms were racing toward us. "Drive!" he yelled, and bending over the seat, slammed the locks shut.

A ski-masked man banged on my window. I screamed something even I couldn't understand.

"Damn it, Chrissy!" Pete yelled. Yanking the keys from my hand, he shoved them into the ignition.

The Saturn roared to life.

"Open the fucking door!"

"Go!" Pete shrieked.

I went, slamming the car into gear and squealing down the street, with three men cursing in our wake.

11

Of course I believe in hell. I have three brothers.

—Chrissy McMullen
to Father Pat

YANKING THE WHEEL AROUND, I screeched onto McVine. Harley and Pete hit the right window, but I didn't care. There was a single headlight in my rearview mirror. I took the next turn at fifty miles an hour and punched the accelerator. We hit a bump. My head struck the ceiling. Pete swore. Harley whimpered. But I sped up and took the next turn, then an alley, wheeled onto Wentworth, and raced toward the 210. The single headlight was long gone. We'd lost them, but my heart was still trying to beat its way out of my chest. A Chevron station appeared on my right. I plowed up to the building, careened to a halt, and attempted to unlock the door, but my fingers wouldn't cooperate.

"What are you doing?" They were Pete's first coherent words since I'd hit the gas.

I gave up the battle with the lock, closed my eyes, and tried to convince my heart to stay within the confines of my chest. "Who were those guys, Pete?"

Perched on the edge of the seat, he stared out the back window. "I think we should keep driving."

"What did they want?"

He never turned from his perusal, reminding me of his earlier nervousness. I considered dragging him out by the hair and demanding answers, but my hands were still shaky, so I concentrated on the lock again, finally conquered it, and rushed stiff-legged into the store.

In a minute I was back. Pete locked the door behind me as I fumbled with the plastic wrapping on my newly purchased pack of Slims.

"I thought you quit," he said. He'd moved into the front seat. Either Harlequin was hiding behind me or my little Saturn was convulsing. My seat shook at erratic intervals.

I could see a trickle of blood snaking down from Pete's hairline.

"Who were they?" I asked again. Our eyes met, but Pete shifted his to the cigarettes, took them from my hand, and dispensed with the packaging. He lit one for me and one for himself. I took a drag and closed my eyes. "Peter—"

"Okay." He took a puff from his own and glanced out the window. "Just . . . let's get the hell out of here."

"Where to?" I stared at him, blinked. "Home? Oh, wait, I can't go home, 'cuz there are three men there waiting to—" But a thought hit me suddenly, knocking me between the eyes like a sledgehammer. "It was you," I hissed.

"What?" He leaned away from me.

"The guy who killed Will." I felt myself go pale, felt my extremities chill. "He was after you."

"What the hell are you talking about? Who's Will? And Jesus . . ." His voice was cranked tight. His eyes were wide and white as he glanced out the window again. "Someone killed him?"

Unless I was mistaken there was honest befuddlement there. I took another drag, exhaled slowly, and found my cell phone.

"What are you doing?"

I was already flipping it open. "Calling the police."

"I don't think that's a great idea."

The sledgehammer again, but this time the feeling was dulled by a queasiness in my stomach. I'd first noticed it when I was four and my brothers had put earthworms in my chicken noodle soup. I stopped my index finger millimeters from the 9. "What have you done?" I asked.

"Let's go. Come on, Chrissy. We can talk while you drive."

His nervousness convinced me. Generally my über-dumb brothers are smart enough to know when to be nervous. Back on the 210 I took a puff of my cigarette. I was looking for my Zen place, but a moron seemed to have taken up residence. "Why shouldn't I call the police, Peter?"

He blew smoke toward the windshield. "You know the Vette?"

"Your friend's car that you're thinking of buying?" I crushed out my cigarette with rattly fingers and pulled out another.

"I borrowed it."

"Borrowed, as in . . ." I closed my eyes for a second, but when I opened them, he was still there. ". . . can I use your car for the week, buddy? Or as in . . . stealing?" I stabbed him with a glare.

"I didn't steal it . . . exactly."

"Well, what the hell did you do?" I yelled.

"If you'll quit shrieking at me, I'll tell you."

"Listen, Peter," I said, "I'm considering drop-kicking you onto Rivera's sidewalk. If there's some reason I shouldn't do that, you'd better pry open your pea-sized brain and tell me the—"

"Rivera? The cop?" His tone was gleeful, his grin sudden. "You still seeing him?"

I ground my teeth.

"I always thought you'd end up with one of them geeky—"

"Damn it, Peter!" I snarled.

"Her name's Alice."

My mouth was still open. I tried to use it to good advantage. "Whose name?"

"The girl I was seeing." He exhaled heavily and stubbed his cigarette out in my mini-ashtray. "I met her at the bowling alley. Wasn't like I was looking for no action or nothing. But she was wearing this little—"

"Oh God!" I said, and saw the sleazy tale roll out before my eyes like a cheesy B movie.

"Oh, don't get all high and mighty. I remember not so long ago you woulda given up dessert to be asked to go—" he began, but I rounded on him.

"What about Holly?"

He held my glare for a moment, then glanced out the window. "Holly and I were taking a break."

"When?"

"What?"

I felt a headache coming on. I gritted my teeth against it. "Did you know she was pregnant at the time?"

"It wasn't my idea. Swear to God, Chrissy. She was tired of me. Said as much. Said she didn't want to see me no more."

"So?" I shrieked. "I've said that a thousand times."

"So I hooked up with Alice. But Holly . . ." He shrugged. "I couldn't forget about her, even though . . ." He chuckled. "I shit you not, that Alice had—"

"Shut up!" I said, then shook my head, trying to rid it of the stupids. "What are you talking about? Are you saying this Alice was so distraught about your leaving that she's trying to kill you?"

"Well . . ." He grinned. "She probably heard about my reputation in the—"

"Don't!" I may have screamed the word at him. "Don't you dare tell me your stupid reputation. First of all, I'd barf, and secondly . . ." I paused, thinking. "No woman would want you back that bad, unless . . . she was the mother of your fourteen kids or something."

"I don't have any kids. I swear . . . no matter what they say."

I left that alone. "Then, is she . . ." I made a circular movement near my ear.

"A little crazy, yeah," he said.

"Ahh, shit, Peter . . ." I began, then found a smidgen of sanity. "Wait a minute. Wait." I was shaking my head, remembering a hundred fantastical lies from our childhood. "That's ridiculous. Unless you've changed your ways, none of those thugs was named Alice."

"Maybe she had a..." He paused, winced. "...an overly protective brother... or something."

I felt myself pale. "One of them was her brother?"

"I don't know," he snapped. "She seemed kind of normal until—"

"The guy at Vons!" I rasped.

"What?"

"The guy at the fruit stand? Was that her brother?"

"You think we were pen pals or something?"

I shook my head, thinking. "You'd have to be literate."

"Funny. Funny as ever."

"Did you recognize him?"

"Who?"

"The guy at Vons!" I may have been shrieking again, but it seemed appropriate. "Did you recognize him?"

He shook his head, looking honest. Stupid, but honest.

"What else?" I demanded.

"What?"

"What else have you done?"

"Nothing." Now he sounded wounded. Stupid, but wounded.

"Tell me or I'm calling Rivera."

He scowled. "Well, see, Alice is the reason I borrowed the car. We'd been drinking a little... at the Longpoke—"

"The Longpoke?"

"Yeah." He chuckled. "Funny story."

I held up my hand. I wasn't in the mood for funny.

"Long story short, Springer was an old friend of Alice's."

"Springer?"

"The Vette's owner."

I blinked, uncomprehending. Maybe stupid was contagious. "You said you just borrowed it."

"Could be I forgot to tell him I was borrowing it. I mean, shit, the wedding's been coming up so fast and—"

"What else?"

"What?"

"Besides hooking up with a lunatic and stealing your friend's friend's car, what else did you do?"

"Nothing."

I waited, letting myself remember I was talking to a man who had once put a cherry bomb in a blender to see what would happen. "Why'd you need the loan, Pete?"

"I told you—"

"A lie."

"I'm hurt, Chrissy. I—"

"You're going to be if you don't tell me the truth."

He stared at me for a second and then grinned. "Jesus, you were always such a damn hard-ass."

Forget Rivera. I was pulling out the stops, I thought, and flipped open my phone.

"What are you doing?" he asked.

"Calling Mom."

Our eyes locked. He must have been able to tell I wasn't bluffing, 'cuz I think he teared up a little.

"And mean," he said. "You were always mean as a damned wet cat."

"I'm going to tell her you cheated on the mother of her first grandchild."

"Why don't you just hand me over to Guido."

"I—" I began, but then his words came home to me. The world spun into slow motion. I blinked, thinking. "Guido?"

He remained mute. A sign of intelligence . . . or death.

I took a deep breath and kept my hands steady on the wheel. "Peter . . . please. Please tell me you didn't get mixed up with the mob."

He stared at me for several seconds.

"Holy crap." I felt weak and a little disoriented.

"I was trying to do the right thing, Chrissy." His voice was very soft. "I was. For the baby."

"What'd you do?" I asked, but he barely seemed to notice me. He was scowling out the window, lost in his own thoughts . . . not an easy task.

"Our apartment's not big enough for three. The baby's going to need a nursery."

"What did you do?" I asked, each word carefully enunciated.

"Horses," he said, and turned back toward me, expression blank.

"Hor—" I began, then felt my heart stop. "You were gambling?"

"Of course not," he scoffed. "I was going for a bit of a gallop on the green and—"

"Don't be a smart-ass."

"Yeah, I was gambling, and I was doing good, too. Then I hit a piece of bad luck. Didn't want to tell Holly. Or Mom." He said the word like someone else might mention the black plague. "So I took out a loan."

I blinked and stared numbly through the windshield. "I didn't think it was possible," I said, kind of to myself.

He frowned, not following.

I nodded. "You're even dumber than I thought you were."

"I didn't know he had mob connections."

I turned on him with a snarl. "Guido? *Guido!* What did you think, Pete? A guy named Guido was a nanny?"

"Hey, not all of us have Ph.D.s."

"But all of us have brains." I paused, thinking back to a dozen events that called that statement into question. "Don't we?"

"Not like yours, though, Chrissy. You're the smart one. I didn't get no fancy education like—"

"Oh, please! Fancy education? I paid my way through Schaumburg Tech, schlepping drinks and showing enough cleavage to hide a battalion of freedom fighters."

He stared at me a second, then grinned. "Yeah. God, I loved the Warthog. Whatever happened to that blond chick who worked there? The one with the legs—"

"I swear to you, Pete, if you change the subject one more time, I'm going to shoot you myself."

There was a moment's hesitation, during which he may have been thinking. "You have a gun?" he asked, words slow.

I shifted my gaze to the roadside. "Maybe," I said.

"Here?" He was staring at me like I was the stupid one. "With you?"

I stared back, but suddenly he was digging through my purse and came up with the Glock, holding it in accusatory fingertips.

"Jesus, why didn't you just shoot them?"

Turning, I snatched the gun from his fingers. "What the hell is wrong with you?" I asked.

"Those guys could have—"

"What? Killed you? Yeah!" I leaned toward him. "And I'm thinking of doing the same thing."

"Listen—"

"And you know why?"

He thought about that for a second. "Does it have something to do with sheep shit?"

"Because you're crazy. And you lied to me. And Christ, Pete, you could have gotten killed. You could have gotten *me* killed. You could have—"

"You're right." He sounded resigned, beaten, sincere.

I narrowed my eyes. "What?"

"You're right," he said again. "And I'm sorry."

I blinked. Stared. Blinked some more. "Did you just apologize?"

"I've apologized before. Geez, Chrissy, I'm not—" he began, but I was already wheeling into the parking lot of the Highland Grill.

"What are you doing?"

"Rivera apologized," I said. "*You* apologized. The apocalypse is obviously coming." Killing the engine, I got out of the car. "I'm not going to die on an empty stomach."

12

What if there's no such thing as PMS, and this is just my personality?

—*Chrissy McMullen,*
who may have plagiarized
a cocktail napkin

PETE STRETCHED HIS ARMS across the back of the booth and grinned at me. He'd cleaned up the blood on his forehead and taken two Advil. He looked as good as new. You could probably take a sledgehammer to his cranium without doing any permanent damage.

Behind him, the Highland Grill was papered in red plaid. A green tam shared the adjacent wall with tasseled bagpipes and a hirsute leather pouch. "Hard to believe Dad used to call you Pork Chop."

I'd finished the fried mozzarella sticks, the cock-a-leekie soup, a loaded baked potato, and a steak the size of a Frisbee. I pushed away the last plate without licking it clean. I always enjoy eating, but when my life's threatened,

I'm one gene short of cannibalistic. "Hard to believe he called you human."

He laughed and leaned forward, sobering a little. "Thanks for . . ." He nodded to the left. "You know. Back there."

"You mean when I saved your ass?" My refined phraseology may have slipped a notch. Calories do for me what ten shots of tequila might do for a normal person.

"You were kind of amazing, actually," he said.

"And you were an idiot."

He grinned again, shrugged, and leaned back. "Can't choose your family."

"But you can move a couple thousand miles away." I finished off my milk. "For all the good it did me."

He sighed, glanced toward the interior of the restaurant. Most of the tables were empty. The chandeliers were made of antlers; the coat hooks, brushed brass. "Truth is . . . Holly had kicked me out. Back then. Right before the Alice episode."

I tensed a little. Truth is, Holly's decision may have had a little something to do with me . . . and the fact that I'd suggested she do just that.

"Said I was too immature. Said she'd worked too hard to make it on her own and she didn't want the baby growing up with someone as infantil as me."

"Infantile," I corrected.

"What?"

"The word . . . Never mind. So what does that have to do with three guys running after my car in the dark?"

"I don't know. Could be Alice decided she couldn't live without me. Like a fatal attraction thing." He sighed, leaned back. "It's the shits, being this charming."

"What's it like being a turd burglar?" Yep, my vocabulary seemed to be slipping back to my childhood days.

He put one elbow on the cushion behind him and grinned. "I know you've always been jealous of me, Chrissy, but . . ."

"Jealous," I said, deadpan.

He glanced across the restaurant at our waitress. She was about two months old, bright as a bauble, and dressed in a tiny plaid skirt with a black sweater stretched tight over her chest.

"Let's face it," he added, turning back toward me. "The McMullen boys get the Irish charm, while the girls get—"

"A brain?"

"I was going to say hips."

"You know it's not too late to shoot you, don't you?" I asked.

He chuckled, glanced at the approaching waitress, and leaned forward conspiratorially. "I can't help it if the lassies find me irresistible."

"Can I get you anything else?" the waitress asked, smiling. "Coffee, tea . . ."

If she said "or me," I was more than willing to shoot her, too.

"I'm stuffed," Peter said, leaning back. "But maybe my sister here would like another cow to gnaw on."

I smiled, stood up. "Drink your water, Pete. Fluids are very important for STDs," I said, and trundled outside, leaving him with the bill.

He was still grinning when he sauntered out of the restaurant and slid into the passenger seat. "Good one, Chrissy."

"You're a doofus," I said, and stroked Harlequin's ears.

He'd poked his head up over the armrest a couple seconds after I'd entered the car, and whimpered now.

"Am not."

"Are, too."

"Listen." He took a deep breath. "I really am sorry, but I think, maybe, you shouldn't go home for a few days, until I get this straightened out."

"Getting it straightened out suggests you have some kind of plan," I said, tone nonchalant, stomach twisty.

He shrugged, but he looked a little pale. "I'll talk to Harvey. He owes me a favor."

"Harvey?"

"He's a . . . businessman, in Chicago."

"A businessman." I said the words slowly, thinking. "So this doesn't have anything to do with Alice."

He glanced away, looking uncomfortable. "Might have more to do with that twenty thousand."

I nodded, reminding myself not to kill him. Killing him would be wrong. "Tell me you're not going to borrow from the mob to pay the mob."

"Harvey's not the mob . . . exactly."

I gave him a look.

"Anymore."

"God help me," I said, and started the car. In a minute we'd arrived at a modest little motel I hoped wouldn't have roaches bigger than my dog. I checked in, pulling out my credit card, but at the last minute changed my mind and paid with cash. It seemed unlikely that the mob would be aware of my electronic transactions—but then, it didn't seem all that conceivable that I'd be on the run with my dimwit brother, either. Sometimes life's just a kick in the ass.

It was almost midnight by the time I stepped into the motel room. Pete and Harlequin had already taken the far bed and were grinning in tandem at the TV screen. A laugh track flared up. I felt neither abandoned nor jealous at the fact that Harlequin had chosen to share Pete's bed. Dogs can't be blamed for seeking their own kind.

Kicking off my sandals, I punched the OFF button on the boob tube.

"Hey," complained one of the two.

"We need a plan," I said.

"I told you, I'm gonna contact Harvey and—"

"I was thinking more of a plan that wouldn't make Mom blame me for your untimely demise."

"Chrissy . . ." He bunched the pillow up behind him and propped his back against the headboard. Above the bed there was a picture of a prairie. I think. Although it might have been a seascape. The hotels I tend to patronize like to keep their art options open. "I'm flattered."

"Shut up," I said. I was dropping rapidly to his level, so I straightened my back, smoothed my spiced orange sheath over my thighs, and sat primly down on the available bed, facing him. "From whom did you borrow the money?"

"I think I told you about Guido."

"Was he the one who actually handed over the cash?"

"No. Her name was Charlene."

I suppose I shouldn't have been surprised by the gender but I was. "Charlene who?"

"It doesn't matter," he said. He sounded defeated and tired. Well, join the frickin' club. "She got the money from someone else."

"Who?"

He thought about that for a moment, then, "D."

"As in A, B, C . . . ?"

"Yeah."

"Does he have a last name?"

"He doesn't need one."

"How about a middle initial."

"This isn't someone you want to make fun of, Christopher. Not if you still have an attachment to your liver."

I thought about that for a second. The McMullens make fun of everyone. But I *was* rather fond of my liver. "How'd you meet him?" I asked.

"D?" He inhaled slowly. "I never did. He doesn't like to be bothered. Not by men anyhow."

"What does that mean?"

"Listen, Chrissy, it's been a long day. I'd like to—"

"Yeah, they seem long when folks start shooting at you, don't they?"

He stared at me, scowled a little. "Who was this Will guy?"

As it turned out, I wasn't all that excited to tell my older brother that I'd invited a paid killer to rebuild my garage. "Don't change the subject," I said.

"Somebody killed him? In your yard?"

I didn't say anything.

"How'd you know him?"

"Let's just stick to the subject."

"But what if you were right?" he asked. "What if it was because of me?"

Fear was creeping up from my belly again. "I'd rather not talk about it."

"What did he look like?"

I drew a deep breath and tried to be a big girl. Which, after the cow I'd just ingested, would seem fairly simple. "Five-eleven or so. Wire-rim glasses. Dark hair."

"About a hundred and eighty pounds? Green eyes? Wears a silver watch on his left wrist?"

I felt numb, slow. "You know him?"

He stared at me in solemn silence for an instant, then, "Nope. Doesn't ring a bell," he said, and zapped the TV back into operation. "But for a minute there you looked like you'd swallowed a goldfish...or sheep shit." He laughed.

I felt sick to my stomach, not unlike the sheep-dropping incident. But I was no longer ten years old and wasn't about to stoop to his degraded level. Instead, I stood up, lifted my chin, and glided haughtily toward the bathroom. Pete was staring at the TV, still chuckling as I passed him. It was so tempting to snatch the remote from his hand and flush it down the toilet. So tempting. But I was a grown-up. I was mature.

But I wasn't stupid enough to neglect that opportunity. The remote hit the water with a splash, sank like a stone, and sat at the bottom of the bowl like a dead guppy.

I locked the door, brushed my teeth with my finger, and smiled for the first time all day.

13

You don't know how many friends you have till you buy a big-ass house on the beach.

—*Eddie Friar, who just bought a big-ass house on the beach*

"HELLO?" I FELT GROGGY and disoriented when I answered my cell.

"Mac?"

I closed my eyes and refrained from weeping with joy at the sound of Laney's voice, even though I was holed up in a subpar motel with a brother who failed to register on the IQ test. "Hi."

"Where are you? I called you three times yesterday. You never answered."

"Oh." My mind spun into action. Elaine had become my best friend in fifth grade and has remained so through pubescent insanity, hormonal overdose, and the disappointment associated with adulthood. She's a genius who happens to be gorgeous and had shipped off to Idaho some weeks ago for filming. I may be an insensitive clod who habitually causes people to want to off me, but I had no intention of destroying her chances at stardom. "My phone's on the fritz."

In the bed next to mine, Pete rustled to life. Harlequin had abandoned him sometime during the night. I refused to feel vindicated. He was just a stupid dog. I stroked his head and mentally promised a T-bone when and if I ever returned home alive.

"Who is it?" Pete asked, sitting up.

The line went silent for a minute, then: "Do you have company?"

"What?" I asked, pressing the receiver more firmly to my ear and trying to muffle the abrasive sound of my sibling's awakening.

"I thought I heard a voice."

"No. I . . ." . . . wasn't going to make her worried about my continued survival. Laney is the nicest person on the planet and likely to risk life and limb in an attempt to make certain I was not only safe, but happy to be so. "I just had the television on." I winced, remembering the fate of the remote and promising myself that today I would remain refined and mature no matter how poopy my stupid brother acted.

"Yeah? What's showing?"

"What?"

"On the television. What's showing?" she asked.

"Um . . . I already turned it off."

There was one of those pauses that always comes before Laney starts thinking circles around me. "What's going on, Mac?"

"Nothing," I said, but my voice had already taken on that hard-edge quality prompted by an infusion of guilt. Apparently, attempts on my life make me feel somehow culpable.

She didn't respond. I felt horrible. Elaine has bailed me out of more jams than a certified bondsman. "You still there?" I asked.

"Yeah. Sure." Another pause. "Say, do you have Lieutenant Rivera's phone number, Mac? I can't seem to find it right now."

I felt my stomach drop. It was a blatant threat from the nicest person on the planet. "Everything's fine, Laney. Really."

"Uh-huh. Oh, here's his number." I heard her fumbling in the background. "I'll just give him a call. Ask him to check up on you when he gets—"

"Okay!" I said, and covered my eyes with my hand. My fingers felt a little quaky. "Holy crap, you should be registered with the FBI or something."

"What happened?"

I exhaled. Peter threw back the covers and traipsed into the bathroom. He was wearing boxer shorts and nothing else. I rolled my eyes toward the ceiling and refrained from giving him a wedgie.

"Mac?"

"I've had a little trouble."

She might have been holding her breath, but she let it out now. Laney is kick-ass at Zen. "A little trouble is when your houseplant has aphids," she said. "Real trouble is when the earth explodes, thereby liquefying your houseplant." Another pause. "To which of these examples would you compare your trouble, Mac?"

I tightened my grip on the phone. I wanted quite desperately for her to ride in on a white charger and save me, but I couldn't bear for her to risk her life. "This is somewhere between aphid infestation and the destruction of life as we know it."

"How does it compare to being attacked by an insane psychiatrist with a butcher knife?"

I remembered that incident pretty well. "It's . . . umm, less than that. I think."

"How about being poisoned by a wealthy octogenarian?"

It's funny, but both of those things have actually happened to me.

"Is that Laney?" Pete asked, emerging from the bathroom and scratching his belly. It was as flat as a drum. I have never hated him more.

"The TV sounds like Peter John," Laney said.

I closed my eyes. "It's not as bad as you think."

"Are you staying in a cheap motel with a brother who once fed you sheep droppings?"

If Laney would invest in some purple eye shadow and maybe a jewel-tone head scarf, she could be a card-carrying psychic. Still, I should have lied. I should have lied well and immediately to save her, to do the right thing. But I wanted to see her something terrible. "Maybe," I said.

"I'll be in L.A. by noon. Where should I meet you?"

I realized suddenly that I had been holding my breath, but just hearing her say it made me exhale slowly and smile a little. Despite Will Swanson and his dead eyes. Despite thugs. Despite having overdosed on fried foods just eight hours before. "I love you, Laney," I said.

"Uh-huh. Where are you?"

I shifted my eyes toward Pete. I was alone in a motel with a good-looking man who was eighty percent naked. And he was my brother. The irony of the situation wasn't lost on me. It just wasn't very funny. He yawned, stretched, looked about as bright as a pet rock. I sighed. Yeah, he may be as dumb as a bag of hammers, but he was my bag of hammers. "I need a favor," I said.

I wouldn't allow Laney to return to L.A. on my behalf. But I did accept the money she wired and had subsequently stowed it in my purse. By noon I was at LAX. I had learned all I could about the mystery initial man from my brother and was armed with knowledge. D was in his late thirties, disliked men, and owned a high-rise on State and Seward, where he ran a possibly legitimate software business. I felt about as prepared as a turd in a toilet.

As for Rivera, I had called him from my cell and lied my ass off, saying I was flying to Chicago for an emergency maid of honor fitting. The last thing I needed was for him to drop by my house and find me missing. Making him believe I'd been murdered on my way home from work would almost be as bad as letting him know I was winging my way to Chi-town to pay off a felon with only one initial. Besides, if he knew my intentions, there was no way in hell he'd let me go. For a minute I had been kind of tempted to tell him.

"I don't like it," Pete said. He had taken on his big brother tone despite the fact that he'd be hiding out, Glock in hand, at cheap motels until I returned with the all-clear message from D.

"This isn't exactly the best day of my life, either," I said. We were striding through the airport together. I'd purchased a backpack and stuffed it with a few newly acquired essentials. Nothing fancy. I still wore the spiced orange sheath from the day before. It was a little wrinkled, but considering it had been slept in... and shot at... it didn't look half-bad.

"This is stupid," Pete said, stopping beside the rotary belt that shuffled travelers' worldly possessions into another realm. "Don't go."

I faced him, stomach doughy. "Have any better ideas how to keep D from exterminating you?"

He stared at me a minute, then, "Have fun," he said.

I rolled my eyes, set my carry-on in a plastic tray, took off my shoes, and did the same with them. Airports have been kind of edgy ever since the rash of terror threats. Had the shoe bomber been thinking, he would have put the explosives in his underwear. That would have really livened up air travel.

Taking a deep breath, I gave Peter a wave and marched bravely through the scanner and headed toward the gate.

The flight was bumpy, noisy, and crowded. I slept like the dead. If the dead drool. By the time I awoke, the landing gear was screeching out of its hidden compartment and the right corner of my mouth was crusty. We touched down like a meteorite, bumping and grinding.

Despite gummy fatigue and rancid terror, memories assailed me. Chicago may be filthy, windy, and dangerous, but it's also the place where I had been spawned, sworn off boys, and donned cutoff overalls to work the crowd at the Warthog. In short, Chicago sucks.

I hailed a cab like a veteran, gave him an address, and

closed my eyes against my own stupidity. Afternoon traffic was bumper-to-taillight. Even so, it didn't take long to reach my destination, a concrete high-rise located squarely on Chicago's famous Gold Coast. There was no coast in view, however, just endless gray buildings towering over me like disapproving gargoyles, dark against a bumpy, overcast sky.

Shutting down any good sense that may have the nerve to show in the terrifying light of day, I opened the door and stepped into the lobby. Marble walls greeted me on all sides, as gray as the exterior. According to Pete, D owned the entire building, but security didn't seem particularly heavy. A handsome woman with black hair slicked back in a bun manned the desk. There was a pale leather couch where two supermodel-tall women discussed a fashion magazine. One was a redhead, one brunette. The rent-a-cop that lounged near the steel elevator was approximately half their height, but they may have been the same species.

I went straight for the desk, stomach churning. "I'd like to see D," I said. My tone was no-nonsense, my demeanor the same.

The dark-haired beauty gave me a tight, professional smile. "I beg your pardon?"

"D," I said, nerves clattering like wind chimes, sweat glands laboring like overachieving workaholics. "I'm here on business."

A little line formed between the receptionist's perfectly groomed brows. "Would D be the first or last name of the person with whom you hope to converse?"

I was starting to feel ridiculous. And relieved. I had obviously made a mistake. Or more likely, Pete had made a mistake. D didn't reside here at all. Perhaps he didn't even exist. But then I noticed the veins in Dark Beauty's wrists. They were swollen like spring tributaries. I'd once dated a bodybuilder and knew the signs. She'd been pumping iron and popping steroids, which meant she wasn't just some pretty bimbo trained to man the desk. She was some pretty bimbo strong enough to toss me out on my ass.

"Just D," I said.

Her gaze held mine for an instant. It was like staring down steel. "I'm sorry, there is no one here by that name."

"He tried to kill my brother," I said, raising my voice.

That got her attention. Hers and every other person's in the place. But suddenly I realized that everyone was female . . . and watching me with narrow-eyed expressions. The tall pair of superwomen put down their magazine and rose deliberately to their feet. There were identical lumps just above the waistbands beneath their jackets. I had a sneaking suspicion it wasn't cellulite.

"Listen, I don't want to cause any trouble," I said, but the Amazon Pair was already moving toward me. One was reaching for the lump behind her back. See how I was right about that cellulite thing? "I just want to pay back what I owe—"

"Will you come with me, please?" said the brunette. The redhead stood a few feet back, legs spread beneath a pencil-thin, ivory skirt. Below the hem, her legs looked like something from a James Bond trailer.

"StairMaster or aerobics class?" I asked.

The supermodels glanced at each other, then at me. "Come with me," repeated the brunette.

"This is a misunderstanding," I said, but everyone was

on their feet now, watching me, absolutely still. My hair was starting to sweat.

"Please," repeated the brunette, clasping my arm. I jerked away, and that's when the guns came out.

My bladder quivered in concert with my knees. The room was absolutely silent, and then the elevator doors opened and someone laughed. We turned toward the noise in breathless unison.

A man with curly hair and dark sideburns stood in the very center of the conveyance. He was wearing an ivory-toned Western shirt and dark blue jeans that someone else had labored to wear out. He was in his mid-thirties and had his arm wrapped around a curvy black woman's back. They were both smiling. "Well," he said, brows rising as he took in the scene, "this looks interesting."

"Please, sir," said the receptionist, hand hidden beneath the desk, "I think it would be best if you returned to your office for the time being."

He looked at her for an instant, then glanced at me and smiled. "Who are you?"

I tried to speak. Nothing came out but a squeak, so I cleared my throat. But it didn't do much good. "Are you D?"

"That your first name or your last name?" he asked. The African American woman laughed. Everyone else was sober as Sunday. I felt like I was going to faint.

"My name is Christina," I said.

His smile brightened a little. If Pete hadn't told me he was a mobster with a liver fetish, I would have thought him kind of handsome in an urban cowboy kind of way. His boots seemed to be snakeskin.

"Christina McMullen," I added, and waited for the

bomb to drop. But apparently I'd neglected to light the fuse, because he finally shook his head, looking lost.

"Do I know you?"

"Sir," repeated the receptionist, and he laughed.

"Tanya here seems in a terrible hurry to shoot you," he said, "so I'm going to have to assume I should recognize your name, but I'm afraid I don't."

I felt weak and stupid. "You tried to kill my brother."

He tilted his head at me, then, "Goldy, honey, it looks like I'm going to be detained for a short time. Why don't you go on to lunch without me?"

Goldy was as black as the inside of my eyelids. "You sure?" she asked.

He nodded and looked back toward me. "Would you care to step into my office?"

"Sir—"

"She armed?" he asked.

"I don't know, sir. I haven't had time to ascertain—"

"You armed?" he asked me.

I shook my head. "Airport security frowns on handguns in carry-ons," I said, and realized in that moment that I had kind of bonded with the Glock and missed it something fierce.

"Then come on up," he said, motioning toward the elevator. Something inside me told me not to go. I think it was my liver. My feet concurred, but I still tripped forward.

The elevator was absolutely silent as it slid upward. The doors were just as quiet when they opened. He motioned me out. For a moment I couldn't seem to convince my legs to carry me through, but finally one knee bent and the other was obliged to do the same.

His office was as big as Wrigley Field. Photographs lined the walls. I stared at them, expecting celebrities, but saw that every picture featured him with a costumed Disney character. Cinderella seemed to have lifted him into her arms.

"So who is your undead brother?"

I jerked my gaze from a photograph of him wrestling with Minnie Mouse. He motioned me toward a chair, but my brain had gone numb.

"I say 'undead' because you said 'tried,'" he urged, but my dura mater was still struggling with the seven dwarfs. Had they been throwing darts at him?

"I say 'brother' because you indicated he was your—"

"Peter," I said, grappling my thoughts into submission.

He raised his brows, sank into a chair the shape of a satellite, and made a stronger motion toward the one that stood opposite him. I managed to take the few steps to it and settle in, nerves jumping like wet cats.

He stared at me for a long second, then shook his head. "Nope. Sorry. Doesn't ring a bell."

"Three of your thugs attacked him in L.A."

He made a face and laid his left ankle over his right knee. I'd been right about the snakeskin. "Thugs," he said. "Kind of politically incorrect, don't you think? I like to call them collection engineers."

He was making light of it. Making fun of me. And his clothes looked wrinkle-free. I wasn't sure which one of those things made me more teed off, but I held my temper and my stomach. "I've come to return your money," I said.

"And you are Christina?" He settled back in his chair and cocked his head. "Pretty name. What do you do, Christina?"

"I don't see what that has to do with—"

"I'm just making small talk. Trying to prevent you from peeing in your . . . dress. Nice color, by the way. Great with your skin tone."

I considered telling him he didn't scare me, but I'm not that good a liar. "I'm a psychologist," I said.

"Really?" He leaned forward suddenly, making me jump. "That's fascinating. Do you practice here in Chicago? 'Cuz I gotta tell you, we've got a shitload of nut-cases in this little burg."

I blinked, wanting to look at the picture of him and Snow White something terrible. I think they'd been making out. "As I said, I've come to return the money my brother borrowed from you."

"Oh, yeah. That's right. Peter . . . ?"

"McMullen."

"McMullen. Good Irish name. Are you Irish? Hey! Can I get you a drink?"

He was obviously right; there *were* nuts in Chicago. "No. Thank you," I said, then: "Lieutenant Jack Rivera is expecting me back in L.A. this afternoon." I was gripping my armrests as if I were prepared to blast off. "He's a . . . police officer."

He stared.

"LAPD," I added.

He raised his brows at me, then reached for his pocket. I neglected to breathe, but he only pulled out a razor phone and punched in a number. "Sandy." He gave me a grin. "Do we know a . . ." He paused, shifted his gaze to me, brows raised.

"Peter," I supplied.

He shook his head with a grin for his own forgetfulness. "Peter . . ."

"McMullen."

"Great name," he said, then back to Sandy. "McMullen." After that he narrowed his eyes and listened. "Really? No kidding. Uh-huh." He tilted his head up and scratched his neck. "Fuck *me,*" he said, and hung up.

I shifted in my chair, barely breathing.

He snapped his phone shut and stared at me. "You sure you're a psychologist? 'Cuz your brother sounds like kind of a fucktard."

Fucktard! That's exactly what he was, and I'd just started to worry about running low on insulting nomenclatures. "He *is* a . . ." I paused, finding I couldn't quite say the word. It was all well and good to ridicule Pete myself, but that sort of thing should be kept among family. "He's going through some hard times," I said.

"Yeah? Like what?" he asked, and rising, went to polish a picture of himself and Belle with his sleeve.

"Like . . ." I tried to focus, but damn it, Belle seemed to be wearing combat boots. "Why all the pictures with cartoon characters?"

He stared at me an instant. "Minnie'll never let you down," he said. "Are you married, Ms. McMullen?"

I shook my head.

"Engaged?"

"Listen—"

"Twenty thousand dollars is a lot of money. Do you make a lot of money as a psychiatrist?"

"Psychologist," I corrected, which seemed to prompt him to return to the seat across from me and smile.

"Are you busy tonight?"

I felt breathless and kind of loopy. "Like I said—" I began, but he waved away my protest.

"Your flight. I know. But you could go back tomorrow."

"I don't think Rivera—"

"Lieutenant Rivera," he said, nodding. "LAPD. Policeman. He your boyfriend?"

My mind was starting to spin. "Boy—"

He laughed. "It's a god-awful term, isn't it? Boyfriend. He's probably some muscle-bound gym junkie with a six-shooter in one fist and handcuffs in the other, and I'm calling him— Hey, you ever been handcuffed?"

My head felt cottony, but I managed to pull the check from my purse and wobble to my well-shod feet. My sandals matched my sheath to perfection. "I'm paying my brother's bill."

"Bill." He laughed again. "Sounds like I'm a greengrocer or something."

I handed the paper to him, but he didn't look at it. Instead, he was staring at me, first my legs, then my face, then everything in between.

I swallowed my heart. "Do you promise to call off your thugs now that—"

"As I said, they like to be called—"

"Collection engineers," I corrected.

He stood up, smiling. "I don't think your brother deserves you."

I prepared to disagree, but I couldn't force out the words. "He made me eat sheep droppings." I was, quite obviously, losing my mind.

He raised his brows. "And you still don't want me to kill him?"

"My mother would blame me."

He laughed. We were standing uncomfortably close. "Where'd you get the cash, Christina?"

"A friend loaned it to me."

"The muscle-bound lieutenant?"

"A girlfriend."

He raised his brows a little. "Her legs as notable as yours?"

I drew a steadying breath, trying to keep up. "If her legs were here, you'd toss mine out the door."

His brows dipped a little, but his eyes were laughing. "What's her name?"

I opened my mouth to tell him, but she was the one unsullied person in my life, a gleaming paragon of sanity. "I can't say."

His brow furrowed as he studied me, thinking. "Have dinner with me," he said.

For a moment I couldn't get any words out, then, "I'm afraid I can't do—"

"Have dinner with me and I'll say this check is good."

My heart clunked in my chest. "It *is* good."

He glanced at it. "Twenty thousand."

"That's what he said he owed you."

He stared at me, letting me think, and the truth sank in slowly, freezing my mind.

"Interest," I murmured.

He tilted his head. "Bingo."

"I'm sorry. I—"

"I promise not to eat you."

"What?"

"If you dine with me, I promise not to eat you."

I blinked. He laughed.

"Really," I said. "I can't."

"One meal," he said, "and you're off the hook."

I paused, thinking, *No, no, no.* "And Pete?"

"He really make you eat sheep turds?"

"Put them in my cereal. Said they were raisins."

He shook his head.

"He's going to be a father," I said, and he shrugged.

"All the more reason to have two functioning knees."

"Okay," I said.

"Yeah? You'll do it?"

"Yes," I said, and knew I hadn't been adopted after all. Retardation obviously ran in the genes.

14

A guy's got to get a license to drive a Geo, but any doofus with a few good swimmers can be a father.

—*Dagwood Dean Daly,*
better known as D to those
who want to keep their livers

WE NEVER LEFT the building, just took the elevator up to the top floor. From there I could see a long, tawny stretch of Oak Street Beach. Despite the fact that the beach is man-made and had been laboriously hauled in from more tropical climes, the beach was nearly deserted. The restaurant was just as empty.

"So what does it take to become a licensed psychologist? A master's? A bachelor's?" he asked.

I drank my strawberry margarita and set it back on its leather coaster. The whole restaurant had a Western motif, making me wonder if he matched it or if it matched him. "I have a Ph.D."

"Really? Even though your father called you Pork

Chop?" We'd been there a while. And maybe I had talked too much. "Or maybe *because* he called you Pork Chop."

"How do you mean?"

He shrugged. "You needed to prove your value. To vindicate yourself. Some people succeed because of their heritage. Some despite it." He drank his daiquiri. You don't usually see men drink daiquiris. Especially pseudo cowboys in snakeskin boots. "Maybe you should thank him."

"For calling me a slab of meat?"

He laughed. "I happen to love pork."

He was looking at me funny, maybe the way mobsters look at people they're planning to fit for cement boots, maybe like they look at folks they want to get in the sack. I guess I don't know much about mobsters.

"And complicated women," he added.

"Complicated." I shook my head. "I'm pretty straightforward."

"So you adore your brother," he said, leaning back in the booth. "Admire the hell out of him. In fact, you adore him so much that you agreed to borrow twenty thousand dollars from a friend you won't even name and bring me said money to get him off the proverbial hook."

I fiddled with the coaster. It felt kind of like suede. Those crazy cowboys.

"Or could it be that you think your brother's a first-rate peckerhead but you still agreed to bring the check?" He tilted his head, thinking, then: "No," he said. "It was your idea."

I didn't say anything.

He chuckled and leaned back against the rust-colored cushions of our booth, steepling his fingers. "Still trying to impress your father after all these years, Ms. McMullen?"

"I just didn't want to read about Peter in the morning news."

"Your parents wouldn't understand, then, if you let him sink because of his own moronic decisions?"

I snorted. It didn't sound very ladylike. Or human. But he'd insisted I have a drink.

"Don't tell me your mom called you Pork Chop, too."

I made a smiley face in the condensation on my glass. "What did your parents call you?"

He eyed me for a minute. "Funny, isn't it? You need a damned license for the privilege of driving a Geo Metro, but any doofus with a couple good swimmers can be a father."

I had said as much myself in the past. What did it mean that I shared life philosophy with a guy with a cowboy fetish and one initial?

"So you ran away to L.A. in the hopes of . . ." He paused, waiting for me to finish the sentence.

"I didn't run away."

"Okay." He tilted his head a little. Except for the muttonchops, he was clean-shaven, had a nice jaw and okay ears. "You *transferred* to L.A., hoping to leave your past behind. To build a new and better Christina McMullen."

"I'm not seeking parental approval, if that's what you think."

"Which brings us back to the adoring brother scenario, and I don't know . . . that seems like kind of a long shot. Does he have some redeeming qualities that aren't readily apparent?"

I thought about it a second. "He didn't call me Pork Chop," I said.

He laughed. "One point for Peter John. Why didn't he go to his brothers?"

"What?"

"With his financial problems. Why didn't he enlist his brothers' help?"

That was a good question. One I hadn't really had time to delve into, what with the shootings and all.

"Might it be because they're fucktards, too? That Christina is the only familial member with the wherewithal to remove him from his current crisis?"

"Mom would have kicked his ass and washed his mouth out with soap," I said.

"She would have left him to me?"

I thought about that for a minute. "No," I said finally. "She would have kicked your ass, too."

He laughed. "I'd like to meet her."

I gave him a disbelieving glance.

"She sounds fascinating."

"Why do you dislike men?" I asked.

He raised a brow, at which time I remembered he was the kind of guy who makes people's livers disappear.

"Have you met many?" he asked.

I scowled.

"Men," he explained, and I had to give him my "You've got a point" expression.

The world went quiet for a while, then: "How come you don't have a minivan and two and a half snot-nosed kids?" he asked finally.

"Global warming," I said.

He raised a brow.

"Those gas hogs get about three miles to the gallon. Shove them full of kids, it probably cuts the mileage in half."

He was staring at me. "I think it's because you don't believe you deserve it."

I took a drink. "I had to get a license to shovel that kind of crap," I said.

He laughed and leaned forward. "This Rivera, tell me about him."

"He's a cop."

"I think you might have mentioned that."

"Sorry."

He grinned. "He's a lieutenant?"

"Yes."

"He *your* lieutenant?"

I ceased my nodding, not sure where to go from there, but not wanting to imply that I was without a lieutenant.

"Kind of," I said.

"Is he a fucktard, too?"

I tilted my head.

"Why the hell did he let you go?"

I blinked and fiddled with my glass and he smiled, leaning back indulgently.

"You didn't tell him. Because . . . because . . ." He narrowed his eyes. "He would have gone all macho and refused to let you board the plane."

"It's not his decision—" I began, but he laughed.

I bristled a little.

"So maybe you came here to spite him," he suggested.

I was getting kind of pissed. "Why is it so hard for you to believe that I just didn't want Pete killed?"

"I think it was the passion with which you told the sheep-droppings story."

That deflated me a little. Near the wall, a waitress with a face like a China doll and a body like Miss USA watched our table. I didn't know if that should make me feel more or less secure. "They didn't really taste that bad," I said.

His eyes were laughing. "I'm starting to think this Rivera might be dumber than your brother."

I wiped the condensation from my glass. "Wouldn't be easy."

"He ask you to marry him yet?"

I shot him a wide-eyed glance, and he shrugged, giving me a "Well, there you go" expression.

"Thank you for dinner," I said, and cleared my throat. "But—"

"You have to go."

"I think I should," I said, and stood up.

He rose, too. Even in his boots, he wasn't much bigger than I was, but his lean frame made him seem taller, even when he stepped up close. "But you haven't fulfilled your part of the bargain yet, Christina McMullen."

I snapped my gaze to his face.

His eyes were shining. "You haven't slept with me yet."

My well-filled stomach dropped to floor level. "I didn't say anything to indicate—"

"Well . . ." He shrugged. "Not in so many words. I just assumed it was agreed upon."

"I can't—"

He leaned closer, all laughter suddenly gone, eyes intense. "Even for your brother?" he asked, and let the words fall into silence.

My gut twisted.

"What would your mother say?" he asked.

"Maybe I could . . . maybe I could collect the interest," I said.

He shook his head, looking sad. "The money is already overdue, Ms. McMullen. If I gave you clemency I'd look weak, then everyone who owes me would be shagging their sisters at me to hand in late payments. I'd be a laughingstock."

I blinked, feeling breathless. The restaurant seemed eerily silent. "You have pictures of cartoon characters on your walls," I said.

He smiled, his lips inches from mine. "What do you say?" he asked. "Surely even Peter John's life is worth one night."

He was my brother, but . . . "I just . . ." I was stuttering. "I can't," I whispered, but even my voice was pale.

"You know what, Ms. McMullen?" he murmured, eyes steady on mine. My knees felt wobbly. I was holding my breath. "I think you have an overdeveloped sense of duty."

I pulled back an inch. "What?"

He grinned a little. "Christ, he's what?" he asked, tone suddenly brusque. "Forty?"

"Forty-two," I said.

He spread his hands. "And you're still saving his bacon?"

I said nothing. His grin slanted up another notch.

"Did you really think I was going to force you to sleep with me?"

"Umm . . ."

He shook his head, laughed, and offered his hand. "That would be rather unethical, don't you think?" His palm felt narrow but strong.

"So I'm . . . I'm free to go?"

He nudged me playfully with his shoulder. "Unless you *want* to sleep with me."

"No. No. That's all right," I said, but as he tucked me into a cab, I was a little depressed. Because honestly, I kind of did.

15

Sometimes we succeed because of our upbringing, sometimes we do so in spite of it.

—*Dagwood Dean Daly,*
aka D, who never forgave
his parents for his name

"MR. LEPINSKI," I SAID by way of greeting.

I had taken the red-eye home. My flight was unspectacular. But then, what isn't when you've just turned over twenty thousand dollars to a liver-stealing cowboy. Pete had looked a little pale when he'd picked me up at the airport, but he had recouped enough to tell me I looked like hell. I'd slept through Saturday and most of Sunday. Now it was Monday morning and I was back at work, wearing a sleeveless linen dress with Battenberg lace. It was a little girlier than I usually wear, but then, I'm a girl. "How are you this morning?"

"I think I have Legionnaire's disease," he said. Mr. Lepinski had been one of my very first clients. He's a scrawny little man with glasses, yellow socks, and a twitch.

"Legionnaire's disease." I gave him an intelligent look as I settled into my chair. It was good to be back. Okay, it wasn't as if I'd survived a tour in Beirut or anything, but I *had* survived Chicago. In fact, I felt, oddly, that I had beaten it. Returned to the land of my forebearers and proven my mettle. Plus, I'd gotten Pete, the fucktard, off the hook. And honestly, the trip was probably worth the trouble just to learn that new and really quite lovely insult. "What makes you think so?"

Lepinski gave me a list of symptoms as long as my desk. I stared at him for a moment, still going for intelligent. "Have you gone to a doctor?"

"No." He looked a little sullen about it, though I wouldn't have thought it was my fault.

"Can I ask why?"

"Because . . ." He glanced out the window. "I've probably fictionalized maladies in an attempt to help me forget about Sheila."

I had suggested that to him a few months back when he'd been sure he had West Nile virus. He had remembered. I've never felt more powerful.

"And what about Sheila?" I asked. "Have you seen her lately?"

"Saturday."

"Really?" This was news. Usually after a meeting with his estranged wife, he looked as wrung dry as a dishrag. "So tell me about that."

He remained silent for a while, glanced out the window again. His knees were pressed primly together and his lips were pursed, but there was something a little different about him today. Something I couldn't quite put my finger on. "She was . . ." He scowled. "She said she was sorry. Started to cry."

I refrained from gasping. Gasping is considered unprofessional in the shrink business, even though, according to Mr. Lepinski, Sheila never cried. Apparently she lacks tear ducts or something. Most reptiles do. Maybe you've guessed that I'm not crazy about Sheila. I mean, Mr. Lepinski isn't exactly Prince Charming with a vacuum in one hand and a doctorate in the other, but Sheila wasn't even the vacuum.

"She still wants to get back together," he said.

I refrained from screaming, despite the fact that I knew the story of their estrangement and thought he'd be dumber than a box of walnuts to reunite. "And?" Melodic. My tone was nothing if not melodic.

"Mom thinks I should take her back."

I crossed one leg over the other. But they both looked good, a little pale, maybe, but stylish and kind of flirty in their ankle-tie espadrilles. "Your mother."

"Yes."

I processed this for a moment. My gut instinct is generally to assume mothers are wrong, but maybe that's shortsighted. I'm told some moms have no discernible desire to eat their young.

"Is she aware that Sheila cheated on you . . . with the meat guy?"

He nodded primly.

"In your pajamas?" Somehow that made it worse. Not sure why, and I'm a professional.

"I may not have told her about the pajamas," he said.

Good to know. "Did she say why she thought you should reunite?"

He shrugged, glanced away again, increasingly tense. "Marriage, you know. It's a holy sacrament. What God has joined together, and all that."

"And what do you think?"

"It would make Mom happy." He paused. "And Sheila."

"Would it?"

"What?"

The two women in his life were perpetual whiners. Like undersized dogs and squeaky ceiling fans. "I mean to say, were they tittering ecstatically when you two were together?"

"Well . . ." He thought about that for a minute. "No."

"Maybe it's time to consider the fact that you can't make them happy." He was scowling. I let him lean into it, then, "Maybe . . . just this once . . . you should focus on trying to make *you* happy."

He turned his myopic scowl on me. "Isn't that kind of . . . selfish?"

"Yes," I said. "I think it may be. But while some people succeed because of their upbringing, others have to do so despite it."

When we called it quits a few minutes later, I felt pretty good. I mean, we hadn't exactly found the cure for male-pattern baldness or anything, but I thought we were making progress. And even if I had borrowed a few lines from a mobster who scorned most of the alphabet, what I did seemed to have purpose.

The rest of the day went pretty well, too. I saw four more clients. None of them tried to kill me.

Laney called. I told her she'd probably saved Pete's life, but I'd try to forgive her. I hung up with a smile.

Micky Goldenstone left a message saying that, per my request, he had gotten me an audience with David Hawkins in Lancaster on Tuesday morning. I considered contacting him to let him know I would no longer need that particularly painful favor, but life kept me hopping.

The phone rang at 7:17. I picked it up, secure in the fact that Mandy wouldn't bother to do so. It had been a good day, why ruin it with unrealistic expectations.

"L.A. Counseling," I said.

There was a moment of silence and then dead air. I stared at the phone a second, then settled the receiver back into its cradle, reminding myself that everything was okay. Things were straightened out. But when the phone rang again, I jumped a little.

"L.A. Counseling," I repeated.

"Hey." Rivera's voice sounded deep and strangely homey. It was a little embarrassing how happy I was to hear it. Apparently I had forgiven him for neglecting to tell me about Swanson being connected to David Hawkins. All that was behind me now.

"Hey yourself," I said, easing back in my chair.

"How was Chicago?"

I straightened a little, trying to divine how a normal person might answer that. Something about Mom's new wallpaper or how Dad had cried he was so happy to see me. But for all Rivera's faults, he's not stupid.

"Dad called me Round Steak and Mom told me to stand up straight," I said.

He laughed and I felt myself relax. Things were going to be okay after all.

"How's the bridesmaid's dress?"

"Not as bad as the last three."

There was a pause. "You sound pretty laid-back."

"Why shouldn't I be?"

"Some folks tend to get jumpy when they get shot at in their backyards."

For a moment I was stunned that he knew, but then I realized he was referring to the first time.

"Oh." I refrained from adding "that." I mean, I didn't want to seem too relaxed, thereby making him suspicious that I had borrowed twenty thousand from my best friend, hopped the first flight to Chicago, and met a guy named D who could talk about breaking people's knees and trying to fulfill futile familial expectations without a proper segue. "Well, that was almost a week ago. Ancient history."

He paused again. "What's going on, McMullen?"

I tensed, scowled a little. Did he know something? I mean, it wasn't as if I were talking to Laney. This was Rivera. He may be no idiot, but he's about as sensitive as a sledgehammer. "What do you mean?"

"You seem happy."

I relaxed a smidgen. "I'm happy a lot."

He snorted. It sounded wood-smoke masculine and almost friendly.

I smiled. "I was happy just last month."

"Were you drinking with my mother at the time?" he asked.

I put my feet up on my trash can and admired my shoes. "Very funny, Lieutenant," I said, tone chock-full of conviviality.

But he's not called Bloodhound Rivera for nothing. Okay, he's not called Bloodhound Rivera at all.

"So why the good mood?" he asked.

I shrugged. "There are no current high-risk pollution advisories, Harlequin has stayed off the counter for three whole days." Well, two. "And no one has tried to kill me in more than twenty-four consecutive hours."

"I'll put out a bulletin. Have you learned something about Swanson?" he asked.

His tone was blasé. But I was careful. "I don't think it had anything to do with me. I mean, the man was a convicted felon. Besides, isn't there some kind of governmental department paid to do that investigative stuff?"

"About that . . ." he said. "I think you might be right: Swanson's death may not have had anything to do with you."

"What? Why?"

"I have reason to believe there was a hit out on Swanson. Guy named Hank was pretty pissed at him."

"Hank." I felt a little breathless. "That was his brother's name."

"He was an only child. Hank was his partner. They ran some small-time cons down South. Then one day they went for the gusto. Got away with almost fifty grand. That's when Swanson disappeared."

"With the money?"

"That's what I hear."

"From whom?"

"I'm paid to do that investigative stuff, remember?"

"So you think Hank killed him."

"I've still got some leads to check out."

So none of my troubles had anything to do with me.

Will's murderer had not been trying to off me. Pete's attackers bore me no ill will. I was simply an innocent bystander...in the wrong place at the wrong time. At another time that may have made me mad. But just then I felt nothing but relief. "So I'm safe," I said.

"Just keep your doors locked."

"Yes sir, Officer," I said, but I felt a little giddy.

He snorted. "Want to know something funny?"

"What?"

"I kind of miss you. You free tomorrow night?"

"Free from what?"

"Christ, McMullen, are you on drugs?"

"It's not as if you've been Mr. Congeniality in the past, Rivera."

"This is the new me, remember? Starting over. Wooing."

"There's going to be wooing?"

"You bet your sweet ass, sugar cakes."

"Wow. Sweet talk, too. I feel flushed already."

He chuckled. "I'll leave my cell phone at home."

"Is that allowed?"

"I've hired a sitter."

"Shall I expect roses and chocolate, too?"

"Nothing that mundane."

"You shut your dirty little mouth," I said, putting my feet on the floor and sitting up straight. "Chocolate is never mundane."

"My apologies to the Hershey Company."

"I should think so."

"In fact, I have a recipe for a kick-ass fondue."

Rivera is a spectacular cook. It's one of the things about life that makes me think maybe God is up there laughing his head off about the world at large. Rivera looks about as much like your typical chef as I look like lobster bisque. And I hardly ever do.

"Messy," he said, "but what you can't lick off will usually come clean in the shower."

I blinked. I actually *was* feeling flushed now. "Good Lord," I said, and he chuckled, low and quiet.

"See you tomorrow night."

"Umm, Pete came to visit for a few days."

"Your brother?" His voice had already roughened toward suspicious. He knew my familial history pretty well. "Why?"

I ran a few possible scenarios through my head about overly protective brothers and discarded them out of hand. "He's probably planning a few days of L.A. debauchery before the big day. But I'll try to get rid of him by tomorrow."

He thought about that for a second, then: "Don't worry about it. You can come to my place. My shower's bigger anyway," he said, and hung up.

Grouchy-looking clouds were boiling over the San Gabriels when I headed home. I made a stop at Yum Yum for Tuesday's breakfast, ate a small donut hole, then remembered no one was currently threatening my life and added a fritter to the celebratory menu. Darkness was just settling in by the time I reached home, but I was still happy. The Corvette was nowhere in sight. I skipped up my crumbling walkway and inserted my key.

I didn't hear a thing until an instant before I was grabbed from behind and yanked backward.

I tried to scream, but a hand crushed my mouth. Terror shot through me like an electrical current.

The man behind me snarled something, but I couldn't understand, couldn't think. I tried to shake my head.

"Unlock it!" he gritted, and crowded close against me. He was big, hard. Terror choked me as much as his hand, but my mind was clattering along nonstop. What if I let him inside? Whatever he was going to do would be that much more likely to get me killed. I tried to shake my head again, but he was cutting off my air.

"Open up," he snarled, and shoved me forward. I felt something solid nudge my spine. "It's hard as hell getting blood out of linen."

My hand shook on the key, but I tried to turn it, tried to save myself.

"Hey," called a voice from the street. "Is everything all right there?"

"Fuck it!" he said, and dropped his arm around my shoulder. "Get rid of her," he ordered, and twisted toward the street, turning me with him.

An elderly woman stood on the sidewalk. She was wearing a dented straw hat, long blue shorts, and a red sleeveless shirt. "You okay?" she asked.

He squeezed my arm hard.

"Everything's fine." My voice cracked. I tried to swallow, tried to think. "Mrs. . . . Mrs. Fischer, isn't it?"

"What? No. I'm Doris. Doris Blanchard. From down the street." She cocked her head to the left. "House with the blue shutters."

"Oh. Sure. Hello." I lifted my hand in a stiff-fingered wave. He squeezed my arm. "I'm Christina and this is . . ."

I paused, desperate, terrified. I didn't want to die. There was chocolate fondue. And showers.

"Don't try anything stupid," he growled, but I'm terrible at taking orders.

"What was your name again?" I asked him. My voice sounded rusty. My knees were frozen.

Doris was squinting. "Are you the fellow that lives on Ruby Street? The one with the dog that looks like Gentle Ben?"

I could feel his attention shifting from me, and in that instant I swung my hand up over my shoulder, stabbing with my keys.

Sheer luck landed it in his eye. He stumbled back, cursing, but I was already running, sprinting toward the street and screaming bloody murder.

"Run! Run!" I shrieked, but Doris remained as she was, probably frozen with fear.

I shot up to the gate, but I couldn't get it open. My hands were out of control. Something sounded behind me. I spun around, ready to fight, but just then a gun fired. I screamed, waiting for the pain, but it didn't come. I jerked my gaze toward my house just in time to see my attacker race around the corner and out of sight.

Another shot popped off practically in my ear. I jerked back toward Doris. She stood, jaw jutted forward, gun smoking.

"Holy shit," I said, and collapsed, dragging my hand down the black bars and falling in a wilted heap on my decrepit walkway.

16

Tact is for people with too much damned time on their hands.

—*Lieutenant Jack Rivera*

"CAN YOU DESCRIBE your attacker?" The officer who asked the question was tall and sparse. His partner looked a little like a young Michael J. Fox. Short, cute, blond. I was sitting on my couch, feeling discombobulated and kind of dented. I think I shook my head.

"He was a yellow belly," said Doris Blanchard. She was still standing, apparently unimpressed by fleeing banditos and smoking guns. "Run off soon as I snapped off a shot."

The cute officer shook his head in disbelief, but apparently the gun was legally registered in Doris's name. That had already been determined. The same couldn't be said for much else.

Across the room, Pete stared at me, eyes hollow, mouth

turned down. He'd been in the house the whole time, coming out moments after the second shot, to find me in a misty heap on my disintegrating concrete. Apparently, the Vette was in my garage.

He'd thought it might be best not to call the police, but Mrs. Blanchard wasn't one to fool around. Armed with six-shooter, dagger-sharp wits, and a cell phone, she'd dialed 911 before I'd managed to hobble shakily into my living room.

"Any idea what he was after?" asked Slim.

I stared at Pete. He disconnected our gazes and paced. I tried another head shake. It was easier now that I'd had a little practice. Harlequin laid his head on my knee and sighed.

"Do you keep any valuables in the house?"

"Valuables?" I was trying to think. Really I was. But mostly I was thinking that I'd just spent three hundred and eleven dollars on a plane ticket to meet with the mob, and men were still accosting me at my front door. The idea made me kind of angry, in a hazy sort of way.

"High-end items," Slim continued, and glanced around. "Stereo systems, computers, that sort of thing."

Pete had disappeared into the kitchen.

"I have a nice blender," I said.

Both officers were staring at me.

"Makes great smoothies." Life is complicated. Smoothies make it simpler. "I like mine with bananas."

The officers glanced at each other.

"Did you hit your head when you fell, Ms. McMullen?"

"What happened?"

I turned my head at the question. Rivera was just striding into the living room, eyes dark as hell, brows low.

"Lieutenant," Slim said. "Seems there was another incident."

Rivera sat down beside me. "You okay?"

I was becoming aces at nodding.

"I couldn't see exactly what was happening on account of my cataracts and the bad light, but when she come galloping toward me shrieking like a scalded cat, I snapped a shot off at the perp. Thought I might of winged him, but they say there ain't no blood." Doris shook her head, mourning.

Rivera stared at her an instant, then shifted his hawkish gaze toward the other officers.

"Mrs. Doris Blanchard," said Cutie. "Said she was out for her evening walk."

"Osteoporosis," she said. "It's a bear-cat. Use it or lose it, but I don't go unarmed no more."

"Ruger P85 9mm," said Slim, lifting the pistol.

Rivera looked like he was about to masticate nails, but when he spoke, he was all business. "Did you get a description of the bastard?" Okay, maybe not all business.

Cutie shook his head, but Doris spoke up.

"Like I says, it was already getting dark and my eyesight ain't what it used to be."

Rivera snapped his gaze back toward me. I shook my head. "He was behind me." My throat was closing up again. "All of a sudden. I didn't see him." Maybe I should have. Maybe I would have, if I'd been careful. The thought prompted strange fragments of guilt. "He just . . ." I swallowed, nerves jittery. ". . . grabbed me. Out of nowhere."

A muscle jumped in Rivera's jaw. "How long ago was that?"

"Twenty-seven minutes," Doris said. He glanced at her. "I keep a pretty tight schedule. Gladys always knows my whereabouts, case something happens to me. I gotta get home in time for *Gunsmoke*."

Rivera turned toward Slim. "Have you gotten a statement from Ms. . . ."

"Miss," she corrected. "Miss Blanchard. I ain't never married. But not for lack of offers, if you know what I mean. I was a looker in my day."

"We just got here a couple of minutes ago," Slim said. "Made sure the victim was safe, took a look around the backyard."

"And?"

Slim shook his head. It was the size of a small cantaloupe. The muscle jumped in Rivera's jaw again. "Officer Williams, take Miss Blanchard home. Make sure she's safe, then—"

"I can find my own way home," she countered, tone roughening. "Ain't dead yet."

He shifted his gaze from Slim to Doris. "I'm afraid we'll need a formal statement," he said, "if you're not too upset."

"Upset!" She scoffed. "Ain't no yellow-belly sidewinder gonna upset me. Come on," she said, eyeing Slim and jerking her head toward the door. "I'll tell you about the time I shot my cousin in the hinder."

The door slammed behind them.

"You need anything?" Rivera asked. Had his eyes not been hard-ass cop, I might have fallen into his lap. Instead, I lifted my chin and drew a deep breath.

"No." My hand shook a little on Harlequin's head. "I'm fine."

He narrowed his eyes. My ninny-headed brother shuffled back into the living room. Rivera glanced at him. "Get her something to drink."

Pete nodded, disappeared. Seems even dumb-ass practical-joking brothers are compliant when a couple shots are fired.

In a moment, Pete returned with two tumblers. He tucked one of them into my hand. It was full of whiskey. Whiskey tastes something like battery acid to me. I drank half a glass. Pete did the same.

"Tell me what happened," Rivera said.

"He grabbed me." The glass shook. If I chugged the whole thing, how long would it take before I slid under the couch in a blessedly catatonic state? Nyquil might be a shorter route.

"Start at the beginning," Rivera said.

I tried another fortifying breath, nodded once, and thought about calling D. His business card was in my purse, tucked in my wallet between twelve thousand receipts and two five-dollar bills. When I'd heard it wasn't safe to carry a lot of cash, I had taken it to heart.

"I had a full day of clients. I left shortly after I spoke to you."

"You came straight home?" he asked.

I nodded, intentionally neglecting to tell him about Yum Yum's.

"Anybody follow you?"

"No. I mean, I don't think so."

He didn't like my answer. Rivera's kind prefers a circuitous course home. Something resembling Celtic knot work. Just in case. If I listened to him, I would have to allow four hours a day to commute. Of course, maybe I'd be unscathed when I arrived at my door . . . *if* I arrived at my door.

"You didn't look behind you?" he asked.

"I didn't think—" I began, tone already defensive, but he stopped me.

"Were there any unknown vehicles on your street?"

I shook my head. But there might have been a herd of pachyderms hobbled in my driveway. I wouldn't have necessarily noticed. The Vette was gone. I'd been euphoric.

"Okay. Go on."

"I exited my vehicle and proceeded up my walkway."

He gave me a strange look for my phraseology, but sometimes I feel better if I use educated language. Turns out, I could have employed the word "sesquipedalian" juxtaposed beside "somnambulism" and I would have still felt like crap. But it was worth a try. "Did you notice anything unusual?" he asked.

"No."

"Was your gate open? Was the security light off?"

I shook my head. His scowl deepened.

"Go on."

"I had just inserted my key into the lock when he . . ." My voice shook. I took another drink to cover it, but I'm afraid it didn't work very well, 'cuz my hand was still shaking, too. "He grabbed me," I said.

"How?"

"From behind."

"Show me." He stood up. I stared at him, lost.

"Come on." He took my drink, set it on the end table, and pulled me to my feet. "This'll be over in a minute."

I nodded numbly.

"Grab me," he said.

"He . . . he put his hand over my mouth."

"Do it."

I thought for a moment, then reached up and covered his lips. They were warm, a little chapped. He remained motionless, head tilted toward me, then reached up and pulled my fingers from his face.

"Where was his other hand?"

I swallowed and poked him in the back.

"Like that?"

"Yes."

"Are you sure?"

"Yes."

"Positive?"

I scowled, tired. "Yes."

He exchanged glances with the other officer.

"Left-handed," Cutie said. "Only one-in-ten chance."

Rivera nodded once. "Okay. Good. What happened next?"

"He told me to open the door. I—"

"How did he say it?"

I thought again. It made my head hurt. "He said something initially that I couldn't understand. I tried to shake my head." I did the same thing now. "But his grip was too tight." I swallowed.

"It's okay," Rivera said, voice softening, eyes unreadable. "You're doing good."

"Then he said, 'Unlock it.' "

"Here." He pulled away, moved around behind me. "We'll reenact it. I'm like this, right?" He put his right hand over my mouth, his left against my back. I tried not to throw up.

"Yes," I said.

"You're positive."

"Yes."

"Okay. You have your keys out?"

"In the lock."

He nodded. "So he told you to unlock it. What'd you do?"

I had frozen. Frozen like a Popsicle. Not shot him in the balls like I wish to hell I had. "I didn't . . ." I drew a shaky breath. ". . . I didn't want to go inside. I mean, it seemed safer out where people might see. Where . . ." My voice failed me. "But then he threatened me."

His hand tightened almost imperceptibly against my mouth, but he eased up in an instant. "What'd he say?"

I cleared my throat. "Said something . . . something about how hard it is to get blood out of clothes. And I thought, *'He's going to kill me.'* But maybe he wouldn't know I had a security system. If I didn't unman it, maybe the cops would come."

He seemed tense. "What did you do?"

"I tried to open the door." I jiggled my right hand, imagining, remembering. "But it was stuck. That's when Doris showed up."

"Doris Blanchard."

"She asked if everything was all right. He swore, put his arm around my shoulders and . . ." It was playing through my mind in hazy slow motion. "He turned me toward her." I pivoted. Rivera went with me, playing along. "I didn't know what to do. But I thought, maybe if I kept her talking . . . She introduced herself, so I told her my name and . . ." I faltered. Fear was trying to eat its way through my esophagus.

"What?"

"I asked him what his name was."

He swore very softly under his breath. "Then what?"

"He told me not to do anything stupid."

For a moment I thought Rivera might comment on the unlikelihood of that scenario, but he didn't.

"Doris said hi and waved and he . . . I thought I felt his hand lift from my shoulder for a second so I . . ." My heart was pounding dully in my constricted chest. I licked my lips. They were parched. "I still had my keys in my hand."

He waited.

"So I stabbed him."

"Did you make contact?"

I managed a nod. "In his eye, I think."

His mouth quirked a little. Maybe he was smiling. Maybe he was snarling. Damned if I know. "And then?"

"Then I ran."

He released his hold. "Did he follow?"

"No. But I thought he would. I couldn't get the gate open. Couldn't . . ." It was hard to breathe. "But when I turned he was already running away." I fell silent, remembering.

"What was he wearing?"

I shook my head. I hadn't noticed anything except that all my body parts were still intact and nothing seemed to be bleeding profusely.

"Think back."

"I am."

"Think harder. What color skin?"

"White, I think white."

"Because of his voice or because you saw him?"

I shook my head. "Just an impression. But I don't think his hair was dark."

"Okay. Where was he when you saw him."

"Running away. I only saw his back."

He nodded, took my hand, and tugged me toward the front door.

"Where are we going?"

"Just outside. It'll be okay." He led me down my walkway and deposited me by my front gate. "You were here?"

"Yes. About here."

"Okay. Stay there," he ordered, and strode back to my stoop. "Where was he?"

I shook my head. It was difficult. I felt like there were eyes staring at me from behind every bush, every rock. Officer Cutie stepped outside, watching. Pete followed. Harlequin peeked past his thigh.

"He was running away," Rivera urged.

"Yes."

"Could you see his hair clearly, as if it was contrasted against the evergreen, or indistinct, against the stucco?"

I scowled. "Against the arborvitae, I think."

He nodded. "Good. Good. How about his shirt?"

"White," I said, getting a flash of memory. "I think it was white."

"Long sleeves or—"

"Long. The cuff . . ." I stopped breathing for a second. "I felt the cuff scrape my chin when he grabbed me. It was kind of stiff. Like it'd been starched. A dress shirt maybe."

"How about pants?"

"Yes."

"He was wearing pants?"

I felt myself go pale. "Why the hell wouldn't he be?"

He scowled at me. "Was he wearing long pants or shorts?"

"Oh." I felt weak, strained. "Long pants."

"Are you sure?"

For a second I had an image of the bottom of his shoe as he tromped around the corner of the house. "Yes. They were light, I think. Different than his soles."

He gave me a weird look.

"He was running," I said. "I saw the bottom of his shoe."

"Tread or smooth?"

But there I drew a blank.

He nodded. "What happened after that?"

I drew a steadying breath. "He was gone."

"Running fast or . . ."

"Stumbling, kind of bent over."

He glanced at the other officer.

"We didn't see any blood," he said.

"Look again," Rivera ordered.

Cutie nodded and disappeared around the corner of the house.

"And that's the last you saw of him?"

I drew a shuddering breath. "I was kind of out of it. Didn't really . . . I wasn't really very aware until Pete came running out."

Rivera shifted his dark eyes to my brother, then touched my back, ushering me inside. Pete shuffled into the kitchen, hands in his hip pockets. "You scared the shit out of me, Christopher."

"You were here?" Rivera's voice was deep and low.

We turned our attention toward him in unison.

"Huh?" Pete said in typical Pete style.

"You were here in the house the whole time?"

"I didn't know there was any trouble," he said. "Not until it was too late."

"You must have seen the bastard."

"No."

Rivera remained silent for a fraction of a second, eyes narrowed. "There were two shots before he ran off. You must have gone to the window when you heard the first one."

"I had the television on. Thought I heard something, but . . ." He shrugged. "If I had known Chrissy was home, I would have gone to check, but—"

"So you did hear the shots."

"Maybe. It's hard to say. But like I said, I didn't know she was out there."

"It was late. What time did you think she'd get home?"

"I wasn't expecting any trouble," Pete said, sounding agitated. "I thought everything was all cleared up after Chicago."

The room went absolutely silent. I jerked my gaze from Pete to Rivera, breath held.

"What about Chicago?" Rivera said, and I felt like throwing up.

17

Expect stupid. It's everywhere.

—*Unknown East Hollywood graffiti artist*

I WAS FROZEN like a winter salamander. I mean, yeah, some guy had just tried to kill me on my doorstep, but that seemed tame compared to the flames that suddenly shot out of Rivera's nostrils.

"What happened in Chicago?" he asked, staring at Pete.

My brother snapped his gaze to me and back, but Rivera stepped between us, breaking our eye contact.

"What about Chicago?" he asked again.

"Not much," Pete said. "There was just a little trouble with—"

"With Mom," I spouted, breaking out of my trance. "But we thought everything was okay now."

"What was wrong with your mom?"

"Oh, she was just a little . . . upset."

"About?"

"Peter leaving." I nodded to the rhythm of my lies. "So close to the nuptials. She thought he should stay home . . . with Holly."

"So you thought . . ."—Rivera turned his searing gaze on Peter—". . . it might be your mother threatening Chrissy on her stoop."

"Never know," Pete said. "Mom's full-blooded Irish."

I laughed. It sounded like the guffaw of a certified nutcase. Rivera turned on me. I sucked in my breath and felt the blood rush from my face.

"Want to tell me what's going on, McMullen?"

"Uhhh," Pete and I said in unison. We glanced at each other, pale-faced, before my brother realized Rivera had been addressing me. Even Pete wasn't stupid enough to protest.

"Someone grabbed me," I said. "I don't know who or why." I sounded panicked. Like I was going to pee in my pants and didn't know quite what I was saying. I'm a hell of an actress.

"What does that have to do with Chicago?" he asked.

"Nothing." My voice cracked. "Nothing. But . . ." I tried a shrug. It came off fairly well. ". . . things have been pretty scary and I didn't want to tell Mom. But I didn't want to stay here alone, either, so . . ." I let the sentence trail off and tried a wimpy shrug.

"Are you saying you asked your brother to come here and protect you?"

This was not going to be an easy sale, but I gave it a go. "I was frightened. You can't blame me for that. I didn't know—"

"Jesus!" he said, and stepped forward, but in that instant the door opened and Officer Cutie entered. Rivera turned toward him, expression crackling with disapproval. "Well?"

Cutie shook his head. "Sorry."

Rage sparked in Rivera's eyes as he looked at me. For a moment I thought he would swear or rant or spit, but finally he said, "I think we're done here for tonight," and pulled his gaze from mine. "I'll get back to you. After I look into things."

Maybe to some innocent and somewhat naïve bystander that might have sounded like a promise. To me it was a threat, plain and simple. Nevertheless, I managed a thank-you as Cutie stepped out the door.

Rivera turned, speared Pete with his lightning eyes, and returned his gaze to me. "Lock the damned door," he said, and left.

I locked the damned door and dropped my head against the rotting wood.

"Holy fuck!" Peter said from behind me.

I turned on him with a snarl. "What the hell is wrong with you?"

He pulled his head back as if affronted. "What'd I do?"

"I was just about killed."

"And that's my fault?"

"Of course it's your fault," I snarled, and charged toward him like a storm trooper. "Who was it?"

"What?" He didn't back down. The McMullen brothers may be a trio of cement-headed buffoons, but never let it be said that they're cowardly buffoons. "How the hell would I know?"

"You must have seen him."

"I didn't. I swear."

"You heard the shots."

"Well, yeah, but shit, I was watching *24*. They're always shooting someone. When I realized there was trouble, I went straight to the door. My damn heart just about stopped when I saw you—"

"Who was it?" My voice sounded crazed.

"You think I'm lying?" His tone was wounded, and for a moment I felt guilt shift through me. Then I remembered the droppings. The dead rodents. The gigantic bloomers.

"I went to Chicago," I growled. I was panting a little. "Paid three hundred dollars for a ticket on a plane flown by a pilot with the sensitivity of a road mender. And why? What for? So I can be attacked on my own stoop?"

"Maybe D didn't get the word out yet. You only just got back. Maybe he hasn't been able to get a hold of his knee-breakers yet."

That made a certain amount of sense. Maybe too much for Peter, but I couldn't think of any other explanations. Finding my purse, I sat down on a chair in the kitchen, dug out D's card, took a deep breath, and found my cell phone. Long distance was free. I dialed. It rang four times before it was picked up.

"I got to tell you, Christina, I didn't think you'd call."

I was temporarily speechless, then, "D?"

"How are you?"

"I'm . . . fine."

"Good. Safe trip back to L.A., I hope."

"It was a little bumpy but—" I stopped myself, realizing my flagging sanity, and let the surreal dialogue wash over me. "Listen, D . . ." I cleared my throat, remembering he was the kind of guy who threatened livers. "I don't mean to bother you, but I was wondering, did you get a chance to call off your hit guys?"

He delayed a second as if thinking. "I believe we discussed this before, Christina."

My mind felt moldy. "What's that?"

"That's a rather antiquated term."

I closed my eyes. "Right. Sorry. Did you get a chance to talk to your . . . ahh, collection engineers?"

"Why?" I could hear his chair squeak, imagined him sitting up, putting the leather soles of his snakeskin boots on the floor. "What happened?"

I shot my gaze to Pete. He was standing perfectly still, suspended in stupidity.

"I, um . . . I had a little trouble," I said.

"What kind of trouble?" His tone sounded concerned. The kind of concern a brother should have for his sister.

"Someone threatened me on my doorstep."

There was a moment of silence, then, "I'm sorry. Truly I am."

"Yes." I cleared my throat. "Well . . . thank you."

"Maybe you should move back to Chicago. I can guarantee you protection here."

God help me. "Well, I'll think about that, but I was wondering if you would mind calling off your guys. You know, while I'm still in L.A."

There was another instant of silence, then, "I hate to admit this. I mean, it's embarrassing as hell, but the truth is . . . my contractors haven't been outside of the greater Chicago area for several months."

My world ground to a halt. "What's that?"

He sighed. "It's been crazy busy. What with the economy like it is. Loans late everywhere. I planned to get around to your brother, but . . ." I could almost hear his shrug.

"You . . ." I shot my gaze to Pete again. He remained as he was . . . stupid. "You mean, you didn't try to kill my brother?"

"Honey, I don't mean to be vain or anything, but we don't *try* to kill people."

"So you didn't try to drag him into a van."

He chuckled, quietly amused. "If we want someone dead, he's dead, Christina. If we want someone in a van, he's in the van . . . and maybe dead, too."

I felt sick and a little light-headed. "Oh."

"I hope I haven't disappointed you. I mean, it could have been my guys. It just wasn't. But your brother was on the docket. I hope you don't think your trip here was a waste of time. It was very nice meeting you."

It hadn't been D. So who the hell had it been? "Thank you," I intoned.

"We would have gotten around to his knees eventually, had you not shown up with the cash. It was very brave of you."

"Okay."

"You sound a little hazy. Are you all right?

"Sure. Yes, I'm all right."

"Have you been eating?"

"What? Oh, yes, eating."

"People don't take hypoglycemia seriously enough," he said. I rather foggily remembered telling him about my blood sugar problem. "It's nothing to fool around with."

"I'll remember."

Pete was scowling. Did he know more than he was saying? It seemed unlikely, and yet . . .

"... want, I can send someone down there."

I snagged my attention from Pete to the phone, senses fully focused once again. "What's that?"

He paused as if surprised by my tone, then, "I'm a little busy to come myself, but if someone's bothering you, I could send a guy to—"

"No!"

There was a pause. "Are you sure?"

"Yes. But thank you." I meant it quite sincerely.

"No problem. You take care of yourself, Christina."

"I will."

"Good. And if you change your mind, let me know."

"About the ... the engineer?"

"That or sleeping with me. Either one."

"Oh." I cleared my throat. "Thank you. I'll do that. Well ... good-bye."

The distance between us was silent for a moment, then, "Christina?"

"Yeah?"

"Your brother doesn't deserve you."

I clicked the phone shut.

Pete shuffled to his other foot. "What'd he say?"

I blinked at nothing. "He said you're a fucktard."

"What?"

"And I should watch my sugar level."

"Did you drink that whole glass of whiskey?"

"It wasn't him," I said. "Not at the van. Not in the supermarket. Not at my door."

"Huh! Do you think he was telling—" he began, but I didn't let him finish.

"So who was it?" I asked.

"How the hell would I know? Maybe D's lying."

"Maybe *you're* lying," I said, and stood up.

"Damn it, Chrissy," he said, "You think this is my fault."

"Your fault? Your fault!" I was starting to scream a little and gesture rather wildly. "Everything's your fault, Peter. I haven't been able to look at raisin bread since I was ten."

"What the hell . . ." he began, then laughed as he caught my drift. "Shit, Chrissy," he said, finishing off his drink and setting the glass on the table. "If I thought that little prank would make you so crazy, I would have . . . tried it again later."

I think it was then that I went totally bonkers, because that's when I snatched my purse from the counter and pulled out the Glock.

18

The trouble with insanity is it can flare up at the most inconvenient moments.

—*Dr. Frank Meister, Chrissy's Psychotropic Medication professor, after doing a little freelance marijuana testing . . . again*

I POINTED THE PISTOL at Pete. He stared at me, expression blank.

"Who was it?" I asked.

"What the hell?" He was still grinning a little and sounded only mildly surprised that I was pointing a gun at his left eyeball. What should that tell me?

"I tried to save your sorry ass," I said. "Spent the day with a mobster." I nodded. "He propositioned me. Did you know that?"

"No kidding? D?" His grin lit up a little. "Shit, he's worth a damn fortune. You didn't turn him down, did you?"

I stared at him in stupefaction for a moment, then:

"Does this thing have a safety?" I asked, remembering a dozen past movies. I didn't want to be one of those hapless bimbos who couldn't shoot her brother because the safety was on.

"You can't shoot me, Chrissy."

"Not until the safety's off," I said, still searching.

"Mom would be madder than hell."

"You know . . ." I lifted the muzzle and pointed it at him again. ". . . I don't think she likes you any more than I do."

"You kidding?" His grin had amped up a couple more watts. Maybe some women would find it infectious. I found I wanted to slap him silly. But that seemed kind of anticlimactic when I was pointing a gun at him. "*Everyone* likes me more than you do."

"Tell me what just happened," I said.

"You think I know?"

"Yes."

"Well, you're wrong. I told Robocop the truth. I thought everything was all hunky-dory after you came back from Chicago."

I narrowed my eyes. "I borrowed twenty thousand dollars from my best friend in the universe. Wore the same underwear for days."

He made a face. Apparently even a half-witted barbarian sets his standards above recycled underwear.

"But I figured it was all worth it when D promised asylum."

"Asylum?" His lips twitched.

"If you laugh, I'm going to shoot your ear off your head," I said, tone neutral.

He snorted. "You couldn't hit my ear with a baseball bat."

"Then maybe I'll shoot your head off your ear."

He was starting to scowl a little. "Listen, Chrissy, you got a right to be pissed. Hell, I'd be shitting bricks. But I don't know what's going on no more than you do. That guy *must* have been one of D's boys."

"He promised—"

"Asylum. Yeah, I know," he said, struggling with his grin again. "But maybe he lied."

Mob bosses could lie? I shifted my weight. My feet were sore. Perhaps I wasn't wearing the proper shoes for being attacked in. "Maybe *you* lied," I said.

"I'm your brother."

"My point exactly," I said, and widening my stance like I'd seen on the cop shows, embraced the Glock with both hands.

"Holy crap, Chrissy, are you out of your fucking gourd?" Pete asked.

I scowled, giving that some judicious consideration, nodding finally. "There are some fairly reliable indicators."

He was starting to look worried.

"I'm going to count to three," I said.

"Mom'll tan your hide. I'm giving her her first grandchild, you know. She's going to be really torqued if you kill me."

"You're probably right," I said, and tilting my head thoughtfully, lowered the muzzle a little, looking for the most shootable part of his anatomy. "I believe tradition insists that I shoot out your kneecaps in this situation."

"Ahh, hell." He shuffled his feet, looking irritable, then: "Okay. Fine. Maybe it was Springer."

I squinted at him. "What's a Springer?"

"The guy at the door just now. One of the guys who tried to drag me into the van. Maybe it was Bill Springer, the Vette's owner. I told you about him before. Springer."

"Was it?"

He threw up his hands, looking peeved and frustrated. But I wasn't all that jolly, either. "Could be. How would I know? It was darker than shit out there."

I thought about that for a second. "Did he ask for the keys?"

And now he just looked confused, but it seemed like a fairly straightforward question. I wanted to shoot him just for his stupid-ass expression. "When he was dragging you toward the van. Did he ask for the keys?"

"I don't know. How the hell would I know? I was busy bleeding from my head. Remember? Shit, you're such an—"

"Did he?" I repeated, voice dropping an octave.

There was a pause, then, "No."

"You're sure?"

"Yes."

"Doesn't that seem like an obvious first step if he wanted his car back?"

"I don't know. He loves that car like a kid. Maybe he wanted to kill me first. Get the keys later."

"How?"

"What?"

"How's he going to get the keys if you're . . ." I closed my eyes but kept the gun trained on him . . . kind of. "Never mind. Who else have you pissed off?"

"No one."

"You know how I know that's a lie?"

"Damn it, Chrissy—"

"Because I've met you."

"Put that thing down before—"

"Talked to you," I continued.

"This isn't funny."

"Neither was the time you locked me out of the bathroom after the Kool-Aid drinking contest. Who else wants to kill you?" I asked, squinting at him with one eye.

"Besides you?"

"Besides me."

He tilted back his head and released a long-suffering sigh. "Joey's kind of ticked."

"Joey . . ."

"Petras. He's in the department with me."

"A firefighter?" I was surprised. Pete was a firefighter down to his asbestos underwear. And those firefighters always look so chummy . . . at least on the calendars.

"Yeah."

I twisted my mind away from the thought of calendars, even though sometimes they don't wear much more than suspenders. "What'd you do to piss him off?"

"Nothing."

"What else?"

He exhaled dramatically, slumped over to the couch, and flopped diagonally onto the cushions, head draped over the armrest. "Charlene . . ." He shook his head. "She is so damned hot. Swear to God, you could cook an egg on her—"

"Please." I closed my eyes. I wanted to keep threatening him, but his current position was awfully discouraging. It didn't seem right to kill him while he was just lying there looking pathetic. I let the pistol drop to arm's length. "Please tell me you didn't seduce Petras's wife."

"No! No." He sat up abruptly. "She seduced *me*. I swear it."

I groaned and plopped into the La-Z-Boy.

"Besides, I didn't even sleep with her."

"Right." I dropped my head against the cushion. "So it's all just a big misunderstanding."

"Yeah. It is."

"I should have shot you while I was in the mood."

"It *is*," he repeated.

I sat up, glaring. "So you never slept with her."

"Well . . ."

"God help me." I dropped my head into one hand. I was holding the Glock with the other . . . just in case I came to my senses.

"Well, technically, we were in bed, but we didn't do nothing."

"Just tired?"

"Well, no." He grinned. "We was gonna go at it like adolescent squirrels. I mean, shit, this chick was smoking—"

I put the gun to my temple in one smooth motion.

He stopped.

"Honest to God," I said. "If you tell me how hot she was, you're going to have to clean up the mess."

He scowled, then shook his head. "You're so damn dramatic." Sliding forward, he took the gun from my hand, stood up, and put it on the end table. "Anyway, Joey walked in on us before—"

"I don't want to hear this."

"*Before*," he repeated, raising his voice, "we did anything."

I shrugged, made a face. "So everything's okay."

"Sure." He emulated the shrug and the face. "Why not? Hell, she still had her panties on. A thong. Red with little—"

"Sometimes I fantasize that you were adopted."

He grinned. "Mom says she was in labor with me for fourteen hours. Reminds me every time she irons my jeans."

"She irons your jeans?"

"Yeah. Not Holly, though." He whistled low. "She doesn't even own an iron. Burned herself once or something. Guess I'll have to learn to—"

"Maybe *I* was adopted."

He shook his head. "Saw you when you come home. You were wearing the same ugly-ass expression then that you got now."

"I'm sorry. Is my mood ruining your day?"

He bounced to his feet. "Hey, I know I screwed up with Petras. It was a dumb-ass thing to do. You think I don't know that?"

"I do sort of wonder."

He stared out my window. It was nightmarishly dark beyond the feeble light of my security lamp. "Been thinking about . . ." He paused. ". . . about what it will be like to have a daughter."

I remembered now that he was going to be a dad. It made me want to run out and buy a package deal of tubal ligations.

"She'll grow up. Get boobs." He swallowed and made a face I'd never seen him make while referring to the female anatomy. "Get married." He was scowling at his imaginings. "Probably to some asshole who . . ." His mouth twitched. ". . . who will cheat on her." He sighed. "Then I'll have to kill him." His tone was introspective, making me think he was maybe growing up, but I yanked myself out of that fantasy before it could get me killed.

"When did this all happen?" I asked.

"What?"

"The Joey Petras debacle. How long ago?"

He shook his head. "Half a year, but Joey's still cranked."

"Go figure. So you were dating Holly then?"

He wobbled his head. "Off and on."

"Did she think it was on?"

He plopped back down on the couch. "Naw. She didn't want to get serious. Holly, she's . . ." He scowled. "She's funny. Says she's crazy about me 'cuz I don't have a fit if she goes out with her friends and I can make her laugh even when she's barfing up her breakfast. Which happened a lot a while back, and of course I'm great in—"

I put my finger to my head in lieu of the Glock.

He flapped a dismissive hand in my general direction and continued. "Anyway, she says I'm the opposite of her tight-ass ex who watched her every move, but . . ."

"But she still wants someone who doesn't forget she exists every time she steps out of the house?"

"I know I fucked up," he said. "I just didn't think . . ."

"What?"

"Didn't think Joey would take it this far. Shit, I fed you sheep droppings and you never tried to kill me."

"Until now."

"Till now," he conceded.

"So you think it was him . . . on my stoop?" I stifled a shiver.

"Joey? No." He shook his head and sighed. "But his old man owns a string of clubs."

I stared at him, not comprehending. "Clubs?"

"Exotic dancers, that sort of thing. Got a couple in L.A.," he added.

The truth was beginning to dawn on me. "You think his father might have paid one of his employees to avenge his son?"

"Them bouncers ain't exactly clean as Sunday laundry. You know what I mean?"

I picked up the receiver, dialed 411, and asked for Chicago, Illinois.

He scowled. "Who you calling?"

I ignored him and spoke clearly into the phone. "Petras," I said. "Joseph Petras."

19

If men weren't necessary in the procreation process, they'd have gone the way of the dodo bird long ago.

—*Cindy Peichel, environmental guru*

"WHAT THE HELL are you doing?" Pete hissed, but the operator was already rattling off the number.

I wrote it down on a rumpled napkin, hung up the phone, and handed him the misshapen numerals. "Call him," I said.

"What?"

"Call Petras."

"And say what? 'Shit, man, I'm sorry your old lady couldn't keep her hands off me'?"

For a second I was tempted, almost uncontrollably, to knock him over the head with the phone. I'd tried it on others with favorable results.

"You're going to call him," I said, "and apologize."

"You're off your rocker 'bout a mile and a half."

"You're going to call him," I said, "or I swear to God I'll tell Rivera you stole the Corvette from—"

He snorted, but I raised my voice and continued.

"—from a man named Bill Springer, whom I will subsequently call to inform about the whereabouts of said beloved Corvette."

He stared at me. "I don't know how the hell you got so mean."

"Think livestock," I said, and dialed Petras's number. The phone rang on the other end. I handed it to Pete.

He took the receiver grudgingly.

"Yeah." I could hear Petras's muffled voice on the far end of the line.

Pete shuffled his feet, shoved a hand in the back pocket of his jeans. "Hey, Joey," he said.

There was a full five seconds of silence before the phone went dead. Pete glanced at the receiver, then handed it back to me.

I shook my head and hit REDIAL.

He stared at me and swore with impressive sentiment, but didn't hang up.

The phone rang four times, then: "God damn it, McMullen, I should fucking kill you."

I could hear Petras pretty clearly now.

Pete looked a little pale.

"Apologize," I said, but Joey wasn't giving him a lot of time. In fact, there wasn't really a pause between the curse words and the threats of dismemberment, some of which were fairly creative. But I was merciless. I took the cell out of my purse, holding it up like a weapon of mass destruction. "I've got Rivera on speed dial," I said.

Peter John gritted his teeth and ran splayed fingers through his hair. "You're right," he said, talking over Petras's rant. "I'm a shit."

There was a moment of silence, then, "And an asshole."

Pete nodded, sighed. "Yeah. And a fucktard." What? He already knew the word? Damn it! "Sorry."

"And a damned head case. What the hell were you thinking? You know I come home for lunch."

Peter dropped into the nearest chair. "Yeah."

"Should have shot your damn balls off soon as I walked in the door."

He sloughed lower. "I would have if she was my wife. She's—"

I could hear the word "smoking" about to launch from his lips and poised my finger over my cell's 4.

Pete's mouth remained open for a moment, then, ". . . your wife," he finished. "She's your wife." He exhaled. "You'd have had every right to smoke my—"

"Not anymore."

"Huh?"

The sigh came from the other end of the line now. "I threw her out, and all her crap with her. Shoes, spider plant, and fucking eyelash curler."

"No shit?" Pete sat up straight, eyes suddenly bright, mouth starting to quirk at the corners. "So she's single?"

I stared at him. The initial grin suggested I was going to need more firepower than a cell phone and an idle threat. I reached out and slapped him on the side of the head.

Pete's brows lowered. His mouth turned down. "I mean . . ." He sloughed back again. "I'm sorry to hear that."

"Well, you sure as hell should be. Girl has an ass like a time bomb. Second Chico hired her, I couldn't think of nothing else. Shoulda known she'd bag every loose bastard that came along."

"Loose . . . There were others?"

He snorted. "Goddamn amazing you could get mattress time."

Pete looked peeved. "She told me she was only doing me 'cuz I was so—"

I laid the gun carefully on my lap.

He opened his mouth, closed it, glanced out the window. "Listen, Joey, I'm sorry. I ain't been much of a friend."

"No shit!"

He looked at the gun in my lap, scowled, and sighed. "But my sister ain't got nothing to do with this."

There was a moment of silence, then, "What the hell are you talking about?"

"She's a royal pain in the ass," he explained, scowling at me, "holds a grudge like a damned pit bull, but—"

"Have you been sparring without headgear again?"

"You want to take a shot at me, man, you got a right, but leave Christopher out of this."

Petras laughed, long and satisfied, before pausing. I could imagine him smiling on the other end of the phone. "So someone's finally punching you full of holes, huh, McMullen?"

"Call off your dogs," he said. "I'll meet you—"

"It wasn't me."

"It ain't going to look good when the LAPD finds out your bouncers are taking potshots at the locals."

"Bouncers . . ." He paused, managing to put two and two together. "Pop sold the L.A. clubs."

"What's that?"

"Too hard to manage them from here. Sold them to some developer in Inglewood. Gonna be some spa where they give mud baths and facials and shit."

Pete made a face. "No kidding?"

Silence stretched out for a second.

"So you're in L.A., huh?"

For a moment I thought Pete might give him the address and possibly directions, but apparently even reason-challenged dimwits can think if they're shot at enough times.

"Hiding out at your sister's," Joey said, and chuckled. "Bob said you were headed down there. Hey, how's she doing? They still call her Pork Chop?"

"Naw," Peter said, and glanced at me, seeming to think. "Now they call her Dirty Harry."

"I like the sound of that. She married?"

Pete snorted. I wondered what it would cost to get a silencer for the Glock.

"Shacking up?"

"Hang up the phone," I said, and after a few more bean-headed comments, he did.

I stared at him. He shook his head. "Can't believe he kicked her out. Charlene . . ." He said her name with some reverence. "When things get slow at the station, we pin her picture up in the can. Shit." He slouched back again, stretching out his legs. "Joey's right; she's got an ass could make a boob man reconsider his—"

"Who was it, then?" I snapped.

He narrowed his eyes by way of question, drawn from his intellectual ponderings.

"Besides stealing a Corvette and cuckolding a friend," I said, "who did you screw over?"

"Cuckolding?" He grinned.

I gave him a dry look. "It's amazing you've survived this long."

"You've got to loosen up, sis."

"Who else?"

He shook his head, but the movement bobbled to a halt. His expression became a little pained.

"What?"

"Some guys don't have no sort of sense of humor whatsoever."

I braced myself. "What specifically do they fail to find amusing?"

"Shit!" He leaned forward, his eager expression reminding me a little of Harlequin, without the sloppy-jowled charm. "It was the funniest thing. See, Dehn's got this '71 Camaro Z28. Rally wheels, Detroit locker rear end. Chrome center caps with—"

"Dehn?"

"Name's actually Daryl. Daryl Dehn. He was a bowling buddy."

"Of course."

"Oh!" He shook his head and gave me a disapproving look. "Don't go getting all snotty. When we was kids you woulda given up dessert for some guy to take you bowling. Anyhow, he's got this car he's always bragging about. Like he built it himself from scrap metal and a rubber tree. Fucking Henry Ford or something. Truth is, he don't know shit about engines. But he's got to act like some Harley stud. Steroids, pumping iron, the works. Overcompensation's what it is."

I think I looked at him as if he'd just sprouted an extra head.

"I watched *Frasier,*" he said, then, "anyway, I guess he was a scrawny little runt when he was a kid. Asthma or something. So he's always saying how his Camaro is better than my Mustang. And fuck, everyone knows the Mustang's got twice the—"

I held up a weary hand. "I haven't had a cigarette for three days, you're an ass, and I have a gun."

He stopped, mouth open, then shut it and grinned. Which may be the only reason he's still alive today. It's hard to kill a guy who thinks everything's funny. "Okay, the kicker is, I tucked a little smoke bomb under his hood. Stuffed it under the coil wire by the distributor cap."

I stared, uncomprehending.

"See, it doesn't do no damage, just smokes like hell on fire. But Daryl . . ." He chuckled. ". . . he thinks his engine is about to blow, so he pulls off on the shoulder like a pussy, gets it hauled to the shop, and damn—here's the funniest part—them geniuses at AutoMart can't figure it out, neither." He shook his head. "Bunch of college boys sitting around scratching their asses. Can't let nobody think they don't know a carburetor from a lug nut, so they tear the whole damn engine apart, only to find my little bomb tucked up tighter than a freshman's—"

"You ruined his car?"

"Ruined it? Hell, no." He waved a hand at me. "It's fine." He chuckled. "It just cost him a thousand bucks to figure that out."

"And he knew you were to blame?"

He thought about that for a second. Either that or he had indigestion. "Could be he guessed."

"It seems a little drastic for him to try to kill you over it."

"Yeah, well . . ." He squirmed a little. ". . . there was that other part."

I felt old and kind of crunchy. "What other part?"

He cleared his throat. "See, he was so damned worried about his car, he told the mechanics to call soon as they learned something. Day or night, didn't make no difference."

"Uh-huh."

"Only, old Daryl doesn't always spend his nights at home."

I shook my head.

"He gave them his contact numbers . . . home, cell, work, stupid sidekicks, girlfriend." He had to stop and laugh. "Anyway, they got the numbers screwed up and asked for Kimmie instead of Daphne when they called his house."

"So his wife found out."

"Other girlfriend, actually. Daphne. Chick's got legs up to her eyeballs. And . . ." He paused without me even threatening him. "Anyhow, she was way too good for old Daryl. And she's got herself a temper. Still . . ." He looked almost serious, almost sad. ". . . . don't know how she could bust out his windows like she did. Even a Chevy don't deserve that."

"Tell me, Peter, have you ever heard the expression 'Water will seek its own level'?"

He glanced impatiently toward the kitchen. "If this little lecture is going to be as god-awful boring as I think it is, I'm going to get myself another drink. You want anything?"

"I want you out of my house."

"Yeah, well, I wanna win the lottery," he said, and disappeared from sight.

I dialed 411 again, made my request, and wrote down the number.

Pete stopped short, drink in hand as he headed out of the kitchen. "What the hell now?"

"Daryl," I said. "You're going to call him, tell him you're putting the check in the mail today."

"What check?"

"For the damage to his car."

"There wasn't no damage."

"Well, there's going to be a good deal of damage," I said, "if you don't make things right. And if I remember my anatomy correctly, the patella doesn't mend very well."

"Fuck," he said, taking the phone. "I should have smothered you soon as you first come home from the hospital." He dialed. "Ugly little shit anyway."

I smiled. "I hope your daughter's just like you," I said.

He blanched a little at the suggestion.

On the other end of the line a woman answered the phone.

He jerked his gaze from me. "Yeah, hi. Is Daryl there?"

I heard a mumbling but nothing distinct.

He thought about that for a second. "Is this . . ." He waited, possibly thinking. "Kimmie?"

More mumbling.

He paced closer. "Pete. Pete McMullen."

"Petey?" The volume was rising.

"Yeah." He relaxed a little, maybe because she wasn't

swearing at him yet. It had to be an unexpected relief. "How you doing?"

"Good. Good." Silence. "Daryl's pretty steamed at you, Petey."

"Yeah, sorry. That's why I called. You know where he is?"

"He just . . . he just stepped out for a few minutes." Another pause, long and uncomfortable. "For cigarettes or something."

"You know when he'll be back?"

The volume was dropping again.

"Can you tell him I called?" Another pause, then: "Thanks," Pete said, and glanced at me as he hung up. "He's not there."

I scowled. "Does Daryl have a criminal record?"

"Daryl? Naw. Well, nothing serious. He likes to act tough, but he's really just a white-collar pansy. Might have busted up a bar once, though. Some guys can't hold their liquor."

"Uh-huh. And you thought he was a prime candidate for a little leg-pulling, did you?"

"He was being an ass."

I nodded. "So he went out for cigarettes?"

He shrugged. "Guess so."

"Is Daryl dumber than, say . . ." I glanced around, looking for a point of reference. ". . . my couch?"

"What the hell are you talking about now?"

"You said he had asthma as a child. How stupid would he have to be to smoke after spending his childhood with an inhaler shoved in his esophagus?"

He was thinking again. I hoped he didn't hurt himself. Kind of. "You think Kimmie's lying?"

"Was she jealous of Daphne?"

"Huh?"

I thought for a second. "What's Daphne's last name?"

"Leifer."

"How about Kimmie?"

He shook his head. "No idea."

"So her legs weren't good enough to ensure her a surname."

"Do I want to know what the hell you're talking about?"

"I think Kimmie is worried that Daryl left her."

"What?"

"He cheated on Daphne with her. Maybe she thinks he's cheating on her with Daphne." I squinted into the distance. "Maybe she's right."

He made a face that suggested he saw my logic.

I picked up the receiver. "Where does she live?"

He shrugged. "Last I knew she was with Daryl. Who you calling?"

"Directory assistance," I said, but they couldn't find a listing for Daphne. They did have a Harold and Evelyn Leifer in Naperville, however. I gave them a call. A wobbly female voice answered.

"Hi," I said, using my chipper tone. "Is Daphne there?"

"Who?"

"Daphne."

"Who's this?"

I tensed, excited. I didn't usually hit pay dirt on the first dozen calls. "My name's Karen. I'm a friend of hers from work."

"Oh? Where do you work?"

I glanced at Pete. He shook his head, leaving me on my own.

"Well . . ." I laughed. ". . . this was years ago—that we worked together, I mean."

"So you've known her a long time?"

"Quite a while."

"That's nice." The phone went quiet.

"Is she there?"

"Did you say Daphne or Danny?" she asked.

I scowled at the phone. "Daphne." My voice was still chipper but it was wearing a little. "Daphne Leifer."

"I'm afraid I don't know anybody by that name. Harry has a niece named Pamela, though. Isn't that a lovely name? Pamela Fender. *Beckinson* now actually. She had to get married. Has two little girls. The oldest one's kind of going to fat, but they're both pretty in the face."

"Well, tell them hi," I said, and hung up.

Pete was staring at me like I'd lost my mind. "What now, Karen?"

I ignored his facetious tone. "Do you think Daphne's still living in Chicago?"

He tilted his head. "Daphne or Danny?"

"It's not too late to shoot you, you know."

He laughed. "Her sister married a guy named Milt Oslo."

I was already dialing. "You couldn't have told me that before?"

"I could have, but then I would have missed seeing your Girl Genius act."

In a moment I was connected to Chicago, once again asking for Daphne. I waited for a rejection, but the man cupped the phone and yelled. I glanced at Pete. Maybe he was trying to look cool. But he seemed kind of fidgety.

"Hello?" The voice on the other end sounded young and surprisingly sweet, considering her supposed temper.

"Yes, Daphne Leifer?"

"Who's this?" She still sounded young, but a little suspicious now, too. I reminded myself that Daphne had been around the block. Nothing grows women up faster than finding out men are scum.

"This is Officer Spencer. I was wondering if I could ask you a few questions."

"Is there some kind of trouble?"

"Perhaps." I paused as if checking my notes. "Do you know a Mr. Daryl Dehn, ma'am?"

There was a heartbeat of silence, and when she next spoke the sweetness in her voice had been replaced by something sounding like fingernails on rusty metal.

"Whatever he's accused of, I'm sure he's guilty," she said.

I blinked, felt my heart lurch, and improvised madly. "When was the last time you saw Mr. Dehn, ma'am?"

"It was when I kicked him in the balls and busted out the windows on his goddamn car."

Wow. "Do you know his current whereabouts?"

"Don't know and don't care."

Okay. "We have reason to believe he's in the L.A. area." I paused, hoping she'd respond. She didn't. "Do you know where he might be staying while in that region?"

"With Dickhead and Nickhead."

"I beg your pardon?"

"He's got a couple of friends." Her tone indicated she wasn't any more fond of the friends than she was of her ex. "They might even be dumber than Daryl."

"And their names are—"

"Richard Parker and Nick . . . somebody."

"And these two gentlemen live in L.A.?"

"No. They live over in St. Charles. But . . ." She snorted and changed her tone to a kind of hillbilly chant. ". . . they're skatin' down the superslab, hauling go-go girls down to Shakeytown."

"Huh?"

"What?"

I cleared my throat. "I beg your pardon?"

"They're truck drivers. In other words, they're sitting on their brains all day and staring cross-eyed at a white line, but to hear them talk, you'd think they'd invented air or something."

"You seem to know them pretty well."

"Too well. Dick's my cousin."

I wasn't sure condolences would be appropriate. "Do you happen to have Mr. Parker's phone number?"

"Yeah, I could probably chase it down, but it wouldn't do you any good. Janine says he's been gone all week."

"Janine?"

"Dickhead's sister."

"Could I get his number anyway?"

She paused. Ratting on the guy who'd cheated on her was one thing, but family ties are strong, even if you'd like to sever those ties with a butcher knife and run like hell. Just ask me.

"What did you say your name was?" she asked.

I squirmed a little. "Officer Spencer."

"Well, Officer Spencer," she said, "if Daryl's doing something stupid, it was his idea and he'll drag the Heads along with him." She paused. "And he's always doing something stupid."

She hung up a couple seconds later. I turned toward Peter John.

"She thinks he might be with Richard Parker."

"Who?"

"Richard—"

"Oh, shit!" He scraped his fingers through his hair. "Dickhead?"

Hmmff. "You know him?"

"Nickhead and Dickhead! They're truckers."

"Do you think they'd assist Daryl if he was bent on revenge?"

"You kidding? If Daryl declared himself king, those two clowns would buy him a crown."

20

I'd love to go out with you, but I'd hate to deprive some village of its idiot.

—*Emily Atkinson, one of Peter McMullen's more sensible acquaintances*

THE DOORBELL RANG. Harlequin went into hyper-squirrel mode. It was late. Well into the wee hours of the morning. I'd been talking to Pete for a lifetime . . . or at least a couple of hours. I'd also called Richard Parker, aka Dickhead, but I'd gotten his answering machine, which had spouted some trucker gibberish I couldn't quite decipher. I was tired, grouchy, and smokeless, but took a deep breath and opened the door. Rivera stood on the stoop, looking even grouchier than I was. We stared at each other for a good five seconds.

"Decided to try something new and tell me the truth?" he asked.

I opened the door wide. I hadn't told him much on the

phone. Just that Peter John was in some trouble and ready to talk. "You want to come in or just stand there doing your Terminator impression?"

A muscle jumped in his jaw, but he stepped inside.

Pete shoved his hands into his back pockets and shuffled his bare feet. He wasn't thrilled about the idea of coming clean to the LAPD. Neither was I. It meant Pete would probably be around for a while.

As for Rivera, he leaned his shoulder against the wall in the living room and watched us.

"You want something to drink?" I asked.

He turned his gaze slowly toward Pete. "You got something to tell me?"

"Listen." Pete was scowling. "I didn't do nothing wrong. Just a little practical joke, is all."

"So you think grand theft auto amusing?"

Pete opened his mouth, thought better of speaking, and shifted his gaze from Rivera to me.

I shrugged one shoulder.

"Want to tell me about the Corvette?" Rivera asked.

Pete scowled, a petulant expression that should have been left behind in the '80s. "It can do zero to sixty in six-point-five seconds."

Rivera straightened. "You find that out after stealing it from William Springer?"

Pete glanced at me again.

"I ran the plates," Rivera said.

"*I* need a drink," Pete said.

"Then get it," I suggested.

Pete snorted, but took the opportunity to leave the room. Maybe he's not as dumb as he looks. Maybe that goes without saying.

Rivera turned his simmering attention toward me. "Is now when you tell me your brother's really a good guy?"

"My brother's an über-dunce," I said.

He stared at me.

"I'm running out of names. Suffice it to say, he's a moron."

"Gotta tell you, McMullen, you're not looking all that brilliant, either."

I was just about to figure out a way to deny it, but he spoke first.

"Why didn't you tell me he'd stolen the Vette?"

"I didn't steal it . . . exactly," Pete said, reentering, beer bottle in hand. I couldn't help but notice that he didn't deny being a moron. "Bill owed me a favor."

"I don't believe Mr. Springer was aware of that."

Pete looked a little pale. "You called him?"

Rivera remained mute.

"I'm going to return it," Pete said.

Rivera snorted. "Like hell."

We stared at him.

"The department's funny about allowing people to stay in possession of stolen property."

"It's not stolen. It's—"

"Is he in L.A.?"

Pete shifted his gaze to me.

"Springer," Rivera said. "Is that who was here tonight?"

"He didn't ask for the keys."

Rivera turned his scowl on me as if I could intrepret the native language of the morons. "We think it might be a man named Daryl Dehn."

He waited.

So did I. After my illuminating conversation with

Daphne, everything had seemed perfectly clear. But now, with Rivera staring at me as if I were a few smokes short of a full pack, I wasn't so sure.

"He's a friend of Peter John's," I said.

"The kind of friend who accosts your sister on her doorstep?"

My knees felt a little weak, remembering. "Maybe."

Pushing away from the wall, Rivera pointed at my La-Z-Boy and glared at Pete. "Sit down," he said.

For a moment I thought Pete would refuse, but he didn't. Rivera sat down on the edge of the couch, elbows on knees, tips of his dark fingers pressed together. "Talk," he said.

And Pete did. Starting with how he and Daryl had been on opposing baseball teams and ending with the smoke bomb episode.

Rivera didn't look any happier at the tale's end.

I refused to fidget.

"And you think that was enough to bring Mr. Dehn all the way to L.A. from Chicago?"

"He was pretty pissed."

"But you said there was no damage."

"Tell him the rest," I urged. So Pete finished up the story by telling how Daphne had found out about Kimmie.

"Any other friends you think might want you dead?" Rivera asked.

Pete opened his mouth, but I didn't really think we needed all the McMullen laundry aired at once.

"I called Daphne," I said.

Rivera turned his midnight gaze on me and waited.

"After, ummm . . ." I cleared my throat. ". . . after Kimmie said Daryl wasn't around."

"And?"

"She thought Daryl might be with a Richard Parker and a Nick somebody."

"Dickhead and Nickhead," Pete added.

The edge of a feral grin lifted Rivera's mouth. "Hard to believe you wanted to leave Chicago, McMullen."

I gritted my teeth. Yes, I had been raised by a redneck subspecies, but damn it, who was he to talk? We may be a bunch of half-conscious Celts, but I'd met his family, and they weren't going to be immortalized in the Sistine Chapel anytime soon.

"Daphne said Dick's been gone all week," Pete said.

"Gone where?"

I rubbed my forehead. It was beginning to throb. Maybe I needed another quart of Nyquil. Or maybe I was just sick to death of stupid. "Skating down the supersub, taking go-go girls to Frisco?"

"Are you drunk again?" Rivera asked.

"I don't know what the hell it meant," I said. "I have a Ph.D. I don't speak—"

"Super*slab*," Peter corrected.

Rivera and I glared at him in tandem.

"They're skating down the superslab . . . the interstate. Hauling a load of livestock to San Francisco."

I blinked. Rivera stared.

Pete scowled. "Frisco's only—what?—couple hundred miles from here?"

"You think they came here?" Rivera asked.

I shrugged. "Could be. I don't think it was Springer," I said, remembering the Vette's owner.

"It wasn't," Rivera said.

I opened my mouth to ask how he knew, but Pete spoke first.

"Joey said it wasn't *him.*"

Rivera turned his slow gaze on my brother. "You put a bomb in his car, too?"

"No."

"Steal his car?"

"Listen—" Pete began, but this time I spoke first.

"He and Joseph Petras had a . . . misunderstanding."

"Yeah?" Rivera turned his gaze from me to stupid brother number *deux.* "What did you misunderstand?"

"Regarding a woman," I said. "But Pete spoke to him earlier. I don't think he's involved."

"That your professional opinion, or did you divine that?"

"Don't be a smart—" I began, but it was Pete's turn to interrupt.

"The fuckers smelled like shit."

"What?" Rivera said.

"What?" I repeated.

"The night I was grabbed. The three of 'em smelled like cow shit."

The house went quiet. "Grabbed you?" Rivera's voice was as deep and dark as the night outside my window.

I opened my mouth to explain, but nothing came out.

"We'd just come back from getting groceries," Pete explained. "Hell. It was all I could do to drag Chrissy out of there. Ever see her in the snack aisle? She's a Twinkie's worst nightmare. Anyway, we was carrying stuff out of the car, and all of a sudden some asshole clonks me on the head and starts dragging me off."

Rivera turned his slow-burn gaze toward me. "So many threats on your life that you forgot this little episode, McMullen?"

"We thought we had taken care of it," Peter said.

"Yeah?"

I shot my gaze toward Pete. Or rather, I shot Pete with my gaze. He scratched the side of his neck.

"I been having some girl trouble," Peter said. "Thought that was the problem. But we got that cleared up and then this shit happened."

"How?"

"What?"

"How did you clear it up?"

Pete shrugged, glanced at me again. "Just called and apologized."

If Rivera was buying it, you couldn't see it in his eyes. "Aren't you supposed to be getting married?"

"Almost two weeks," he said. "At—"

"What's her name?"

Pete narrowed his eyes a little. "Holly," he said. "Holly Oldman. We met—"

"She know someone's taking potshots at you?"

"I don't want to worry her. She hates violence. Even a scuffle makes her nervous. She's expecting a baby in—" he began, then stopped, mouth still open as we saw the trap in tandem.

"So you were shot at." Rivera's words fell dismally into the silence. He turned toward me.

I opened my mouth, hoping something intelligent would fall out. No such luck. I'd been struck dumb. Or maybe I'd always been dumb.

"And you didn't report it," he said. "Not to the department. Not to me."

"Back off," Pete said. "She's had a shitty week."

Rivera speared him with a glare and jerked to his feet. "And you! What the hell are you doing endangering your sister?"

"He didn't know he was—" I began.

"God damn it," he said, rounding on me, "why the fuck didn't you tell me?"

"You're not my father, Rivera."

"If I were, I'd get a damned vasectomy and put you over my knee twice a week just for—"

Maybe sleep deprivation and terror were conniving against me, because I think I said, "Just try it, Rivera. You won't need a vasectomy if you so much as—"

"Shit." Pete rustled to his feet, still scowling. "Maybe you two can get on with the foreplay after we're done here, huh? I think someone's trying to kill me."

Rivera drew a deep breath and turned back toward him with stiff composure. "What day was this?"

"The shooting?"

A muscle jumped in Rivera's jaw. He nodded.

"Thursday."

"You think there were three of them?"

Pete nodded. "One was dragging me. One had a gun. There was someone by the van. I could hear him talking."

"What color was the van?"

"Don't know. White or silver. Maybe tan."

"Make?"

"Ford. Least the assholes buy American."

"Model?"

"Maybe a Windstar, '02."

I stared. I wasn't sure Pete could name the president, but he damned sure could tell the make and model of a car in the dark.

"Does Dehn own a van?" Rivera asked.

Pete shook his head. "Not as far as I know. Just that dumb-ass Camero. You know it has a 350 engine?"

Rivera glanced at me. I shrugged, not sure which of them I hated more. He turned back toward Pete.

"How about his buddies? One of them have a van?"

"Don't know."

"Did you recognize their voices?"

Pete touched his head, made a face. "Felt like they hit me with their damned Peterbilt. I was pretty out of it."

Anger flashed in Rivera's eyes. I wasn't sure if it was the thought of crime or the thought of me hiding the crime that caused it. It's a common problem.

"When you were accosted on your doorstep," he said, looking at me, "did you smell anything unusual?"

I thought back, shook my head.

"Were there any strange cars parked on your street?"

"I don't think so."

"How about the cross streets?"

I gave him a look.

A muscle jumped in his jaw. "How about you?" he asked, glancing at Peter. "Did you notice anything unusual?"

"Like I said before, I was watching—"

"Do you think your assailant was alone?" he asked me, cutting Pete off at the pass.

"What?" Once he got rolling, it was hard to keep up.

"Did you hear anyone else? See anyone?"

"No."

"Think back."

I was tired of thinking back. And just plain tired. "I don't remember anything."

"Maybe a car starting as he was running away."

"I thought you had a witness."

"Didn't pan out. What do you remember?"

"A guy had just attacked me on my front stoop, Rivera. Mrs. Blanchard fired a gun in my ear. I might not have been at the top of my investigative game."

He stared at me for a moment, then, "I'll need names, spellings, and phone numbers."

I looked at Pete. He nodded, found a scrap of paper on the counter, and started copying numbers from the napkin near the phone.

"What else can you tell me?" Rivera asked, voice hard.

"I'm tired of being shot at?"

He snorted as he scanned the list Pete handed over. "Is that a one or a seven?"

Pete leaned down. "It's a zero."

The muscle in Rivera's jaw was getting a workout. He looked a little like he wanted to slap someone upside the head. I hoped it was Pete.

"What's Nick's last name?"

"I don't know."

"First name Nicholas?"

Pete shrugged. "Maybe. I've heard him called Claus."

Rivera stared.

"Belly like a bowl full of jelly."

Rivera stood up. "What aren't you telling me?"

Pete shrugged. The motion was stiff. "That's all I got."

Rivera turned toward me. "How about you?"

I cleared my throat, remembering D and his female entourage. "If I think of anything, I'll call."

A softer expression flickered in Rivera's eyes and for a moment I thought he might say something decent, might even reach out and touch me, but the moment passed. "I want you to lock your doors, arm your system, and stay in the damned house."

I considered arguing, but his eyes were already burning like Satan's. Not that I've ever actually seen Satan, but it felt like I was in hell. "Sure," I said.

He stabbed me with a glare for another few seconds, then lifted his gaze to Pete. "Can you keep her here?"

Peter shrugged. "Depends how much ice cream we got."

I thought about calling him a dork-faced perv, but resisted.

Rivera straightened, stalked over to Peter, and leaned close.

Their conversation was short. I didn't hear a word of it until Rivera pulled back.

"Got it?" he asked.

Pete nodded. He looked shaken. It takes a lot to shake up Pete, so it could be I was wrong. Could also be that I didn't hate Rivera quite as much as I thought I did.

I followed him to the door, where he turned.

"What'd you say to him?" I asked, needing rather desperately to know that someone had gotten under my stupid brother's skin.

The muscle again. "The senator's in D.C.," he said.

"What?"

"The old man always leaves town when he's got something planned."

"Something planned? You can't seriously believe your father wants me dead."

He stared at me.

"I just told you about Nick and Dick and—"

"I don't want you seeing Manderos."

I laughed. Actually laughed. "Because he's good-looking or because—"

"Because he's got a fucking gun!"

I opened my mouth to argue, then closed it demurely.

The tic danced in his jaw. "Just stay in the damned house and keep your legs together until I get this worked out, then you and Manderos can have a fucking orgy."

"Bite me," I suggested. Not quite so demure.

"Not until I'm done wooing you," he said, and left.

21

Maybe knowledge is power, but it ain't nearly as satisfying as punching some smart-ass in the chops.

—*One of the McMullen troglodytes . . . it doesn't really matter which one*

I WOKE UP AT FOUR in the morning. My head was stuffy. My eyes felt as if they'd been scrubbed with lye and left in the sun to think about what they'd done wrong. I rubbed them, sat up, thought of the previous night and wanted rather desperately to crawl under my bed. Harlequin raised his flop-eared head and gazed at me. His eyes didn't look a whole lot better than mine felt.

Maybe he'd been dreaming of masked guys dragging him into the shadows, too. More likely he'd been dreaming about pork chops, though. He'd stolen two off the counter three weeks ago and had looked kind of dreamy ever since. My own nocturnal meanderings hadn't been nearly so enjoyable.

Slipping out of bed, I used the bathroom, then wandered groggily into my atom-sized office.

Closing the door quietly behind me, I popped onto the Internet and googled Daryl Dehn. The image that finally appeared was a complete surprise. He wasn't the flat-faced goon I had expected, but a relatively handsome Caucasian in his late thirties. He had a neatly cropped head of dusky blond hair, was wearing a pale blue dress shirt with dark pants, and accepting an award for high automobile sales. He worked at a dealership called Stiller Chevrolet.

But it was the other pictures that truly fascinated me. The pictures of Daryl harnessed to a truck. Daryl Dehn, it said, was competing in Sheboygan's Regional Strongman Championship.

He was wearing a gray, ribbed wife-beater and straining against a rope that attached him to a large, cherry red vehicle with rounded fenders. Behind him, a crowd cheered. But it was difficult to notice anything besides the muscle. It bulged out of his shirt, past his baggy shorts, and up his straining neck.

There were more pictures. Some of him flipping tractor tires, some doing what was called the farmer's walk. One of him holding a trophy while his buddies beamed and dumped liquids on his head. I couldn't look away, Was this the guy who had dragged Pete into the darkness? Who had grabbed me by my front door?

Or had one of the Heads accosted me?

I did a new search but found nothing about the Heads.

And that was the extent of my investigative skills. So after a few seconds of intense soul-searching, I clicked off the Internet and dialed the phone.

J. D. Solberg answered on the first ring, sharp-toned and instantly alert.

"What's wrong?"

I scowled at the receiver. It was 4:53 in the morning. "Solberg?"

"Is Laney okay?"

"What?" My stomach twisted, my heart went wild. "What's going on?" Had I somehow endangered her by asking for the loan? Had D made the connection between us? It seemed unlikely, but not so long ago my own tortured existence had involved Laney in a dangerous plot. In that moment I had realized her life was worth a couple of mine.

"I haven't heard from her," Solberg said. "Do you think I should fly out there?"

A hundred nasty scenarios skimmed through my head... crazed strongmen, irate husbands, moronic brothers. "What happened? When was the last time you spoke to her?"

"Last night. I think I should fly out there. I could be there by noon if I don't pack—"

"Is she in trouble? Why didn't you call me?"

"She's still filming in the mountains, but if I took a cab straight from the airport—"

"Wait a minute." My heart rate slowed a little. I took a deep breath, closed my eyes, remembered who I was talking to. This was Solberg. And Solberg wasn't always the most stable of nutcases. "*When* did you speak to her last night?"

There was a moment of silence that somehow managed to sound defensive, then: "Anything could have happened in the last six hours, Chrissy."

I stared numbly at my computer monitor. A picture of

Laney and me graced the screen. We were in the lobby of the Actors Guild Theatre, just about ready to view the premiere of some movie I'd forgotten long ago. Behind us a dozen glamorous stars-in-training preened in their finery. Laney was wearing blue jeans and a tank top. She shone like a meteorite.

There was a reason the Geekster was obsessed. Still, I didn't feel quite ready for his paranoia.

"Solberg . . ." I closed my eyes again and rubbed them. I was tired and maybe a little bit cranky. "Do you have some shred of a reason to believe Elaine's in trouble?"

"They've got her riding a horse." He sounded whiny and a little nuts. Well, join the fricking freak show. "Did you know that? Did you know they're risking her life? Big monster of an animal. What if he gets hungry?"

"Horses are not carnivorous, Solberg."

"Okay. What if he bucks her off? He's big as—"

"It's a gelding?"

"What?"

"The horse, is it male?"

"Yeah. I guess so. Why?"

I leaned into my chair. Things were back in perspective. "No self-respecting male would hurt Laney, Solberg."

"It's a horse."

"You think Laney's appeal stops at Homo sapiens?" Maybe I meant it as a joke, but Harlequin couldn't look at her without getting a loopy look in his eyes. Of course, the pork chops had had something of the same effect.

Another pause, long and agonized. "She's out there with all those men, Chrissy." His voice was little more than a murmur now. "Good-looking, young, muscley guys with teeth and hair and . . ." He stalled, the line went cold with his dread. "Do you think she's met someone else?"

I smiled at the wallpaper on my screen. Laney smiled back. "Since last night?"

"This isn't funny, Chrissy."

I sighed. "Lots of things aren't. Did she say she met someone else, Solberg?"

A pause. It might have been pregnant. I've never been sure how to tell if a silence has conceived or not. "No."

"What did she say?"

I could hear him squirming in his chair and tried not to imagine his scrawny ass plopped down in his office amidst a thousand pictures of my best friend. It just so happens I had broken into his house once. Had even gone through his underwear drawer. I've sanitized my hands with bleach since, but the memory remains.

He drew a deep breath. "She said she misses me."

I dropped my head back and thought of the inconsistencies of the cosmos: The sun looks like a pinpoint of light, yet it's bigger than the earth; something as inspiring as a hot fudge brownie volcano can actually be considered detrimental to your health; and Brainy Laney Butterfield had fallen for the Geek God. "Tell me the truth," I said, "did you make some kind of pact with the devil?"

He paused, sighed. "I know I'm a lucky son of a— Sorry." He halted, reworded. "I know I'm the luckiest bugger that ever lived. I know it. That's why it's so difficult."

I nodded, making my chair rock a little. "You know you can swear if you like, Solberg," I said. "I won't tell Laney."

There was a moment's silence, then, "But if she knew, she'd be disappointed."

And there it was—the beating, pulsing, aching heart of

the matter. He had given up swearing, drinking, and acting like a . . . well, like himself. And he'd done it all for her. He was, in short, her knight in shining armor. So what if he was half her height, balding, myopic, and psychotic. He was hers. My eyes felt kind of wet suddenly. Funny, L.A. isn't usually humid, but it couldn't have been tears. I'm not the sentimental type.

"I'm going to tell you something, Solberg," I said, "and after I say it, you'll never hear it from my lips again, and if you repeat it, I'll have to call a hit man, and I've got him on speed dial." I took a deep breath. "Are you ready?"

There was dead air for a second, but he pulled himself together enough to answer in the affirmative.

"Laney loves you," I said, knowing it was as true as it was unlikely. "She loves you, and when Laney loves, it's forever."

I think I could hear his heart beating on the other end of the line before he spoke. "It was with God," he said finally, his voice barely a whisper.

"What?"

"The pact," he said. "It was with God. I promised to do everything in my power to make her happy for as long as I live."

And suddenly my cheeks felt wet. Damned humidity. I swallowed and wiped the condensation off my face with my knuckles. I'd been considerably more comfortable when Solberg had been a cocky little chicken-legged perv. "Well, you'd better," I said. "So that's why you haven't already raced out there, huh?"

"This is her dream. I think she needs to live it alone. At least for a while."

"Could be you're not such a bad egg, Solberg," I said, and cleared my throat.

He might have misunderstood my emotion, though, because his tone softened. "What's going on, babekins?"

I sniffled a little. "Maybe I miss Laney, too."

"That why you called me at 4:47 in the morning?"

"I was awake."

"Me, too."

I smiled a little, feeling wobbly. Solberg and I on the same track. Terrifying. "I could use a favor."

"From the Geek God?"

The name made me feel stronger. "I've just gotten so I don't gag when I hear your voice, Solberg. Don't blow it now."

He laughed, sounding more like the scrawny dweeb I'd met a thousand years ago at the Warthog, where the urine smelled like beer and vice versa. "What can I do you for?"

"I need information."

"Excellent."

I scowled. "Are you feeling okay?" Usually, he whines like a spanked mule when I ask him for favors. At which time I threaten him with unspeakable tortures and he concedes.

"Been a long night. What do you need info about?"

"They're whos," I explained.

"Even better."

I rattled off the names of the three men most likely to kill me.

"Wait a minute," he said. I could hear him shuffle around in the background. "I gotta get my Mini Rex fired up."

"Do I want to know what you're talking about?"

"A new system I'm working on. Powerful as a dinosaur, but tiny as a cricket. Get it? You can wear it in your ear. Say the words you want to look up. It checks its database, then reads back what it finds.

"Bored, Solberg?" I asked.

"I've had some free time in the past couple months," he admitted. "Say the names again."

I did.

"What do you want to know about them?"

"Anything you can find out. But mostly their current whereabouts."

"Anything else?"

I scowled, thinking back. "Whether they're right-handed or left-handed."

He didn't skip a beat. "And?"

"How much time do you have?"

"Twenty-seven days, six hours, forty-two minutes and . . . four seconds."

Till Elaine came home. "You're one sick puppy, Solberg," I said.

"Don't tell her, okay?"

I agreed, but I was pretty sure she already knew. Knew, and loved him anyway. I stifled a girly sigh and trudged on.

"There's also a Joseph Petras and a William Springer."

"Okay . . ."

He waited for me to go on, and I thought, *Oh, what the hell.* "Peter John McMullen," I added.

I could hear him pause. "Your brother?"

"Yes."

"What's going on, Chrissy?"

"Nothing I want Laney to worry about."

I thought I could hear his face scrunch into a frown. "I'm not real comfortable about keeping secrets from her," he said.

I thought about that for a second. "Laney's not the kind to stay safely in Idaho if she thinks I'm in trouble, Solberg."

"What do you want to know about Pete?"

"Everything," I said. "Everything you can find out."

22

A person without regrets is called a corpse.

—*Doris Blanchard, the liveliest octogenarian in the three-state area*

I WENT BACK TO BED after that, but gifted though I am in the sleep department, even I couldn't relax.

At six-fifty I gave up and stumbled into the shower. It was the smartest thing I'd done in days. By the time I stepped out of the steam I felt almost human.

Everything was going to be okay. I wasn't going to let these goons scare me. Well, okay, they were going to scare me whether I liked it or not, but I wasn't going to become paralyzed with fear. Even Solberg, oddball extraordinaire, had managed to be productive under stress. In fact, he'd created some kind of ear-sized contraption that would probably net him a couple zillion dollars in profits during the next few years. If he could manage that, maybe I shouldn't be cowering under my bed. True, Rivera had been rather emphatic about my staying home, but Micky Goldenstone had gone out on a limb to get me a visitation to Lancaster's state prison and I could no longer afford to pass it up.

Still, the thought of visiting my former mentor made me feel cold and a little nauseated. I considered hiding behind sloppy blue jeans and a baggy sweatshirt, but after my visit to Lancaster I would be going straight to the office.

I'd worked my ass off to build my practice, and I wasn't about to let Mandy scare off my clients at this late date.

On the other hand, I didn't particularly want to get stabbed to death while getting out of my car, either. Pattering barefoot to where my purse lay on the counter, I dipped inside and pulled out the Glock, then scowled at the back of Peter John's tousled head where it lay on a pillow on my faded plaid couch.

In a second I was beside him. "Pete."

"Mffmf."

"Wake up," I said, and nudged him with the gun.

He rolled over, scrubbed his face with his left hand, opened his eyes, and froze. "Oh, hell!" He let his head drop back against the rumbled pillow. "Not again."

"Don't be stupid," I said, knowing it was a long shot. "I just want to know how to use this thing."

He sat up slowly, looking wary and a little like his hair had had a run-in with an industrial Wet Vac. "On who?"

"Whom?" I corrected. "I'm not sure yet."

He was scowling. "When you figure it out, will you let me know?"

"This is the trigger, huh?" I said, fingering the doohickey.

"Shit!" he said, awake now and slurping all the way upright. "Be careful."

"That's my plan."

He squinted at me, then out the window. The sun was just now making its appearance. Lazy-ass sun. "What the hell are you doing up?"

I considered getting on my high horse and telling him that some people had to work for a living, but I remembered him promising to keep me home. Rivera could scare a turnip. Pete's not as bright as a turnip, but still, he may have planned to follow the good lieutenant's orders.

"Couldn't sleep," I said, "but I'm sure I'll do better with this thing under my pillow."

Pete swung his bare feet onto the floor. His legs were bare, too. What is it with men and clothes? You'd think they were allergic to fabric. "If you blow your damn head off, it's not my fault."

"I'll make sure Mom is notified," I said, examining the cool, brushed metal.

He made some sort of *hmmffffing* noise. "You were always her favorite, you know."

"What?" I stopped cold.

He took the pistol. "You know it's true."

"Her favorite *what*?"

He pushed a button and a rectangular piece snapped out of the handle and into his hand. "I think all that schooling actually made you dumber, Christopher."

"I was *not* her favorite."

He stared at me, jaw set. "Who was, then?"

Now, that was a stumper. "I always assumed she hated us all equally."

He snorted and lifted the rectangular thing. "This is the magazine. See the bullets?" I did. They made me feel a little sick. "You keep the magazine separate from the gun if you want to be safe."

"But I can't shoot anyone that way."

"I guess it depends on your definition of safe." He shoved the magazine back into the handle with a sharp *snap* and yanked back the slidey thing at the top of the pistol like they do in the movies. Then he tilted the gun so I could see in the open space. A deadly little cylinder was cradled there, cold and ready. "Now it's loaded."

I swallowed, but managed to nod.

"Push this button," he said, and did so. The slider snapped noisily back into place. I jumped and was surprised when he didn't laugh. "Now it's ready. Long as you leave the magazine in there, you don't have to rack it back again. Just aim and fire."

"What about a safety?"

"There ain't one. Not really. See this little lever in the middle of the trigger?"

I did.

"Long as you have your finger firm on that thing when you fire, it'll discharge."

"That's it?" I asked finally.

"Pretty much. There's a site at the top. You point and shoot. Just like a camera."

"I never was any good at photography," I said distractedly, and rose to my feet.

There was a moment of silence in which I expected Pete to fall back into unconsciousness. I'm not the only McMullen with the much-revered sleep gift. "She expected more from you."

"What?" I asked, staring at the deadly little piece in my hand. If I didn't know its capabilities, it would be kind of cute.

"That's why Mom was so hard on you," he said. When I turned my befuddled frown on him, his expression was somber, almost sad. "The rest of us . . . There wasn't much hope." He was silent for a moment. "But you're special, Christina."

I stared at him, mind free-falling in my cranium as a thousand errant thoughts tumbled about like underwear in an oversize dryer. Could it be true? Had Mom liked me best? Did she expect more? Did she think— But Pete's unusual silence caught me in a sudden stranglehold. This was my ninny-hammer brother talking.

"You're full of crap," I said finally, and he laughed as he swung his feet back onto the couch.

"Shit," he said, still laughing. "I knew the 'you're special' part was over the top, but I had you going for a minute, didn't I?"

I stared at him, trying desperately to think of something caustic to say, but my efforts would have been wasted anyway, because he was already snoring. It took all my considerable maturity to keep from stuffing corks up his nostrils. Peeved, I tromped into my bedroom and shut the door behind me. Harlequin rolled onto his back, showing his bald belly. I sat down beside him and rubbed him absently as my mind did funny things in my head. It might be called thinking.

True, Peter John was a troglodyte, but could he, this once, this singular time . . . be correct? Maybe my parents truly had seen potential in me. Maybe they'd really cared. Wanted the best for me. They simply hadn't known how to show it. It's often the case. Sometimes the offspring in question turns out relatively normal, but sometimes the collateral damage is devastating. According to Rivera, Will Swanson's mother had been a drug addict. Undoubtedly that had had some bearing on Swanson's subsequent life of crime. On the other hand, Julio Manderos had been orphaned, neglected, and abused, yet he'd fought the odds and become a kind and caring individual.

What about the man who had accosted me? Who was he? A dangerous man, certainly. An angry man. But controlled. Disciplined. I remembered the feel of his hand on my mouth. He had had a goal in mind. A mission. And he would see that through. Yet . . . what had he said exactly? *"It's hard to get blood out of clothing."* No, *linen. "It's hard to get blood out of linen."*

My spice orange dress was linen. Had he known that? What kind of man would have that kind of information in his head? An educated man, probably. A well-dressed . . .

Senator Rivera! The name popped into my head. The senator dressed immaculately and . . .

Crazy! This was crazy! His son had put insane ideas in my head. But why *had* Julio stopped by my office the day after Will's death? And why the gun? He was well dressed, too. Well dressed and charming. Too charming to be interested in me. Unless he had ulterior motives. Just as Dr. David Hawkins had.

My phone rang.

I jumped, heart pounding, and reached for it with quivery fingers. "Hello?"

"Chrissy?"

"Mom?" My relief was almost palpable.

"Have you heard from your brother?"

"Wh—"

"Your brother!" Mom's voice sounds like an early-morning James Earl Jones. "Peter John. Did you tell him not to go through with the wedding or something?"

"No. Why would I—"

"Why? How would I know? You tried to convince Holly not to marry him. Remember?"

"I didn't try to convince her not to marry him. I simply said she should think things through so that—"

"What? The last thing we need is for that girl to start thinking."

"Ummm . . ."

"What in the world is wrong with you, missy? Don't you want your brother to be happy?"

It hadn't even taken a full minute and I was feeling like a four-year-old. "He makes people eat excrement."

There was a moment of silence, then, "What on earth are you talking about?"

Good question. I'd never told Mom about the droppings. In the McMullen clan, tattling was tantamount to high treason. And besides, I had no desire for my brothers to spout off about the things I had done or the things I planned to do in the near future. Turnaround was more than fair play; it was smart.

"Besides, he's been married a dozen times," I said. "What makes you think he'll be happy this time?"

"There's a baby."

"That doesn't necessarily mean—"

"He's not supposed to be happy. He's supposed to be a parent."

"But you just said—"

"You don't want to make no more trouble for Holly, do you?"

"What are you talking about? What trouble?"

"This is family, Chrissy. You don't go messing with family."

My head was spinning.

"She's going to be a mother, you know."

"Yes, I—"

"You think it's so simple, but it ain't." Her voice was deepening. I felt that giddy combination of fear and guilt. "You'll find out someday when you have a ten-ounce baby trying to squeeze out of your—"

"Listen, Mom, I'd love to chat, but I have to get to—"

"Have you been knocking marriage again?"

"What are you talking about? I don't knock marriage."

"It's a holy sacrament, ordained by the Church."

"I know that."

"And, by God, this baby will have the McMullen name."

"Why do you think she won't?"

There was a prolonged moment of silence. In the McMullen clan that's more than significant. It generally precedes something humiliating and possibly lethal.

"Because Peter John isn't here. And I think you know where he is."

"How would I—"

"You two was always so chummy. You and him."

"What?"

"Thick as thieves, you two."

"Are you kidding me?"

"You call me first thing if you hear from him."

I felt limp, shell-shocked. "Sure."

"I mean it, missy."

"If he calls, I'll let you know."

"See that you do," she said, and hung up.

I stared at the phone like it was a hand grenade—which, come to think of it, might come in handy. Then I blinked a few times and shook my head, checked my recently dialed calls, and rang Solberg.

"She called," he said after the first ring.

"What?"

"Angel." His voice sounded dreamy. For a moment I wondered if he was high, but then I remembered that he calls Elaine "Angel," and that he'd never get high because it would make Laney sad. "She called."

"Everything okay?"

"She does love me," he said.

I relaxed a little but made my voice firm, even though I'd never be able to match's Mom's terrifying baritone. "I told you never to repeat that."

"She loves me," he said, and laughed giddily.

"I need more help," I said.

He was silent a second, then, "I draw the line at murder."

"I'll keep that in mind. I have another name for you."

"Shoot." He brayed a laugh at his self-supposed wit. He was less irritating when he was depressed. "Metaphorically speaking."

"Her name's Holly," I said. "Holly Oldman."

23

Sometimes it's nice to have a man around the house. But a dog will clean the dishes.

—*Tricia Vandercourt,*
Lieutenant Rivera's ex-wife,
a lover of peace
and golden retrievers

I THOUGHT OF a thousand reasons to change my mind, to stay home, to go straight to work, to hide under my covers like a prepubescent Girl Scout. But in the end I headed north and west, taking the 210 to Highway 14 and trundling along toward Lancaster.

I had bought cherry turnovers the night before and left them in my car for breakfast, but my stomach was more interested in churning.

I'd done everything I could think of to bolster myself for the confrontation with my old mentor. Reminded myself that it was not my fault that he'd tried to kill me. Taking comfort in the fact that he was locked behind bars. I'd pulled my hair back into a smooth knot at the base of my neck. My suit was tobacco brown, brightened with a lacy cami under the short, double-breasted jacket. My shoes were a pair of peek-toe leather pumps with three-inch heels. I looked serious, confident, and successful. Not at all like I was going to puke on my shoes.

By the time I reached the prison, or CSP, as it was called, I was sweating like a sailor. It was 9:48 when I arrived at the outer perimeter. I stopped by the gatehouse and was allowed in by a woman who was probably in her forties but looked as if she'd worked there for a couple lifetimes.

According to the Internet site, the compound covered more than two hundred acres. It took me a full five minutes to find the visitors' parking lot. Turning off the Saturn, I got out and smoothed down my skirt. My hands rustled erratically against the wilted silk that had seemed crisp and professional when I had left home.

"Can I help you, ma'am?"

I jumped, turned, my back pressed against the driver's door.

A young man in a brown uniform was watching me cautiously.

"Yes! Yes," I said, and peeled myself from my car. "I'm . . ." I cleared my throat. "I'm here to see Dr. Hawkins."

"Dr.—"

"He's a murder— an inmate."

His expression was dubious. "I'm sorry, ma'am, visiting days are Saturdays and Sundays. They should have told you that at the front gate."

"Oh, yes." I stood a little straighter, remembering to look confident, or at least sane. "I am well aware of that, but this is a special case. I'm a . . . I'm a therapist. I have a ten o'clock appointment."

He still looked uncertain, but finally he said, "All right," and turned away. "Follow me, please."

We entered a brick building, followed a colorless hall, took a right, and continued on.

"Maggie." My guide rapped on a counter the color of bleached sand. A pretty, fresh-faced young woman appeared, hair pulled back in a spunky ponytail. "We got a visitor."

She scowled. Her face remained entirely unlined. "It's not Saturday."

"She says she has a special appointment."

"I'm a therapist," I said. "A friend of mine called you."

She blinked at me.

"A Mr. Micky Goldenstone," I added, heart stalled, muscles aching with tension.

"Visiting hours are on weekends," she said.

It wasn't the last time I heard that, but finally, after dropping Micky's name about fifteen more times, I was approached by a man of fifty hard years. He was a little taller than myself, built broad but solid, and bald as an onion.

"I'm Mr. Rawlins. You Christy McMullen?" he asked, reading from a blue form.

"Christina," I said.

"What?" He glanced up, mildly irritated.

"Yes," I said, "Christy McMullen. I have an appointment to speak to Dr. David Hawkins." My knees still felt a little like Jell-O.

He nodded. "Why'd you want to see him?"

I didn't know what it said on the form. "I'm a psychologist," I said, lifting my chin a little and pursing my lips. "I'm doing a study on violent behavior of seemingly successful members of our society."

He was nodding again, but when he raised his gaze back to mine, his eyes were narrowed. "Says here you're a victim."

My throat started closing up. "What?"

"Says you was the one Hawkins attacked. That means you're the victim."

"*Was.*" I gritted my teeth at him and the world in general. "I *was* a victim. I'm not anymore."

His lips were no more than a line in his face. "Sorry," he said. "I still can't let you in. We handle victims different than the general public. You're going to have to meet with mediation. They'll walk you through the system, then maybe in a couple months you can meet with him."

"I don't think you understand," I said. "I'm a trained psychologist myself and certainly don't need—"

"I don't make the rules."

"Please . . ." The word sounded wobbly suddenly. I tried to make my voice stronger, but it had been kind of a bad week. "He tried to kill me." I straightened my back and took a deep breath. "Why would he do that?"

He was frowning, scalp shining in the fluorescent lights. "Look, lady—"

"I thought we were friends." My nose was starting to run a little. "I thought . . ."

He rummaged around in his pocket and came up with a tissue. It looked relatively unused. "Wipe your nose."

I did as told.

"You in love with him?"

I blinked. "What?"

"Hawkins. You carrying some kind of torch?"

I tried to process his question, but it wouldn't really compute. "He tried to kill me."

He snorted. "Stranger things happen in this hellhole every single day," he said, and stared at me for another several seconds, then: "We don't usually let visitors wear brown—color of the guards' uniforms. But you don't exactly look like one of the guys. Give me your purse."

I did so. He rummaged around, came up with my wallet. "How much money do you have with you?"

"Ahhh . . ." I was trying to think. Honest.

"You can only take in thirty bucks."

"Okay." I would be lucky if I had half that.

"I'll have to take a look."

"All right."

He rummaged through the bills, then glanced up like I might be pathetic. "You carrying any cigarettes?"

I shook my head, but he searched anyway, and came up empty.

"They're crazy for smokes. California banned 'em, you know. Pack can go for more than a hundred bucks."

"Oh."

He set my purse aside. "Remove your jacket."

I handed it over. He checked the empty pockets, felt along the seams, then set it beside my purse. My shoes were next. I stepped out of them, showed him the soles of my feet. He took a cursory glance and handed back my pumps. "How 'bout your waistband?" I was getting good at blinking. "Run your hand along the inside." I did. "Got any wire in your bra?"

Blink. Blink. "No."

He nodded, stared at me. "He ain't in love with you, you know."

"What?"

"We get women like you in here all the time. Young, pretty . . ." He shook his head. "Don't know what they see in these guys. Maybe it's a thrill or something. Maybe—"

"Did you know a Will Swanson?" I asked.

He canted his head, squinting a little.

"Will Swanson. He also went by the names Elijah Kaplan and Wally Hendricks."

Another head shake.

"He was imprisoned here not so long ago."

"Don't recall."

"He was shot in my backyard. Died by my garage." I was feeling a little shocky, kind of surreal.

"You shoot him?"

"No! No."

"You got some bad luck, girl."

I nodded. Couldn't argue with that. "I thought maybe David could tell me why."

He sighed deeply, as though he couldn't figure out if he should believe me or send me packing, but finally he motioned toward my shoes. I put them back on, slipped into my jacket, and followed him down another endless hall.

A minute later, he opened a door and nodded me inside. I stepped in slowly. It was about the size of my bedroom, almost square, with cream-colored walls, three chairs, and no windows.

"You sure you want to do this?"

No. "Yes," I said, and nodded once for emphasis.

He shook his head. "Sit down," he said, and was gone.

I sat fidgeting and shifting. The room was almost

entirely empty. A camera was mounted on the ceiling in a corner.

I was examining it when the door opened and David Hawkins stepped inside.

My heart slowed to a crawl. He smiled a little. I couldn't have smiled back on a bet. My face had frozen in some kind of hideous grimace.

"Thank you, Mr. Edwards," he said to his blank-faced guard, and proceeded to the chair opposite me. "Christina McMullen," he crooned. "Pit told me to expect you."

I scooted my feet up against my chair, and stared. "Hello, David."

He sat down, settled back, and steepled his fingers like I remembered him doing a dozen times in the past. "You look well."

The world felt tipsy and somewhat short on oxygen. "I'm fine. How are you?"

"I'm locked in a cage like a rabid wolverine," he said. His smile broadened. He looked little changed from the day I'd met him at a posh luncheon in Beverly Hills. But maybe there was an edge of feral anticipation in his gaze. Or maybe it had always been there. I'd just been too enamored to notice.

I glanced toward Mr. Edwards. He had remained inside, back to the door. He wore a brown uniform from which dangled a menagerie of tools that looked like they'd stop a charging bull. In that moment I loved Mr. Edwards more than life.

Still, I was having a little trouble breathing.

"How's your practice doing?" David asked. "Well, I hope."

I opened my mouth to answer him, but stopped myself

and cleared my throat. "I'd like to ask you a few questions."

He lifted a hand. The gesture looked as elegant and graceful as I remembered, the sage practitioner educating a neophyte. "Certainly. How may I help you?"

My stomach twisted. "Did you send Will Swanson to kill me?"

He sat perfectly immobile, staring at me. "Dating still not going well, Christina?"

"You paid him, didn't you? You paid him when you knew he was going to be released." I felt frantic and terrible, but his expression remained serene.

"I'm afraid I don't know anyone by that name, my dear."

"You're lying." I leaned forward. Mr. Edwards was watching me. His eyes were neutral, but his hand was on the butt of some weapon I couldn't identify. I briefly hoped it was a bazooka. "He was here in prison. There are no coincidences. You told me that. You knew he was going to be getting out. You sent him to find me, didn't you?"

Hawkins watched me for a moment, then tilted his head back and laughed quietly.

Goose bumps rippled across my skin.

"Why are you laughing?"

"This Mr. Swanson," he said, "can you describe him for me?"

"You know how he looked."

"I believe I might, but I knew him by a different name." He blinked. "You don't have any cigarettes with you, do you?"

I shook my head.

"So you've kicked that nasty habit again. Good for you. But as it turns out, Hollywood's portrayal of inmates' tobacco lust is quite realistic. They're rather desperate for it."

"Did you pay him?" I asked.

He leaned back and crossed one leg smoothly over the other. He may have lost a little weight, but he was still an attractive man—urbane, sophisticated, handsome. I wished to hell I'd never been attracted to him. "I knew him as Wires," he said, and smiled. "It is quite sophomoric, really, but here in Lancaster many have interesting sobriquets. There's an African American gentleman called Ivory. A young Latino named Spade, and me . . ." He motioned gracefully toward himself. "They call me Doc. Not very inspired, I'm afraid, but it shows a certain amount of esteem, I think. Did you have a nickname as a child, Christina?"

"Did you pay him to kill me?"

His eyes were laughing. I felt sick to my stomach.

"Pay him? No," he said.

"But you suggested it to him."

He uncrossed his legs, leaned forward, expression sober, eyes kind. "Now, why would I do such a thing?"

Because almost two years ago I had figured him out. Had learned his true nature. Had realized, to my horror, that he had killed his wife and others. It was my fault he was here, locked up like an animal. "He knew I was from the Midwest. Knew—"

"I believe his given name was Elijah. Elijah Kaplan, if I'm not mistaken. Did you find him attractive?"

I opened my mouth, and he chuckled. "Chrissy, you really must . . . How shall I say this? They are so indelicate here. But sometimes the beasts of the field know the ways of the world, do they not?"

I stared.

He laughed. "You really must get laid. It's one of the true joys of the outside world. That and a glass of Chardonnay on the veranda when the sun is just about to—"

"You told him to woo me." My voice had all but left me. "Told him to woo me and kill me."

He stared at me for a lifetime, then smiled. "In fact, I did no such thing."

"It's not a coincidence that he found me. It's not."

"No, my dear. I daresay it's not."

"Then, what?"

"As you might imagine, there is not an overabundance of intellectual conversation here."

I stared at him.

"And while Mr. Kaplan was no genius, he was stimulating enough."

"You were . . . friends." I could see it suddenly, two angry, intelligent men, too dynamic to be locked away. "He was seeking revenge on your behalf."

His eyes widened, and then he laughed. "My God, Chrissy, you have a one-track mind. And it's quite smutty." He chuckled again. "No. No, we were not *friends*. Neither were we lovers, as you seem to be insinuating."

I felt crazed. "What, then?"

He canted his head, as if analyzing me. "I believe, my dear, that your Mr. Swanson had an old-fashioned crush on you."

I felt the air leave my lungs.

"Did you know we have access to the Internet here?

Archaic systems, for the most part, but better than staring at the wall until it feels as if your skin is about to crawl off your body and your mind rots in your skull like—" He drew a breath, smiled, settled back. "I told young Mr. Kaplan about you. About our little altercation."

"Altercation!" I felt breathless, crazed. "You tried to kill me."

He chuckled, leaned forward conspiratorially. "Ahh, but that's the operative word, isn't it? *Tried*. Mr. Kaplan was quite impressed by the fact that you dissuaded me."

I had hit him with the telephone and screamed bloody hell. The cops had shown up before I'd bled all over my cheap linoleum.

"I believe he was originally intrigued with your bravado. Your zest for life. But then he saw your picture on the Internet. There is quite a lovely photograph of you in a periwinkle skirt and dove gray silk blouse."

That *was* a good picture. I looked slim, controlled, and intelligent. The magic of photography. "You're saying he . . . liked me?"

He laughed. "Poor Chrissy. Always so insecure."

"That he found me and made up a story just so he could get to know me?"

"How long has it been since you've copulated, my dear?"

I leaned back in my chair. "Not so—" I gritted my teeth and resisted closing my eyes. "That's none of your business."

"So tell me, is young Mr. Kaplan still in your life? Are you simply paranoid and needing to check him out before you take him to your boudoir?"

"He's dead."

His brows dipped the slightest degree, and I watched him, wondering if he was faking his response. If he already knew. If he had hired someone else to do the job at which Swanson had failed. "You jest."

"He's dead. Shot in the head near my garage."

"So his paranoia was not just a psychotic manifestation of his guilt."

"What?"

He puffed a little sigh of disbelief.

"What are you talking about?"

"So he survived this place, only to die a short time later. How ironic. But he always thought he had been born under an unlucky star. Although, knowing his past, I would have to say it's a bit more than bad luck that someone was intent on killing him," he mused, then glanced up as if just remembering I was there. "It appears as if he was right. The two of you did indeed have a good deal in common. As I told your lieutenant."

"What?"

"Lieutenant Rivera, the senator's moody son. He asked much the same questions."

"You knew who Will Swanson was all along."

"Yes, I did."

"You knew he was dead."

He paused, watching me. "In actuality, that I did not know. Your lieutenant can be quite closemouthed. I assumed he was simply checking into Wires's checkered past. He seemed quite zealous. Almost as if you were lovers." His eyes were spookily steady. "Are you two involved?"

"No."

"That's not what I hear."

"From who?"

"Whom."

I jerked to my feet. "Who have you been talking to? You sent the thugs, didn't you?"

His brows rose. "Thugs?"

"You sent them. The three guys with the van. The guy on my stoop."

His brows dipped and then he was laughing. "I am so glad you came, Chrissy. Indeed, I haven't been so entertained for months."

"I know who they are. They'll turn on you. You won't get out of here for a thousand years. You won't—"

He stood up. I jerked back, heart thumping, and he smiled, serene or insane or both.

"You're mistaken," he said softly, and, turning toward Mr. Edwards, nodded serenely. "Quite mistaken."

24

False hope is better than no hope at all.

—*Elmer Brady Chrissy's maternal grandfather, who was supposed to die of lung cancer twenty years before he decided to do so*

I HAD PLANNED TO DRIVE straight to the office from the prison, but my mind was spinning like a dime. If David hadn't hired Will, then whoever had shot Will had probably intended to do just that. Unless . . . unless the shooter had mistaken Will for Pete.

My heart thumped to life at the thought. It would make sense. They looked rather alike, similar height, color, age. But Pete hadn't even arrived yet when Will had been shot. Which meant that whoever had done the deed had known of Peter's impending arrival. How? Petras had known. So it must have been common knowledge at the station. Had Daryl called there and learned of Pete's plans? Or was it somebody else entirely?

Someone was keeping Hawkins informed, telling him about Rivera and me. Telling him about my impending visit. Then again, maybe he knew nothing. Maybe he was just speculating, lying just to make me paranoid. Or maybe he was lying about Will. Maybe he had paid Swanson, then hired someone to replace him when his luck had run out. But I didn't think so. He'd seemed thrilled with the idea that a felon had seen similarities between himself and me. Had been enamored.

I dragged the Yum Yum bag across the seat and took out a turnover. My stomach was still busy churning, but I'd missed breakfast . . . and supper. A little frosting rained down on my skirt. I chewed, thinking.

The process of elimination left the Parker trio. But there had only been one man when I'd been grabbed on my stoop. Where were the other two? Was Daryl Dehn the kind of guy who would work alone? It didn't seem quite right somehow, but what did I know about him, really?

I took another bite and crunched into something hard. Setting the turnover back on the bag, I picked the pit from between my teeth and—

Pit!

I cursed in silence. Hawkins had said Pit had told him to expect me. Micky Goldenstone's childhood nickname had been Pit Bull. Micky, who had been a guard. Micky, who . . . I felt a premonitory tingle in the arches of my feet. Micky had had therapy with a psychiatrist before scheduling appointments with me. A psychiatrist whose name he'd never seen fit to disclose. A psychiatrist who blamed me for his incarceration.

I fumbled my cell out of my purse, dialed directory assistance, and waited, heart thumping as it rang through to the California State Prison.

"Yes." I was holding my breath. "I'd like to speak with Pit, please."

There was a moment's hesitation then, "Is he an inmate here?"

I took a stab in the dark. "An employee."

"Just a minute, please."

I was put on hold. No music played in the background, or maybe it was drowned out by the sound of blood pounding in my ears.

"I'm sorry, it seems Joe already left for the day."

I let out my breath in a whoosh. "Joe?"

"Joseph Pitmore. That's who you wanted, wasn't it?"

"Pit, right? They call him Pit?"

There was a moment's hesitation, then, "Can I ask what this call is concerning?"

"I just . . . I'll call him at home," I rasped, and hung up.

So this had nothing to do with Micky. Nothing at all. Unless . . .

My cell phone rang, causing me heart palpitations and a near collision with an oncoming pickup truck.

"Hello?"

"Good morning, Christina."

It took me a second. "Mr. Manderos."

"I am only calling to see how you are faring this fine day."

"Oh . . ." I swallowed, a little shaky. Why *had* he had a gun? And why bring it to my office? "I'm fine."

"Good. That is good. Everything is well between you and your lieutenant, I hope?"

I vaguely considered reiterating that I didn't claim ownership, but my mind was busy elsewhere. "Yes. Sure. No problems."

"Good. After some thought, I worried that I may have caused trouble between you. It was not my intent."

"No. No trouble." That was just an outright lie. There would always be trouble with Rivera.

"Then it would not be problematic if I stopped by again sometime?"

I remembered Rivera's warning, Julio's affinity for linen, the Glock. "Stopped by?"

"You are not afraid of me again, are you, Christina?"

"No. I . . ." I paused. "Why me, Mr. Manderos?"

"I beg your pardon?"

"You could have your pick of women."

"Surely you are not saying that you think yourself unworthy."

I thought about that for a second. Maybe I kind of was, but I denied it. "No. I just mean, why me? Why now?"

"Because I believe you need a friend."

"How do you know?"

There was a moment of silence, then, "I know what it is like to need a friend. To be in danger. But I shall stay out of your life if that is your wish."

His voice was smooth, melodious, almost hiding the hurt. Guilt flooded me.

"No. I didn't mean that. I would love to see you."

"You are certain?"

"Of course."

"Very well. I shall hope to see you soon."

We hung up a moment later.

My hands were almost steady by the time I reached home, but Julio's phone call had reminded me of the gun. I treaded softly past the couch where Pete still slept and took the Glock from the drawer in the end table. Then I trundled Harlequin into the Saturn and hurried off to the office.

Bruce Lincoln was my first client of the day. He's wealthy, intelligent, and ridiculously good-looking. He stopped dead in his tracks when he saw a dog the size of a brontosaurus tied to the leg of my desk.

"This is Harlequin," I said, tone placid. I had taken two Sudafed for my stuffy head and felt duly hazy. "I hope you don't mind him visiting. I couldn't leave him home today." I had tried to think of an eye-popping lie to explain his presence, but my mind was busy elsewhere. So screw it; this was my office, I could bring in a llama and two Siberian tigers if I wished.

"You having your house fumigated or something?" he asked.

"Nothing so dramatic," I said, and turned the conversation aside. "I haven't seen you for a while. How are you doing?" Good God, I sounded almost normal, as if the material of my bra hadn't been called into question only a couple hours prior. As if a convicted felon hadn't become infatuated with me and subsequently died on my lawn. As if . . .

"Tracy called off the wedding," he said.

I snagged my attention back to Mr. Lincoln. He had

been a client of mine for only a few months, but I'd heard a good deal about the impending nuptials during that time.

I waved in the direction of the couch and swiveled my chair toward him. Despite everything, I had looked pretty decent when I'd left for work that morning.

"Sit down. Tell me what happened."

He didn't sit down, but trolled across my tiny office, looking caged and confused. "I don't know. I thought she loved me. She said she loved me."

He turned toward me, eyes sad enough to make Harlequin look like a piker. "Was it all a lie? Do you think it was all a lie?"

"Take a deep breath, Mr. Lincoln," I said, and took my own advice. "And let's start at the beginning. What's happened since our last session?" I hadn't seen him in two weeks, which wasn't quite the beginning, but seemed like a good place to start.

"I don't know. I thought everything was going fine. We had just ordered the flowers. Yellow roses. She loves yellow roses." He ran his hand through his hair, a nervous gesture I had never noticed in him before. But why should he be nervous? The man had everything. Good job, good sense of humor, good— Wait a minute. Why had he originally sought my services? Something about sexual addictions. I settled back, settled in, put my own silly troubles behind me. So someone had accosted me on my stoop. So a couple guys had taken potshots at Pete and me. This was L.A. What did I expect?

"So she seemed fine while you were at the florist's?" I said, leading the witness.

"Yes. Well . . . yes, I think so."

"You think so? Is there some reason to believe differently? Did she seem distressed about something?"

"No. I mean . . ."

I waited, pointedly not remembering David Hawkins's soundless laughter, or the suffocating feel of a large hand across my mouth, or Will Swanson's dead eyes.

Bruce shook his head, and continued to pace. "It was ridiculous. Just idiotic."

"What was ridiculous?"

"She's not usually the jealous type."

I nodded and waited, but he failed to continue.

"Did she have something to be jealous of?"

"No." This with some emphasis. "I mean, maybe Jenna was flirting a little."

"Jenna?"

"The girl in the flower shop."

I felt the first niggling of understanding.

"Are you usually on a first-name basis with your florist, Mr. Lincoln?"

"Well, she . . ." He was pacing again. Pacing and wringing his hands. "She introduced herself."

"I see."

"Jenna Mann. 'Like Jenna Elfman, but without the Elf,' she said. She's got a great sense of humor."

A side-splitter. Like Roseanne Barr, but something about the look in Bruce's eyes suggested she might be a few sizes smaller.

"So she was flirting with you?"

"Maybe. Maybe a little."

"While your fiancée was present?"

"No. I . . ." He stopped suddenly, deer in the headlights.

I waited, knowing.

"I had another appointment with her."

"An appointment without your fiancée?"

"Tracy asked me to go. She decided she wanted baby's breath after all. Not just roses."

"So you were kind enough to stop in."

"Yes. Yeah, and I . . ." The fingers through the hair again. "Jesus, she's a great girl."

I waited. "Tracy or—"

"Tracy. Jesus, not— Jenna's just a kid."

"So you're not interested in her?"

"No. I mean . . . no . . . absolutely not."

"Did you tell her that?"

"Yes," he said, but his face was red now and his hands clenched into fists.

"Were you in bed with her at the time?" I asked, and that's when he started to cry.

I felt drained by the time he left. Mandy poked her head into my office after the front door announced his departure. "Men suck," she said. "Why do they always want what they can't have? I mean, they rove around like wild Gypsies, but they expect us to keep our legs together till they decide to come wandering back."

Generally true. "You're not really supposed to listen in on client's sessions, Mandy," I said. But why *were* men so territorial?

"Yeah," she agreed, and entered the room. "Client confidentiality and all that. So he really slept with that chick, huh? Do you think his fiancée'll take him back?"

I sighed, and gave up on pretending to update records. "Would you?"

"Naw, I'd kick him in the teeth." She settled onto the couch, put her feet up on the coffee table, next to my magnet with geometric metal pieces stuck to it. She had on fishnet hose and four-inch cork-wedge sandals. "He's got a grade-A ass, though."

"Would that make the fact that he slept with someone else better or worse?"

The doorbell rang. Harlequin lifted his boxy head and issued a bone-jarring bark.

"Good point," Mandy said, and yanking her feet off my table, tromped toward the door. "That's probably why you're the shrink, huh?"

"Maybe. Hey, Mandy?"

"Yeah?" She stopped short.

"Do you carry Mace with you?"

"No. I hate that stuff. Some guy sprayed me in the eyes once when I was at a club." I didn't think I wanted to know why. "I was barfing for an hour."

"Still—"

"I got me a nail gun under the seat in my car, though."

"A nail gun?"

"Yeah. I can hit a bull's-eye from forty feet. And I took a kick-ass self-defense course."

"Oh," I said.

She turned away, but she hadn't made it to the door before it burst open. She shrieked, threw up her hands, fingers straight, edges out, just as Rivera stepped inside.

He didn't seem to notice her. "What the hell are you doing here?" he snarled.

I pulled my gaze from his, put an unsteady hand on Harlequin's head, and turned toward Mandy with smooth aplomb. "That'll be all for now, Amanda."

She lowered her lethal weapons slowly. "You sure?"

"Yes. Thank you."

"You want I should get my nail gun?"

"I don't think that'll be necessary," I said, and she nodded once before skirting the lieutenant with obvious misgivings.

I understood her feelings.

He gave me a look. It wasn't exactly ecstatic, but it wasn't quite as deadly as I expected. "I thought you agreed to stay home today."

"Did you?" I shuffled the files around on my desk.

"You have some kind of death wish?"

"I can take care of myself, Rivera."

He stared at me for an elongated moment, then snorted. "Is that some kind of joke?"

"No, as a matter of fact, it's not."

"So that why you brought the dog? Self-defense?"

"Well, that and the fact that I didn't think my brother was a good influence on an innocent—" I stopped, narrowed my eyes. "Did he tell you I was gone?"

He didn't respond, except for a slight lowering of his brows.

I rose to my feet. "Did Peter John call you?"

He still didn't answer, but watched as I unhooked Harlequin. The dog wriggled like a giant centipede, then galloped to Rivera, who caught him as he reared onto his hind legs. It's hard to look dignified while fending off a thousand-pound carnivore. You can take my word for that.

"I didn't expect him to turn out to be the intelligent McMullen," he said, thumping Harley on the ribs before pushing him down and keeping a hand on his bony head.

"And I didn't expect him to turn out to be a snitch. It was the only bad quality he didn't have."

"This isn't a joke," he said. "You could have been killed."

"That's why I brought the dog, and my Mace, and Mandy has a nail—" I stopped, thinking, heart suddenly lodged in my throat, knees weak. "Could have been?" He was glowering at me. I felt my face go pale. "*Could* have been?"

He said nothing.

"You know something," I breathed.

He watched me in silence.

"What do you know?"

"You tell me."

He knew about D. About the Glock. About . . . I calmed myself, watching his eyes. He looked smug, satisfied, almost relaxed.

"It's not Julio," I said, picturing him as a child, abandoned and wounded and afraid. "It's not. I'm not sure how he knew I was in trouble, and I know he had the Glock and everything, but just because he respects your dad doesn't mean—"

"Glock?"

I blinked, speechless.

"How'd you know it's a Glock? And what the hell do you mean *had*?"

"I . . ." I froze, momentarily speechless. "You found Dehn," I rasped.

He let me sit in breathless silence for a moment, then: "He was in San Francisco."

"*Was?*"

He nodded. "Him and the Heads."

"Holy shit!" I sat down suddenly. "Pete was right? They came here? To my house?"

"I did some legwork. Turns out they have a friend named Deets in Pomona. Friend owned a silver van. I put out an APB. The boys picked them up in East L.A."

"You're kidding." I felt numb.

"Sometimes even the LAPD gets lucky."

If I'd injured his pride, I hadn't noticed it at the time. "Do you think it was them? The guys who attacked Pete? Who grabbed me?"

His eyes were deep and dark, his voice the same. "We found your address in Dehn's pocket."

I felt limp. "How long have they been in town?"

"Since the thirteenth, according to Deets."

"So before Will . . ." I couldn't finish the thought.

"Looks like it."

I felt pale and breathless. Harlequin left Rivera to plop his head on my lap. Next to Laney, he's pretty near the best friend I've ever had.

"Dehn's denying everything," Rivera said. "But the Heads are already looking kind of queasy."

Me, too.

"There's one more thing."

I glanced up.

"Dehn's left-handed."

I remembered the terrifying moments on my stoop. "So it's over."

"Looks like it, but I want you to be careful . . . until everything's cleared up."

I stroked Harlequin's giant head, looked at my Glock-filled purse, considered Mandy's nail gun. "Okay."

"You all right?"

"Yes. Sure. I'm fine."

"You know what I think?"

I glanced up, dazed. "My brother's an ass?"

He gave a single nod.

"Did he call you?"

"It's the only thing he's done right since he hit town."

"An ass and a snitch," I said.

He rested his hips against my desk and scowled. "Could be he cares about you in his own numb-nuts way."

I snorted. "Could be you scared the crap out of him."

"Yeah." He grinned a little. "That, too."

"What now?"

"With the Dick and friends?"

I nodded dimly.

"We can hold them for a couple days, but I think someone will be ready to squeal by morning. We're keeping them separate. Gives them more motivation to talk if they think the others already have."

I thought about that for an instant. "What about Will?"

"What do you mean?"

I meant, had David been right? Did Will's murder have nothing to do with me? But I wasn't ready to admit that I'd ventured alone to Lancaster. "Do you think they shot him?" I asked. "And if so, why?"

"My money's on Hank Cooley. We know he was in town less than a month ago. But I think he might be back in Texas by now." He stared at me a second. "Still, it could have been Dehn."

"Why? Why would he do that?"

"You must have noticed the resemblance."

"What?"

"Will and Pete. Same coloring. Same height. Similar features. Maybe that's why you were attracted to him."

I was lost in my own thoughts for a second, but came to with a start. "What are you talking about?"

"Psychology 101. We're attracted to the type of people we can relate to. There's no shame in looking up to your big brother, McMullen."

I jerked to my feet. "You watch your mouth," I said, and he laughed.

"I have to get back to the station. Thumbscrews to crank," he said, and turned away.

"Rivera."

He glanced back at me, dark eyes sparking.

"Thanks," I said.

"I'd do the same for any psychotic shrink with a great ass," he said, and left.

25

All's well so long as you don't get shot in the hind end with a twenty gauge.

—*Chrissy's cousin Kevin, who didn't like to set his sights too high*

I DIDN'T EXACTLY WHISTLE through the rest of the day. In fact, I felt jittery and numb simultaneously and ached for a cigarette. At four o'clock I calmed my nerves with a yogurt smoothie from Sunset Coffee, then called Pete to tell him the good news, but he had already spoken to Rivera. In the background, my television was chattering about winning a million dollars. In the foreground, I heard Pete pop open a can.

"Should you be drinking?" I asked.

"It's a celebration, sis."

"Uh-huh, but you'll want to be heading back to Chicago straightaway."

He laughed. "Can't take the Vette anyway, remember? Your hard-ass boyfriend took the keys."

I refrained from swearing.

"Looks like you'll have to drive me back."

"No freaking—" I began, but he was already laughing.

"Don't have a shit fit. I'm just kidding. Mom's going to come pick me up."

I made some kind of gurgling noise in the back of my throat. It sounded a little like a phlegm riot.

"Guess she knows you've been trying to talk me out of marrying Holly or something."

"What did you tell—" I rasped, but he was laughing again.

"Jesus, you're easy. I'm just kidding."

I may have snarled a little into the phone. "But you *are* leaving."

"Sure."

"Soon?"

"If I didn't know better I'd think you were all hepped up to get me out of here."

"You don't know better. When are you going?"

"Soon as I get an airline ticket."

"Yeah?"

"You could fake disappointment, you know."

"No, I couldn't. See you tonight."

"Yeah." He laughed, then: "Hey, sis?"

"Uh-huh?"

"If you pick up some fettuccine, I'll make chicken alfredo."

A minute later, I dropped the phone into its cradle.

My brother . . . cooking. Obviously the world had gone mad. My afternoon clients confirmed that notion.

I stepped out of the office at 5:57, left Harlequin in the car as I wandered into Vons. The supermarket was relatively slow. I found the fettuccine noodles, grabbed a gallon of milk and a few other staples, such as M&Ms. I had started through the checkout just as my cell phone rang.

"Hey, babekins."

I had forgotten I'd ever called Solberg, and couldn't dredge up a lot of enthusiasm at the sound of his voice. I felt drained and tired and carnivorous. I put the Snickers on the rotary belt.

"You okay?" he asked.

"Yes." I straightened, rolled my neck, picked up the Sugar Babies. "I'm fine now."

"Yeah? Everything work out all right?"

I drew a deep breath and let it out slowly. "I think so."

"So you can tell me what's going on now?"

I shrugged, retrieved some Heath bars. "Looks like it was some guys with a grudge against Pete. But Rivera got them."

"Holy monkeys, I was afraid it was something like that."

"Why?" I shuffled the Milk Duds onto the rotary belt. "What do you mean?"

"I mean, when you're messing with a psychotic like that, you gotta expect some shit's gonna hit— Sorry. Some excrement's going to strike the proverbial fan."

"Well . . ." I said, fumbling the phone between my shoulder and my ear and digging out seventeen dollars in ones. "Pete's got some problems, I'll be the first to admit, but I don't know if I'd call him psychotic." Although I had. Psychotic and worse.

"I meant Adams."

Something twisted in my gut. The bills trembled in my hand as Vons's teller took them from me. "What are you talking about?"

"Adams," he said. "Holly's ex-husband."

I blinked. "Holly wasn't married before."

"Not after she changed her name."

"You know Laney doesn't like it when you drink, Solberg," I said, but my voice was weak.

"Heather Garnet."

I gathered up my change, trying to make light, to survive. "Ivy Opal?"

"Heather Garnet. That was Holly's name," he said. "She was born in Sacramento. Seven pounds, three ounces."

"That's ridiculous." The change rattled in my palm.

"Bound in holy matrimony on March 6, 1998, to a Gordon Adams. Or rather, unholy matrimony. He was one sick bas— Sorry. One sick puppy. There are all kinds of hospital reports. Broken ribs, iron burns, lacer—"

"What?" My heart stopped. "What kind of burns?"

"The reports I dug up said they looked like they'd been caused by an iron . . . like an ironing iron. Guess he was kind of a freak about his shirts being starched just right, and when she messed up—"

"Are you sure?"

He snorted. "Am I ever—" he began, but I was already hanging up.

Shoving the grocery bag under one arm, I dialed my home phone. No one answered. I hit the END button and tried again. Pete picked up on the fourth ring.

"Peter!" I was breathing hard, humping the grocery bag toward the car on one hip. "Are you okay?"

"Yes."

"Did you know Holly was married before?"

There was a momentary pause. "Not until quite recently."

"Her husband was abusive. Burned her with an iron. When I was grabbed, I thought the guy was wearing a dress shirt. The sleeves were starched. Why—" My mind spun to a halt. Something was wrong. Pete hadn't used a term like "until recently" in his entire life. "What's going on?"

"Nothing. Listen, honey, I have to go."

"'Honey'? What are you talking about? What's wrong?"

"Good-bye, Christina."

"Wait. What—"

"I love you, Pork Chop."

The phone buzzed in my ear. I stared at it. He loved me? He *loved*—

My mind stumbled to a halt. My hand was suddenly shaky on the phone, stabbing at numbers with fingers gone stiff.

"Rivera." The lieutenant's smoky voice made me feel limp, but I stumbled to the car.

"He's in trouble!" I stuttered, struggling with the groceries and my purse, my car keys and my nerves. "I think Adams is at my house. I'm going—"

"Wait. Slow down." I could hear him sit up. Could hear his chair squeak as he straightened. "What are you doing? What are you talking about?"

"Holly was married before. Guy named Gordon Adams. I think—"

"Don't think, McMullen!" he ordered. "Do you hear me? Do not think. I want you to stop and sit down."

"She changed her name." My hand was almost too unsteady to work the little Saturn's popper. But the locks finally unclicked. I jerked the door open, jammed myself inside, squeezing Harlequin over as I did so. "Domestic violence victims don't talk about it. She didn't tell anyone. Thought she'd lost him. I'm sure of it. Pete didn't know."

"Chrissy, listen to me. I'll take care of this. Don't go—"

"I think Adams is in my house."

"Don't do anything stupid."

"Stupid?" I shook my head. "I'm a trained psychologist. I can figure something out. Outsmart him. He's a control freak. Needs his shirts starched or he goes berserk. I think he was wearing penny loafers when he grabbed—"

"McMullen, listen to me. Don't try any of your dumb-ass plans." I heard a door slam shut in the background. "Remember Peachtree? Remember Black? Your plans almost got you killed."

"Yeah." I thought about that for a moment, shivered, thought again. "But Pete said he loved me," I said, and turned the ignition.

"Are you in your car?"

"He wouldn't have said it if he thought he'd have to face me again."

"I want you to lock your doors and stay where you are."

I closed my eyes for a second and covered them with shaky fingers. "He's a fucktard," I whispered, then drew my hand away. "But he's still family."

Feeling stronger, I shifted into drive.

"McMullen!" I heard an engine roar to life. "I told you to stay put. Do you know what the penalty is for disobeying an officer of the—"

I pulled the phone from my ear and heard him swear right before I clicked off. I felt cold and stiff. Harlequin was staring out the passenger window, tongue lolling, happy as a bluebird.

A cramp hit my stomach, but I ignored it, trying to think. I was a trained therapist, a psychologist. Adams was a bastard, a barbarian, accustomed to taking by force. So what if I refused to be afraid? My hands shook at the thought. Okay, bad idea. I had to think deeper, like a professional. What had made him the animal he was? Pain? Probably. Abuse? Likely. He'd been hurt. As a child. And so he hurt in return.

I would appeal to the little boy in him, tell him everything would be all right. That I'd find him the help he needed.

But what if there was no time for that? What if . . .

My mind was racing, scrambling around slippery corners and up dangerous slopes, but suddenly my time was up. I turned onto Owens Avenue, heart beating like a bunny's.

I pulled up to the curb next to my garage and hugged my purse to my side. Even through the imitation leather I could feel the hard, cold steel of the pistol.

Psychiatry be damned. He's my brother, I thought, and slipped the Glock into my grocery bag.

26

I'm just an everyday kind of hero. If the everyday kind saves babies from burning buildings and looks hotter than hell in bunker gear.

—*Peter John McMullen, firefighter*

I OPENED THE CAR DOOR and stepped out, knees quaking, mind screaming to wait, to think, to hold, to run. But Mom had been madder than hell when I'd neglected to wake Peter John for school; how much worse would it be if I let him be killed in my living room?

Still, I couldn't seem to move.

Harlequin squeezed past me and loped toward the front gate. The normalcy of his attitude woke some lingering demon inside me. It might have been the stupidity demon, but damn it, I deserved to have a normal life, to be happy, maybe even to go about my day-to-day business without some bastard breaking into my house.

Leaving my purse in the car, I juggled my keys and groceries and tried not to throw up.

The walkway crunched noisily under my soles. My breath was coming hard. I put a hand on the doorknob, and that's when I lost my nerve completely. I froze, unable to move, to breathe. Who the hell did I think I was? Freud? Spock? Houdini? I didn't know what Adams was thinking. Hell, I wasn't even sure it was Adams.

But then I imagined Pete's baby-to-be. A girl with dark eyes and a loopy smile. A girl needed a daddy, even if it was Peter John.

I shoved my key in the lock, prayed for fools and hapless psychologists, then thrust my way inside, jabbering something nonsensical and casual.

I tried for *"Hey honey, I'm home"* but may only have managed the "Hey." My voice fell like a rock into the silence.

Harlequin brushed past my legs and loped inside, ears flapping.

I reached for him with one hand, heart thumping in terror. I should have locked him in the car, left him outside where he'd be safe. Where—

But then I noticed it: the weighted silence. It lay in the house like a time bomb, waiting, ticking off the seconds. Not unlike a hundred silences from my past. Silences that preceded dead vermin, sheep droppings, and raucous troglodyte laugher.

Could it be? Could he possibly be playing me again?

And then I heard it—the coup de grâce—an almost silent moan slipping through the house like a ghostly whisper.

I ground my teeth. I had heard that moan before, and

each time I'd been duped. There was no real reason to assume Pete was in danger. Just as he had not been in danger the last dozen times he had made me look like a blathering idiot.

Harlequin hadn't come racing out of the living room, tail between his quivering legs. I thought about that. And then I heard it, the faintest snigger of laughter.

It was all a damned hoax!

I gritted my teeth, remembering all the humiliating instances of missing thumbs and popped eyeballs. And suddenly I knew the truth. I was a patsy again. The fucktard knew I was jittery. Knew I was scared shitless. And he was playing on it. Next thing, I'd be slamming down sheep turds and praying to the porcelain god.

"Damn it, Pete!" I swore, and tried to snatch the gun from the celery bag, but the stalks refused to give way. The whole bag came up. I tried to shake it off as I stormed toward the living room.

But suddenly there was a scraping sound and "Chrissy, get out!"

And then a man stepped into view. It took an instant for me to recognize him as the strawberry guy from the grocery store. Blond hair. Rocking body. Nice clothes. Perfectly groomed. Gun rising.

Gun!

I snapped the celery up to shoulder height and pulled the trigger. Life exploded in a sharp spat.

Adams staggered back and bounced against the table.

I heard feet pounding from the living room, but Adams filled my sights. He stumbled backward, struck the wall of the dinette, and slid onto his ass, legs straddled, eyes wide with shock. Blood trailed along the wall behind him.

He looked down at his ruined shirt, then at me. I watched him slowly raise his gun, but I was frozen, mesmerized by the winding trail of blood on my eggshell paint. How would I clean that? What did one use to remove—

But a noise like thunder interrupted my meandering thoughts, and then something hit me. The gun-loaded celery bag flew out of my hand and into the hallway. I screamed as I crashed onto the floor. Ready to die, to bleed, only to realize that Pete had rammed into me. We were both sprawled on the linoleum, half-hidden behind the counter, but a chair accompanied us. My mind reeled, taking in the duct tape half torn from his mouth, confining his wrists. His face was bruised, one eye swollen.

"Pete," I hissed, but a bullet zinged through the kitchen. Something shattered. I shrieked and covered my head, but Peter was yelling something, giving orders.

"Get over! Holy fuck, move your ass," he bellowed.

My brain broke free. I scrambled deeper into the kitchen on hands and knees. He tried to do the same, but his wrists were still bound to the chair arms. Reaching out, I took him by the shirtfront and yanked him forward. Another bullet pinged into the cupboards overhead.

Pete was swearing. I was either praying or crying. Maybe both.

"Damn female!" someone snarled. It could have been anyone.

I needed a weapon. A gun, a dog, a lieutenant. All gone. I was trapped in my kitchen, where—

Knives! The thought stopped the breath in my throat.

My cutlery was so close. In the drawer just above my head.

"I'm going to kill you. Going to kill you and your adulterous brother."

There was a scraping noise. I jerked my gaze toward the sound, but Adams was hidden from sight. Still, I knew. Knew he was sliding up the wall. For a moment his footsteps faltered. I prayed he would fall, would go down and stay down. My heartbeat stuttered with hope, but the footfalls stumbled erratically toward us. A chair crashed to the floor. I jumped, and then I was on my knees, still low as I ripped open a drawer and snatched out a butcher knife.

My gaze met Peter's as I dropped back down. Maybe he spoke, but I couldn't hear over the pounding in my head as I sawed at the bonds on his top arm.

Adams was coming. I could hear him staggering toward us. Heard him click back the hammer on his pistol, and then he was there.

Blood had soaked his perfectly ironed, button-down shirt, but he raised the gun.

"Lestoil," I gasped, hiding the knife behind the chair. "Lestoil'll do the trick."

He was glaring over his gun. It was long, black, scary as death itself. "What are you babbling about?"

"Your shirt . . . it's probably ruined. I'm sorry. It's my fault. I was . . . scared. Nervous. But your pants. What are they?" A scrap of past dialogue zipped through my brain. "Linen? Lestoil will take out the stain. I can press them. I have an iron in my—"

"Shut up," he growled.

I cowered back and did as I was told.

"Women," he scoffed. "You're all the same. Mouthy harlots until you're slapped up. Then you're all sweetness. Let me iron that for you, honey. Let me get you a beer."

I tightened my grip on the knife, waiting. His mind seemed to be drifting away, but suddenly he refocused, nodded.

"Heather was the same way. Like sugar in my mouth when I met her. Couldn't do enough for me. Couldn't . . ." He smiled. I shivered. "But she changed. You all change, don't you? Soon as you think you got a man where you want him. She was a skinny little runt of a kid. But I was good to her. Treated her like a queen. She didn't have to work. Just keep the house clean. Make my meals. That's all I asked. But she couldn't even manage that." He shook his head. "A man wants his wife looking decent when he comes home. Hair done, a little makeup, dishes properly aligned. Is that too much to ask?"

I managed to shake my head. It wasn't easy.

"I blame her father. He left her, you know. Just like my old man left me. Because he was weak. Too weak to teach her right from wrong. To train her in the ways of a real woman. Made my job that much harder. But then she . . ." He gritted his teeth. "Came home one day and she was gone." There was insanity in his eyes. "No thanks. No note. Just gone. I knew she was ungrateful. But I didn't expect her to—"

"You fucking—" Pete snarled, but I spoke up, jittering.

"Some women don't know when they've got it good."

Adams shifted his slow gaze from Pete to me.

"I'd give up my job," I rambled. "I'd give it up in a minute if someone wanted to pay the bills."

He grimaced. "And I suppose you're willing to spread your legs for that?"

Shit. My mind was reeling.

"That why you were with that man by your garage?"

"What?"

"I was hasty," Adams said. "I know better. Discipline. Got to be disciplined. But I thought he was *him*." He shifted his eerie eyes back to Peter. "Saw the wedding announcement on the Internet. I've been searching for years. Holly Oldman." He gritted a predatory smile. "I knew she had changed her name. Heather's no genius, but even she would think of that. I did some research, though. People have trouble leaving their names behind.

"You didn't know that, did you?" he asked, voice congenial, eyes insane. "It's true. They'll usually keep something about it. Same initials maybe. I tried that, then started broadening my search. Holly . . . Heather. See the connection? Once I found her I wanted to go there right off. Bring home my wife. Her place is by my side. But discipline . . ." He nodded, teaching me. "I waited. Learned what I could about your brother. Called the fire station. Knew he was coming here, right under my nose. Do you believe in fate?"

I opened my mouth.

"I knew what I had to do. Knew it right off." He took a wobbly step closer.

"Please," I said, and scooted a couple inches behind

Pete, cowering there, hiding the knife between us, desperately scraping at the duct tape. "Don't kill us."

"I wouldn't have. Would have left you alone. Men fight men. That's what they do. The way of the world. I could have just taken Heather. Could have walked in and grabbed her, but that wouldn't have been right. A warrior takes care of the other man first," he said, turning his gaze.

"You're a fucking wack-job," Pete snarled.

I lifted my hand. The knife bumped against the chair and fell from my numb fingers. "No. No, he's not." I was nearly shouting, trying to cover the sound of metal against linoleum. "He just values control. Order." I moved my hand, searching. "The world is in chaos. Families broken apart. Fathers leaving. Abuse. Children turning to drugs. Women taking masculine roles. Men devalued."

He was staring at me again, and for a moment I thought he was buying it, but then he spoke. "You're a shrink, aren't you?"

My hands froze. "Psychologist," I whispered.

He nodded. "You think you're smarter than me."

"No," I said. "I think you're hurting. Why don't we—"

"You think you can play me," he snarled, and cocked the pistol. "Nobody plays me."

I don't remember finding the knife. Don't remember throwing it. But suddenly it was soaring, spinning end over end. I watched it fly in slow motion, watched it wing past him and clatter uselessly against the wall.

"You'll pay!" he growled, and aimed.

I ducked, wanting to live, but suddenly there was a crash.

Someone yelled.

Adams twisted away, gun raised. Rivera stood in the hallway, legs spread. The world exploded. I screamed.

And then Adams fell, toppling sideways, dead before he hit the floor.

27

You can't choose your family. Can't shoot 'em, either.

—Glen McMullen,
Chrissy's dad, on child-rearing

IT WAS A WARM Friday afternoon in June when Lieutenant Jack Rivera accompanied me on a flight to Chicago. Maybe he went because he thought it would be pathetic if I attended my brother's wedding sans date again, or maybe he went because he thought someone in Chi-town might want me dead. But I prefer to believe it was because he found me irresistible.

I was beginning to put the past behind me, trying to get back to normal, or what passes as such in my world. In the past week, I had seen my usual clients, including Micky Goldenstone. As it turned out, he had never met David Hawkins, but I still couldn't help but wonder if somehow David knew I had a client who had been called

Pit. Knew and was using the fact to make me paranoid, to ruin my business, my sanity.

As for Micky, he was struggling, battling with guilt, skirmishing with the idea of contacting Keneasha, of spilling his guts and opening his soul. I worried about him. Ached for him.

On the other hand, Julio Manderos seemed to worry about me. He had dropped by unexpectedly after work and gifted me with an iTwin foot massager. It hadn't felt as heavenly as his hands, but his gesture had made me laugh, and the iTwin didn't seem to infuriate Rivera. I hadn't quite figured out if that was a plus or a minus.

Sitting there beside him, flying coach, with our arms almost touching, felt oddly personal. I tried to fill my head with thoughts of the impending nuptials, to forgo the blushing discomfort of skin against skin. I felt as if I were ten years old again, dreaming about my first kiss. Which, by the by, had been long on saliva and short on charm.

"You're nervous," Rivera said. He was watching me. I felt the heat of his dark appeal even before I turned toward him.

We'd just lifted off a few minutes before, and my inner ear was still unhappy about the idea of leaving terra firma.

"It's been a rather trying month," I said.

He nodded, eyes intense. "Daryl and the Heads will be in jail for a while."

"Even though they were firing blanks?" As it turned out, Pete's "friends" hadn't actually wanted him dead. Just to scare the wits out of him. Mission accomplished.

"For being stupid if nothing else. And possession," Rivera said.

"Of..."

"Marijuana. They must have been higher than Cheech when they grabbed him. So you're safe," he added. "You can relax. Unless something else is making you nervous."

"A chauvinistic madman was trying to kill me," I said. "Forgive me if I'm still a bit overwrought."

The scar at the corner of Rivera's mouth twitched a little. He was wearing a sky blue button-down shirt and black dress pants. He looked sharp enough to cut your lips on. If your lips happened to be somewhere on his anatomy. Mine weren't. "Madmen are trying to kill you all the time, McMullen. I don't think that's what's bothering you."

"Shows what you know," I said, and eased up on the armrests.

He leaned a little closer. He smelled good. Like someplace sexy where they don't wear a lot of clothes. "So I figure it's either me or the wedding that's got you all keyed up."

I drew a deep breath and scowled at the head of the blond guy in front of me. His hair had been gelled into peaks resembling meringue. The sight made my stomach rumble.

"Peter John thinks there's nothing in the world more amusing than bodily functions gone awry," I said.

Rivera narrowed his eyes and squinted a little, pondering. "I thought I was beginning to follow the twisted meanderings of your thought processes, but..." He shook his head.

I tapped the armrest, imagining the ugly future. "There's nothing funnier to him than flatulence, unless it's seeing me in some god-awful bridesmaid's dress with layers of—"

"I thought you already took care of the dress."

It was then that I remembered my previous lies about my earlier flight to Chicago. Panic hit me somewhere in the midsection. "What?" I sounded a little squeaky.

He stared at me, dead-on.

"Listen—" I began, but he held up his hand.

"I don't want to know."

"What?"

"Did you kill anyone?"

I thought about that for a second, then shook my head.

"Buy any illegal substances?"

"Umm, no."

"Then I don't want to hear about it. Not till I'm done with the wooing."

Wooing. "Okay."

"So you were saying . . ."

"Oh." It took me a moment to reboot my thoughts. "Nothing makes Pete happier than making me look like a pink tank."

Rivera watched me for a long instant, then dropped his head against the cushion behind him and laughed.

I watched him. I don't like to be laughed at, and he laughed for a long time. So I gritted a careful smile. He was, after all, accompanying me to a frightfully familial occasion that many a brave man wouldn't dare attend. "What's so funny?" I asked.

"You," he said, and grinned as he turned toward me. "Think about it, McMullen. In the past couple weeks you've survived death threats, car chases, and your dumb-ass brother." He chuckled again, low and smoky. "And you're worried about the color of your dress?"

"Not the color," I corrected. Men! "The style. The last wedding I was in I wore a bow the size of Texas stretched across my . . ." I glanced to the right. A silver-haired gentleman was watching me from D14. ". . . derriere," I finished.

"Derriere," Rivera repeated, and took my hand in his. His skin felt warm and rough. His smile looked the same. "That another word for ass?"

I cleared my throat, remembered our vow to take things slow, and gave him a prim glance. "I'm a licensed psychologist."

"Oh, that's right." He nodded. "That's why you could psychoanalyze the crap out of Adams the way you did."

I felt a little pasty at the memory. "My diagnosis was correct," I said. "He was an obsessive-compulsive neurotic with pathological anger issues. Had I been given an opportunity, I could have convinced him to relinquish his—"

"You shot him," Rivera said. "Point-blank in the shoulder. Hell, I could have done that."

I opened my mouth to object, but the truth was, I would have stabbed him, too, given half a chance. That realization did unsteady things to my equilibrium. Made me think maybe I didn't know myself quite as well as I thought I did. Like maybe I wasn't quite as sophisticated as I liked to believe. "I don't know what came over me," I said. "I was thinking of Pete and his practical jokes and—" I shrugged. "Suddenly I was sure it was all some kind of sick game."

"Christ, I'm glad there was no hearing. I'm not sure

a judge would have been real sympathetic when you told him you thought Adams was your brother, so you shot him."

"I didn't say that . . . exactly."

He was grinning a little and scraped his thumb softly across my knuckles, making my innards quiver. "If he shows up unannounced again, I'll shoot him myself."

I cleared my throat and shifted my gaze from his thumb. Thumbs are not sexy. No matter what innards say. "What's that?"

He stared at me, eyes dark as turtle mocha latte. "You're his baby sister. He's supposed to protect you."

I thought it might be my duty as a bright, articulate woman to tug my hand from his and declare the obvious; I was nobody's baby sister. But I was busy trying to calm my innards . . . and my salivary glands. "Isn't that a rather antiquated idea, Rivera?"

"Call me a sentimental moron. But it just doesn't seem right for a grown man to hide behind a woman," he said, and raised my hand to his lips.

The caress was warm and titillating, sparking improper suggestions off in every possible direction.

In actuality, I think I might have been hiding behind *him*, but I said, "I'll, ummm . . . I'll tell him."

He stared into my eyes for several seconds, then, "It doesn't matter anyway."

"What—" I cleared the squeak from my throat again and tried, rather unsuccessfully, not to squirm. I've never felt any particular need to be a member of the mile-high club, but I have to admit, at that precise moment I was considering filling out an application. "What doesn't matter?"

"What you wear."

"You wouldn't say that if you saw the size of the bow on—"

"I'd still imagine you naked."

My mouth fell open. I made a few false verbal starts, then found my way. "I thought we were going to take this dating thing slow for a while."

"This is slow, sweet cheeks," he said, and skimmed his fingers down my thigh to my knee. My left leg was glad I had worn a dress. My right leg was kind of pissed it had been placed on the wrong side of my body.

"Jesus," my lips said.

"Pray now while you have the chance."

"Jesus," I repeated.

The rest of the flight was a blur. Suffice it to say that I felt a little *tense* by the time we touched down, but I did not drag him into the rest room and join the mile-highers.

That would have been tacky. Exciting as hell. And practical. I mean, there's not much else to do on flights these days now that they don't even serve a decent meal. Still, it would have been tacky.

We fought our way through O'Hare with our carry-on luggage in tow, then rented a nondescript, midsize vehicle and proceeded to Holy Name Catholic Church. Rivera watched me as I drove. I could smell the scent of his thoughts. They were raunchy.

"So I get to meet the infamous McMullen clan," he mused.

I refrained from cursing, since I couldn't trust my salivary glands to allow me to do it properly.

We arrived at church seven minutes after the rehearsal was scheduled to begin. The vestibule smelled of smoke and candle wax and echoed with a thousand errant memories. They all assailed me at once. Mean little shits. I fought them off like hungry piranhas. This was a new Christina. A classy version of the old—

"Chrissy!" My mother came storming out of the sanctuary like a wombat on a sugar high. "Where have you been? You're late."

"Hello, Mother," I said, heart racing. "We had a nice—"

"Gerald." She turned toward Rivera. They'd met before. Blessedly, I had been heavily medicated at the time. I should have had such foresight again, but I'd finally fought off my head cold. "You've got to meet Glen." She turned, hair lacquered to her head with enough spray to keep a ship at port. "Michael. Michael," she called. "Where's Chrissy's dress? I'm afraid it's going to be too small. I think she should try it on right away so we can take it out if we need to."

Michael Brian McMullen stepped into view. The darkest of the three Neanderthals, he grinned his slow grin and sauntered over.

"Michael," I began, I'd like to introduce you to—"

"Crazy Chrissy," he said, and wrapping his arms around me, lifted me from the floor and squeezed me like a tube of Crest. "Shit, you don't weigh hardly nothing," he said, and set me back down.

I disengaged, tugged my sleek but classy little black dress back into place, and cleared my throat. "This is—"

"You must be her cop," Michael said, and turned his gaze toward Rivera. They shook like two bears faced off across the tundra. "Been hearing stories."

Rivera's eyes were narrowed. "I've heard a few myself."

They stared at each other. Michael grinned. "She ever tell you 'bout the time she set her pants on fire?"

"I think I missed that one."

"She had a crush on this kid," Michael said. "We called him Scags. I don't know what his real name—"

"That must be the dress!" I shouted, seeing a passing garment bag. I never thought I'd be relieved, but apparently there are worse things than assbows the size of pachyderms: there are stories that begin with "She had a crush on this kid."

Spying the dress, Mom rushed over, snatched it from some hapless woman's hands, and shoved it into mine. I pulled the opaque plastic back with slow deliberation.

The gown looked surprisingly normal. It was mint green. The overskirt was made of a delicate organza and there wasn't a bow in sight.

But I was out of ogling time. Because that's when James burst out of the sanctuary.

"Hey, anyone know when Chrissy's—" He stopped, stared at me, and grinned. "'Bout damned time you showed up. Pete looks like he's gonna piss himself. Come on, they're waiting for you."

The dress was snatched from my hands and I was rushed toward the altar, where Holly turned toward me. Her belly was big enough to gestate a brachiosaur, but she still looked pretty, big-eyed, and delicate. Maybe there was a toughness to her that I'd failed to see before, though. A toughness that had helped her survive an abusive marriage and find a guy who . . . well . . . Okay, Pete may be hell and gone from sainthood, but when I saw him standing near the vigil candles, I thought I recognized something in his eyes that had never been there before. Devotion. Admiration. Maybe even maturity.

"Christina . . ." Holly's little-girl voice drew my attention. Her eyes were round and worried as she took my hand. "I'm so sorry."

"Sorry?" I was trying to keep up. But with Rivera's blinding sexuality and the normal-looking dress and Michael sort of complimenting me, I was feeling kind of discombobulated.

Then I saw Father Pat. As far as I know he may have been one of the original authors of the Old Testament. Still tall and stringy, he glared at me from beneath brows so low you'd think they obscured his vision. But he saw. Oh, he saw. I stared at him, heart beating slowly, wishing like hell I had not, at one juncture, wrapped cellophane around the toilet seat in the rectory.

"I didn't think he'd ever find me," Holly was saying.

I dragged my gaze from the priest's, trying to focus.

"It had been so long," she said. "Seven years since I saw him last."

I squeezed her hand. "He was . . ." A first-rate nutcase. ". . . a troubled man," I said. I could still feel Father's eyes on me.

"Can you forgive me?"

"Forgiveness is . . ." I skittered my gaze to Father Pat. ". . . divine."

I think I heard him snort. I turned back to Holly. Priests are not supposed to snort. Even if someone may have, once upon a time, bought him a personal ad, indicating any species would be acceptable.

"Your daughter's going to give Pete fits," I said. "That's good enough for me."

She put a hand on her belly. "I was wondering if you would mind if we named her Christianna. After you."

I felt my eyes well up unexpectedly.

But I could have sworn I heard, "Oh, for God's sake!" coming from Father's general direction. When I turned toward him, however, he was already clearing his scratchy old voice.

"Let us continue in God's name," he said, but he couldn't ruin my evening. The rehearsal went by in a haze. Even the dinner that followed was stunningly bereft of humiliation.

We relocated to Porter's Chop Block, not ten minutes from my parents' home. The prime rib was rare, the potatoes soaked in butter, and the wine plentiful.

Holly's mother was a still-handsome woman who looked like she'd battled life and won. She occupied one end of the table and didn't seem to have, or miss, a male counterpart. As for my own patriarch, he sat in typical silence, looking angrily constipated, but no angrier or more constipated than usual.

All in all it wasn't a terrible evening. Scary as hell, but not terrible. Rivera sat to my right, making terrifying small talk with Michael. James sat to my left. Glancing down the row of faces, I realized something I had never noticed before; we almost looked normal. Relatively fit, attractive, and all grown up.

A couple of tables away, a dark, blocky man lifted his glass toward us. James gave him a congenial nod and rose to his feet.

I had declined dessert. Partly because I'm one classy

broad and partly because I didn't want to scare Rivera right out of the state. I'd already eaten a small herd of Angus.

"That's Pete's philosophy anyway. Right, Chrissy?" Michael said, raising his voice. He stood up. Mom was talking to Holly, who was nodding rhythmically.

I turned toward my eldest brother, catching the tail end of the conversation. "What?"

"From now on we just come running to you when we screw up."

"Hey, she's just lucky I was there," Pete said, putting a proprietary hand on his fiancée's back.

"Yeah, lucky she could save your sorry ass," James said.

"You kidding me?" Peter had been drinking a little. Okay, for an Irishman, he'd been drinking a little. For anyone else, including all kinds of dromedaries, he'd been drinking quite a lot. "It's just a good thing I showed up when I did or—"

"What are you talking about?" Mom asked. "Was there some kind of trouble in L.A.? I thought you just went to make sure she was coming to the wedding."

We turned to her in unison, eyes wide as lost lambs, and then everyone scattered.

"I'll get the car."

"I better get going."

"I have to get home."

"See you tomorrow."

And suddenly we were standing in the parking lot, people scattering in every direction as the night settled in. It had rained a little. The concrete was wet.

"Hey." Pete touched my arm. "Got a minute?"

Rivera glanced at me, silently asking if I was all right. I gave him the thumbs-up eyebrows. After which he gave Pete the "Don't do anything stupid" glare, and strode off.

Peter John watched him go, then cleared his throat. "I just wanted to . . ." He loosened his tie a little, glanced at his feet. "I'm glad you came."

"I wouldn't have missed it," I said.

He grinned, probably knowing I had planned to do just that. "I'm not going to screw this one up. Even though . . ." He shook his head. "Shit. I'm coming into this kind of blind. Didn't even know she'd been married before."

"She's had a rough time, Pete. Victims of domestic violence . . ." I shrugged, still baffled . . . even with a Ph.D. Go figure. "They blame themselves sometimes. Don't like to talk about it."

His jaw tightened. He glanced toward the Chop Block. The door opened. A few silhouettes could be seen against the soft yellow rectangle of light.

"Almost makes me wish . . ." He paused, cleared his throat, tightened his fists. "I halfway wish he wasn't dead so I could beat the hell out of him."

I smiled a little. Christianna was going to have an interesting childhood. "You're going to be a father," I said. "You'll get plenty of chances to be overprotective."

"Shit," he said again, but a grin was lurking. "A little girl. Maybe she'll be like you."

"I'm impressed you can say that without bolting."

"Naw." He shook his head. "It'd be great." His gaze met mine. I waited for the punch line, but he only shuffled his feet again. "I wanted to thank you."

"For saving your ass?"

He grinned. "'Course, if I hadn't made you eat sheep turds all them years ago, you wouldn't have been ready to shoot me when you thought I was pulling your leg."

"Good thing you were thinking ahead," I said, and he chuckled.

The patrons from the Chop Block were getting closer. The evening was friendly and warm.

"Hey, ain't you Peter McMullen?" It was the bulky guy from the restaurant. The two men behind him were silent. One of them held a bottle in a bag. I gave them a smile.

"Yeah," Pete said. "Do I know you?"

"Brad Stacy. Tiffany's brother."

"Tiffany?"

"Yeah, you remember. You dated her a few years back."

"Oh, sure." Pete shifted his gaze toward me, then away. I had no idea if he remembered her or not. But I didn't care. I was happy, full, and maybe a little bit drunk. "Tiffany. How's she doing?"

"Got two boys now."

"Yeah? That's great. Well, tell her hi, will you, buddy?" Pete said, and turned away.

"You told her you couldn't have no kids."

Pete turned back. "What's that?"

Brad shifted his weight, squared his massive shoulders. "You told her the boy wasn't yours on account of some injury."

Pete barely missed a beat. "Oh, yeah, that's right. That umm . . . bull injury. Remember that bull on Grandma's farm, Chrissy?"

I stared, mind bumbling slowly.

"Remember?" he said again, more pointedly this time.

"Sure. Sure, the . . . bull," I intoned.

"Yeah. Biggest damned horns I've ever seen. Caught me right in the—"

"Looks like your fiancée is pretty damned pregnant, though," Brad said.

Pete narrowed his eyes a little. Lifted his chin. "Listen, buddy, I don't want any trouble. I'm getting married tomorrow."

"Yeah? My little sister never did get hitched."

"Yeah, well . . ." I laughed a little, just coming out of a trance caused by this unusual normalcy. "I'm sure she's too good for my idiot brother," I said, and took a calming step forward.

"Stay out of this," warned Blocky Boy, and pushed me aside.

"Hey," Pete said. "Nobody touches my sister."

"Nobody touches mine, either," snarled Brad, and thumped Pete on the chest with both hands, knocking him backward. "Nobody 'cept you."

"What are you talking about? I haven't seen her in years."

"You're a fucking liar."

"And the baby was black. Hell, she told me she'd been sleeping with a linebacker for the—"

And that's when Brad charged. He hit Pete in the gut with his shoulder. They tumbled to the pavement.

I screamed for them to stop. And suddenly footsteps were running toward us. Michael and James appeared out of nowhere, but Brad's friends were pretty wasted. The closest one took a swing at Michael. The other smashed his bottle against the nearest bumper and advanced.

"Don't do anything stupid, Pal," James said, arms stretched out to his sides, but even I could see that that scenario was unlikely. The glass sliced across the front of James's suit coat. And I think, although I'm not positive, that's when I jumped onto Pal's back.

After that there was a lot of spinning and yelling and cursing. I hung on for dear life, legs wrapped around my mount's waist as I boxed his ears.

Until a shot exploded. Everyone froze. I glanced to my left, past my ride's ear. Rivera stood five feet away, legs spread, gun pointed toward the sky.

"Christina," he said, voice low and perfectly modulated.

"Yes?" I had a pretty good grip in Pal's hair.

"Perhaps you should dismount."

"He had a bottle," I said.

Then everyone started talking at once.

"Shut the fuck up!" Rivera yelled.

We did. I climbed down. Pete scrambled to his feet. Our rivals converged, backing away.

"Peter?" Holly appeared, pale-faced and small-voiced, out of nowhere.

"Yeah, honey?" He wiped his nose with the back of his hand and did his best to look casual.

"Everything okay?"

"Yeah." He shifted his gaze to Brad, who raised his hands and slipped into the darkness. "Yeah," he repeated. "Everything's great."

James and Michael agreed wholeheartedly. There were

a few sheepish grins before they traipsed contentedly back to their cars.

In a minute Rivera and I stood alone in the parking lot.

His brows were low, but his mouth was quirking up a little at the corners.

"They started it," I said, and then he laughed.

About the Author

LOIS GREIMAN lives in Minnesota with her family, some of whom are human. Write to her at lgreiman@earthlink.net. One of her alter egos will probably write back.